May the heart of the Harley beat eternal.
May the roar of the Kings never die.

Copyright Statement

Published on 1st February 2024 by Nik Terry.

The author can be reached by email on
nikterryauthor@gmail.com

Or Facebook https://www.facebook.com/NikTerryAuthor

Or Instagram https://www.instagram.com/nik_terry_author_/

If you enjoyed this book, please encourage your friends and family to download their own copy from Amazon and I would also love it if you could leave a review.

A Note from Nik

This book is a work of fiction, figments of my extremely over-dramatic imagination pieced together. It does not depict any MC or MCC in the north east.

The Northern Kings MC Series are dark stories with scenes of violence and other themes that may be disturbing to some readers.

Specifically in Indie, triggers include but are not limited to:

Violence

Murder

Profanity

Alcohol

Drugs

Assault

Domestic Violence

Cancer and Death

Indie is set in the north east of England, and as such, contains some local dialect. I have listed these below and hope you'll enjoy your introduction to some of our great Geordie-isms.

It is thought that Anglo-Saxon settlers influenced the Geordie dialect, and owing to a lessor Viking occupation than more southern parts of England, this wasn't as diluted over the years. The British Library points out that the existence of the River Tweed provided a significant northern barrier against Scottish influence.

Brief List of my favourite Geordie words and phrases

Canny – Good, nice, pleasant, OK.

Howay—This can mean different things depending on the tone. It can mean come on, hurry up, get off it, leave it alone. "Howay man" or howay over here (come on over here), "howay, man it's freezing" (hurry up, it's freezing).

Divvina (Pronounced div-in-ah) – Means "I don't know".

Fettle – Means in foul mood. "Are ye in a fettle, pet?" (Are you in a bad mood, pet). "He's in a right fettle" (He's in a right mood).

Gannin yem (Pronounced exactly how it looks!) – This means going home. "Gannin yem already?" (Going home already?) or "I'm gannin yem" (I'm going home).

Am Clamming – Means to be starving.

Da (Pronounced Dah) - Dad

Ma (Pronounced Mah – like a sheep but with an M) – Mum/Mother. But in the north east we often say mam.

Not all of these feature in this book, but you will see more in the other books in the Northern Kings MC series and the Northern Sins.

How many can you find? Let me know –

nikterryauthor@gmail.com

Books and reading order in the Northern Kings MC Series:

1. Demon
2. Indie
3. Fury
4. Chaos & Carnage
5. Jazz
6. Reap

Books in the Northern Sins Saga and suggested reading order:

1. Red for Revenge (Eli and Ava)
2. Kiss for a Killer (Cian and Charlie)
3. Devil in the Detail (The Viking and Natalie)
4. Taste of Temptation (Oisin and Ellie)

Chapters

Chapter One

Emmie

She stared back at me. Tired, sunken eyes surrounded by deep shadows, and a frown line forming between her brows, thick and rutted, betraying her twenty-eight years. Little bruises marbling pale skin and scattered across the surface of her chest and arms. Her hair lay limp, strawberry blonde strands dropping onto her shoulders, the mirror cutting off the rest of the body she couldn't face looking at.

"Mam! Mam!" The sweet voice was shrill in an exhausted silence, pulling my attention away from the girl staring back at me in the mirror.

I pulled my dressing gown around me before stepping back, hiding the sagging, stretched skin from my view. The girl in the mirror had changed so much, youth taken from her, happiness stripped away bit by bit. A pang of guilt hit me hard, making my eyes tear and my throat choke up. I shouldn't feel like this. I shouldn't wish my life to be different. There were parts I would never change, but all of it had changed me.

She glanced at me again, her face, my face, reflected in the glass. A little smile. Forced. Sad. Tired.

The breakfast table was littered with little round 'o's. Cereals scattered across the top, milk pooling under the bowl and dripping onto the floor.

"Sorry, Mammy. You were busy," she shrugged.

"It's ok, baby."

I sighed, slowly letting the air leave my lungs so not to show the six-year-old my frustration. That I still had to take a shower, cover the bags under my eyes with make-up and drink a cup of the strongest coffee ever, just to get through the day. Shift number two. I'd had five hours sleep. No where near enough physically, or legally, before starting another shift. But it was extra money. Much needed extra money.

The water pounded the glass of the shower door, persistent and rhythmical. Relaxing. The spray on my skin washing away the tiredness, at least for just a few minutes. And for a few minutes I closed my eyes, listening to the steady patter, the heat enveloping my skin, dampening the constant whirring thoughts cycling through my brain.

"Mam!" The bathroom door banged hard against the toilet bowl. "Mam! Where's my football kit?"

"The dryer. Give me a minute. I'll get it in a minute."

"And Lily's dropped the margarine on the floor."

"Right. Ok. I'll sort it in a minute."

"There's none left. Daisy's eaten it."

"What? All of it?"

"Well, she had her tongue right inside the tub, licking it. I'm not eating it if she's been licking it."

I shut the shower off, heat wicked away by the colder air.

"Ok. Ok. I'm coming. Luke, can you at least put the dog outside, please?"

The kitchen was carnage. Wet clothes strewn across the floor, dragged from the washing machine, the fridge door hanging open and half the contents of the bottom shelf knocked out. I sighed, staring, not sure what to tackle first. The dog barked at the back door and the television blared from the lounge. And still I stared. Unable to do anything.

Glancing at the clock, at the time that counted down, the seconds ticked away. Scooping the margarine off the floor, I surveyed the damage. The once smooth texture now mottled by the tongue that had licked through it. It had been a full tub, a third now gone, but if I scraped off the top layer, it would still be good to use. I pushed it on the bench, stroking it over the bread and then patting down the ham.

"Urgh. No way am I eating that!"

"It'll be fine. I've scraped off the bit she'd licked."

"Nah. No way."

Another sigh. That's all I did these days, sigh.

"Luke, please. There's no more marg."

"Fine. I'll just have it without."

Fine.

The boy looked up at me. Light blue eyes and light brown hair. He would be handsome one day. Like his father. He would be a heart-breaker. Like his father. And I hoped the similarities would end there.

The door handle rattled. Daisy barked from outside. Luke moved to the back door.

"No. Wait. Hang on."

Too late. The dog bounded in, sliding on the laminate floor with wet paws. She jumped up at Luke, muddy paw prints covering his black school trousers. And then, with a sudden attack of the zoomies sped round the kitchen, slip sliding everywhere, crashing through the pile of freshly washed clothes, knocking over a stool and galloping into the lounge and on top of the six-year-old drinking out of her cereal bowl on the sofa.

"Mam! Daisy's knocked my cereals over!"

The tears itched at the back of my eyes. Burning and threatening. But I wouldn't let them fall in front of the kids. Not ever.

*****

I threw the car into a side-street, pushing at the door that stuck in the frame, bent on the outside where an object had collided with it. Multiple times. Rust was already setting into the gouges and scratches, marring the silver paint work. It was more than a T-cut could solve. Probably needed a new panel. But right now, I could still get it open and closed, and so it was not a priority.

Not quite 10am, I was early, but after the school run there was little point going home again. That just used up too much fuel, and the dial was creeping ever closer to the red. I'd parked nearly a ten-minute walk away. Outside of the parking restrictions and pay-to-park requirements in the area that surrounded the hospital.

The clouds ahead gathered, threatening and ominous, a never-ending wet spell even though it was only late summer. And that continued now with drizzle. It blanketed outside, fine, wet spittle soaking you quicker than a sudden shower. From a little way away, a low rumble crept into earshot, slowly growing until it was a vibrating, angry growl. The motorbike grew larger in my rear-view mirror, crawling past, the rider scouring the street for a space and then riding away. I watched him go, the black bike and black leather jacket eventually disappearing around the corner to continue its search.

Pushing a leg out, I reached to grab my handbag from the passenger seat, the handle catching on the handbrake and yanking me backwards before it snapped entirely. Great. That's all I needed. I nudged the door shut, the dent in the car door deepening, clunking like the whole thing may fall off its hinges. It probably wouldn't be long before that happened. For now, though, I looped the synthetic leather strap through the billet and tie a knot in it, hoping the fraying on the other side could just hold out a little longer.

*****

"Hey, Mr Carter," I called, pushing open the door of the little room in front of me. "How are you feeling today?"

"Not too bad, lass. Just wondering when I can get outta here?" the man with the long grey hair greeted me. "And it's Ste. Less of the formalities."

"Well, Ste, I hear you've been being a bad boy," I joked, watching a smile light up his face, a flicker of old character igniting behind eyes of rich chocolate brown.

"Sorry nurse." He pouted before breaking into a wide cheeky smile again.

He was a handsome man, even for his age. His hair was thick white, streaked with darker grey, his arms and hands stained with ink. A tapestry of grey and black pictures etched into his skin, intertwining and joining, telling a story of something.

"I hope you're keeping your hands off the nurses?" A voice rumbled from behind me. Familiar yet alien.

I turned to the sound. To the man standing in the doorway, a padded leather jacket open in the middle, giving way to a plain black t-shirt underneath. He wore sunglasses over his eyes, even though it was raining outside, and a thick grey stubble covered his jaw, but not so much as to hide the groove in the middle of his chin.

“Is he behaving, nurse?” The voice growled again, deep and rich.

I nodded, suddenly self-conscious. A silence filled the room, thick and suffocating.

“Nurse Mills….” Ste started from his bed.

“Emmie,” I corrected, my eyes not leaving the man at the door.

“Emmie here was just doing my obs and telling me it looks like I can get home today.”

I turned to complain, opening my mouth like a fish out of water, and the old man in the hospital bed winked at me. When I turned back to make some attempt to corroborate the story, the man at the door was shaking his head, his arms now folded across his chest.

“I don’t reckon that’s what the nurse was saying at all, dad. She was probably telling you to stop smoking.”

Ste shrugged, "I'm dying. My lungs are shot. Don't reckon a few fags will make things much worse."

"That's not true," I corrected. "It'll help massively. Could even buy you more time."

Ste frowned. Not a playful furrow of his brow, but something darker, and suddenly there was more behind the mask of the old man.

"I'll let you two have some privacy."

The man in the doorway moved sideways, just enough for me to slide out through the space he had created, but not enough that I could avoid brushing right up against him, up against the smell of clean leather and the fresh floral scent drifting off warm skin. I paused, suddenly distracted, glancing up at him as he stared down at me, most of his face lost behind the dark sunglasses. And then I scuttled off, hurrying away from the room, suddenly filled with the heavy presence of both men.

Mid-morning break felt like hours away. My stomach rumbled with every second that ticked by, reminding me of the breakfast I'd not eaten and the lunch I hadn't had time to make. The ward was busy, packed with patients, every room and cubicle taken up. Oncology was a tough place to work, physically and mentally draining, a continual loop of families saying goodbye to loved ones. I don't know why I hadn't asked to be moved. Why I hadn't tried to get away from the continual cycle of death and heartbreak? From the tears and the pain. But there was something about watching families come together, cherishing their last moments, and remembering the good times. And in a small way, if I could contribute something towards making it easier, then that was as fulfilling as it ever got.

It was draining though, and at times I slunk home from my second shift in forty-eight hours and dropped onto the couch and sobbed. Today was feeling like another one of those days and I was so desperately tired. Totally worn out by work and life. Tears constantly pricked at the back of my eyes, burning and itching, and it took every bit of strength left in my feeble body to keep them contained.

The queue for the café was nearly out the door when I got there at lunchtime. Just enough time to grab a sandwich, sink a coffee and get back to my patients. I checked the display of my phone, the screen partially obscured by dashes of lines criss-crossing from the top corner, where it had succumbed to yet another fall from overly full hands. We shuffled forwards, one-by-one, until finally I was at the front of the queue, clutching my sandwich while my stomach complained loudly.

The cashier took it from me, the scanner beeping loudly against the backdrop of people waiting behind me. I tapped my card on the reader. *Not authorised.* I tried again. *Not authorised.* Dread crept over my skin.

"Hang on," I squeaked, embarrassment licking at my cheeks. "Let me try this one."

I reached forwards, holding my breath, praying this card had a few more pounds left before it reached its limit. *Not authorised.* The heat teasing at my face now rushed to assault me, my cheeks burning with a mix of embarrassment and the deep nauseous feeling of worry. I was two weeks from payday and those words meant there was nothing left. Not a penny.

"I'm sorry," I dropped my voice, hoping those behind me wouldn't see what was going on. "I'll just go put it back."

“No, you won’t.”

Someone moved behind me, the voice initially a few steps away now rumbling, rich and deep from right above me.

“Put this on my bill, please.”

I turned, half lifting my head, catching his face for the first time. The rich brown eyes a shade lighter than his father’s now he’d taken his sunglasses off, the cleft in his chin more visible from this angle, the strong, proud jaw and the peppered grey hair, flicked across the side of his head. I gave a half smile, embarrassment still fighting with the worry deep in my stomach, and he half-smiled back.

Chapter Two

Indie

She had very light ginger hair, the little nurse with her back to me. Or maybe it had a hint of blonde depending on which way her head turned, giving it an almost light apricot glow. Strawberry blonde, that's what women liked to call it, when they were in denial that their true colour held the rich fiery strands of red. She was slim from behind, the blue uniform designed not to fall into a curve, or hug anything too tight. Boring and totally unflattering.

But despite the bland blue smock over dark trousers, something about her held me captivated. I didn't think it was the messy bun of hair piled on top of her head, strands already breaking free. Nor was it the crumpled sky-blue shirt and black trousers, or the dark-coloured shoes I could just see the back of.

My father smiled warmly as they talked, his eyes fixed on her face, not travelling over the rest of her body like he normally would, imagining what those clothes might offer underneath. Those deep brown eyes were hooked, his face more animated than I'd seen it in months, and if it wasn't for the grey hue of his skin, I'd have had to question why he was in here.

They hadn't seen me. Neither of them. I stepped in closer. My dad smiled, a boyish giggle slipping out at something she'd said.

"Is he behaving, nurse?" I asked loudly, breaking their connection. Interrupting the moment they were having for no other reason than because I could. And I didn't know why. Why I felt the need to intervene, to interject, to break into the private enjoyment of a dying man and his nurse?

My father looked up and the petite nurse turned, startled. Her eyes were wide, frightened, but quickly relaxing as my father patted her hand comfortingly. And there was no lingering of his hand over hers, no attempt to touch her in any other way than caring reassurance.

"Nurse Mills…."

"Emmie," she corrected quickly.

"Emmie here was just doing my obs and telling me it looks like I can get home today."

She turned back to him, and he winked, the cheeky smile returning, looking alarmingly like a caring grandfather not the president of an MC on the brink of a war. The girl, for that was what she was; young, fresh, turned to look at me, a diluted look of exasperation on her face.

"I don't reckon that's what the nurse was saying at all, dad. She was probably telling you to stop smoking."

He shrugged, the grin fading, the darkness in his brown eyes returning.

"I'm dying. My lungs are shot. Don't reckon a few fags will make things much worse."

"That's not true," the young nurse corrected. "It'll help massively. Could even buy you more time."

He frowned now, something playing between his eyes. And she saw it too, her teeth drawing across the right side of her bottom lip.

"I'll let you two have some privacy," she said softly, edging towards the door.

I didn't move from the space I filled, slipping slightly sideways just enough to allow her slim frame to brush past me. She glanced up for a moment, her chin tipped towards me, sea-green eyes searching for mine behind the dark glasses. Freckles dusted her nose, golden marks colouring the pale skin underneath. She was perfectly vulnerable, and young. Much too young. Yet her eyes held a wealth of years. Years that dulled her face, sadness locked down deep in the depths. I'd seen that look before. In another set of eyes I'd never really got over, despite the owner of those caramel-brown orbs only having eyes for my cousin.

The nurse stepped around me, the lightest brush of her uniform catching the arm of my leather jacket. I shouldn't have been able to feel that. She'd barely touched me, yet instead it felt like she'd dragged something burning hot against my skin, the hairs on my arms prickling. I watched her leave, the slightest sway of her hips, the small feminine steps, no air of confidence, just an endearing plainness. Too young. Much too young.

The man with the grey hair and the smug face smirked at me from the hospital bed in the barren room. Tubes attached to his arms, a drip on either side of him, pumping fluids and anti-biotics. Chemotherapy was inconsistent, persistent infections stopping progress, this last infection taking hold.

"What?" I asked eventually, when the smirk turned to an inane grin.

"Nice little thing, huh?"

"For fuck's sake, Dad. You've said that about nearly everyone, and you're three times their age."

"Women like older men. Just look at Tori."

"No, Dad. Tori's a … never mind."

His face changed, the smirk dissolving and anger rushing to fill the spot.

"Talk about my ol' lady like that again and I'm not too sick to put you on your arse."

He was too sick. And he could never have put me down, anyway. He didn't know that, and he'd never tried, thankfully. Which kept me from the predicament of laying out the Club President and my old man. Today wouldn't be any different, but it didn't mean that I would not be on the receiving end of that temper.

"What news?" he asked, his temper retreating.

"Nothing much. All quiet really."

He harumphed, raising an eyebrow, clearly not believing me. And he was right not to. I'd been keeping stuff from him all week, making sure he stayed in hospital this time, rather than ripping out the tubes attached to his arms and discharging himself against the doctor's wishes. Again.

"We've put up extra cameras in the likely spots. At Demon's shop and outside his place, mainly. And then at the garage. The club house is well covered, anyway. There's been no further incidents of vandalism. Seems petty for the Bloody Hand, even for the Notorious."

"Doesn't mean it wasn't them. They'll be warning us. All those fuckers know I'm in here. They'll be testing every Kings' boundary we have."

I sighed. He was right. There'd been a few more incidents. A raid by the police on one of the cutting shops. Fortunately, we had our own sources, and we'd got the tip-off ten minutes before they landed. We managed to clear our people out. And then a fire in the bins at the back of the clubhouse. None of these were coincidences. Not with The Bloody Hand back on English soil.

"We need more recruits, Indie. We're going to need the numbers."

Foot soldiers were what he wanted. Someone expendable when the first blow was struck. My stomach tightened. A glimmer of a memory irritating at the back of my mind, not quite formed enough to batter back.

"And we need to make sure the other clubs are with us. We cannot afford to lose them," he frowned, glancing down at the tube attached to his arm.

"I'll sort it, dad. I'll keep them together."

"I need to be out of here," he grumbled.

"No. We need you stabilised. We need you well enough to lead."

Ste Carter sighed. A sudden weight descending and then the cough started, catching him hard, till he was clutching the cardboard bowl in his hands and vomiting into it. I watched on, emotions circling inside me like vultures and the dull, oppressive feeling of doom slowly constricting my chest.

"I don't know how long I'm gonna be here, son," he rasped, his chest heaving and the bowl in his hands shaking. "You need to be the leader now, Indie. The minute I draw my last breath, the gavel is yours."

And that was what I dreaded the most. The thing I'd never wanted. But the thing I was always promised like it was some sort of honour. The MC kingdom. President of the Northern Kings' MC. I didn't want it. I'd never wanted it.

Behind me the hinges of the door squeaked, a nurse strolling in, an array of pills and injections in a cardboard tray.

"Looks like they're gonna be busy with you for a while. I'll be back in a bit."

My father nodded, his eyes still fixed on me, as if that might be the last time he'd see me. A look of grief taking over his face. My stomach tightened and my throat went dry.

*****

The queue for the hospital café led almost out of the door. People grumbling in front of me, others shuffling restlessly. At the very front was a woman in a blue shirt and dark trousers, a head of red tinged hair just bobbing, almost unnoticeable where the taller people behind her blocked her from my view.

She hovered at the front of the till, and even from back here she seemed flustered, glancing nervously at the growing queue behind her. The cashier shook her head, and the girl fiddled with her purse, pulling out another card and flashing across the card reader. The cashier shook her head again and the people in front of me muttered a bit more. I crept a little closer.

She dropped her head.

"I'm sorry," she apologised. "I'll just go put those back."

"No, you won't."

I pushed past the people in front of me.

"Put this on my bill, please? I'll take a latte and a bacon butty, too."

The people behind me muttered again, but no one complained, and no one else offered to help the nurse with her lunch. She smiled at me weakly, embarrassment colouring her cheeks. And then she ducked her head and rushed off to a corner of the café, setting down and opening the sandwich.

I watched her from my table, pulling at the bread, nibbling round the crusts, pecking at it like a little sparrow, her eyes never lingering on her lunch too long as she scanned the room, ready to take flight at any second. Then she glanced at me, sheepishly, dropping her eyes to the pulled apart sandwich as quickly as they caught mine.

I should have stopped staring at her. Left her alone to eat. To peck at her food. But every few moments she would glance across, see me watching and divert her eyes, pretending to look across me, or around the room. I picked at the sandwich in front of me too, grateful for the little strawberry blonde distraction, letting myself indulge in thoughts that were misplaced. Because the others in the back of my mind were far darker.

Chapter Three

Emmie

"Really, Emmie? You're expecting me to have them all night and then take them to school in the morning?"

"Please, mam. I can pick up a shift at the garage tonight."

She scowled at me, and then her eyes scanned across the kids who stood on the doorstep cradling their backpacks. Sighing, she pushed the front door open wide, and Luke and Lily disappeared inside.

"Thank you," I whispered, and she frowned in response.

The nights were drawing in fast now, each day becoming shorter and shorter, winter nipping at the heels of autumn. And with the shorter days came a chill in the air once darkness fell. The clock struck

10pm, and I locked the doors, the only service to customers now through the little window that overlooked the forecourt.

"You good if I go, kid?"

Ernie glanced around, checking we were locked safely inside the garage shop.

"Yeah 'course. Thanks for the shift tonight," I added, forcing a weak smile at the owner.

"No problem, Emmie. Just pleased I could help."

He handed me a white envelope. Cash in hand. Better for the books and enough for me to get by for a week, if I ate carefully. Then, slipping out through the back of the shop, he left me to take care of the place till the next shift arrived at 5am the next morning.

It would be a long night.

There'd been a smattering of customers, the odd car filling up late, someone calling in for bread and milk, and cigarettes. From the outside we looked closed, shadows filling the space between the shelves inside the shop, a low glow from the fuel pumps. The night outside was still. No wind. No rain. Just a quietness. I glanced behind me at the clock, the minutes ticking by slowly. It would be a long, boring night. But I was being paid for the boredom, paid enough that my kids could eat for a week, and the dog, and maybe even me if I was frugal enough.

Outside, an engine rumbled. Low vibrations growing louder. And louder. And in the darkness a prick of white light grew to a huge round orb, passing in front of the forecourt and moving away again, the low grumbles of the engine transforming to a purr.

It was 12.45am. Most people would be asleep. Most cuddled up to someone, not perched behind a lonely counter, worrying about where the next week's money was going to come from. A car sped past, breaking the speed limit on the road outside, and then some. And then another, either in pursuit or racing with them. And behind them a motorbike. It whined shrilly; a high-pitched, desperate scream, the engine sounding rough even to my ears. Then the road quieted again, descending to the eery calmness of before and I stayed safely behind my glass, watching the vehicles engulfed in the heavy dark of night.

But less than five minutes later a rumble came again, growing louder by the second, deep and rhythmical. Not like the shriek of the bike just gone, but rich and powerful. The headlight lit up the road, swamping it in bright light, but instead of driving past, it slowed, the engine slowing with it; the sound deepening to a lazy growl.

The bike rolled into the forecourt, coming to a stop at a pump, the yellow glow of the overhead lights illuminating the polished chrome. And under the lights, a man moved. A real-life shadow. Dressed entirely in black, he stalked the darkness. I watched as he fuelled the bike, the pounds on my screen ticking upwards as the tank filled. Then the gauge stopped, the motorbike full.

He moved closer, crossing the forecourt in long steps. But when he got to the window, he didn't remove his helmet, just pushed the visor up. I smiled tentatively.

"Thirty pound forty-five pence, please."

His head cocked sideways, his gaze shifting, fixing on me.

"Emmie?"

His voice was familiar, and now that he'd got my attention, his eyes were too. Rich. Brown. But I still couldn't place him. There was a memory, tucked away somewhere. His eyebrows moved, the sides of his eyes crinkling, and he reached up and pulled the helmet off. Underneath, his greying hair was mussed up, some parts flat, other parts sticking out.

"Oh," I said, realisation flooding me. "You're Ste's son."

"Aye. I'm Indie."

He didn't offer his hand, but the window was only open a small amount, just enough to stick his money through. He pushed it onto the counter, colourful tattoos on the back of his hand. I hadn't noticed those earlier today. But then I'd never seen him with that leather jacket off. My eyes lingered on the patterns, trying to make them out, searching for the gangland shit I'd seen before. But these were all pictures, decorations, nothing that seemed to have any meaning and the cuff of his leather jacket cut them off at his wrist.

"You work here too?"

His voice broke my thoughts, and for a moment I just stared into the rich brown eyes looking back at me.

"Yeah. Sometimes."

"Tough day then, two jobs."

I smiled. He didn't know the half of it. Or the jobs. Or that I'd been working the best part of a forty-eight-hour period, and I still wasn't making ends meet. But the eyes that looked back seemed to hold some level of understanding, even though he couldn't possibly know.

"You in for the night?"

"Till 5am."

"Hope you've a day off tomorrow, then."

"Nope. Sleep's for the weak, anyway." Or the rich.

He frowned slightly, cocking his head to his right, and those eyes focussed on me, making my face heat. Somewhere from outside, a phone rang, muffled but urgent. Indie's eyes flicked to his feet, and he fumbled for the zip of his jacket, pulling it down and digging in the inside pocket.

"S'cuse me," he said, turning away, but not stepping back from the window. "Yeah? Fuck… aye…. I'd seen some…. Yeah, not long ago. Be right there." Then he turned back, looking at me almost apologetically. "Gotta go. Nice seeing you again, Emmie."

"Err…you too, Indie."

And it was. Strangely. There was a calmness about him. A man in control. He was older. Much more worldly wise, I suspected. He pulled the black helmet back on, sliding the visor down over his face, his eyes hidden behind the dark tinted plastic. I watched him stride back to the bike, cocking his leg over the mass of leather. And suddenly it was alive, an angry roar tearing through the quiet forecourt, making me jump even though I'd expected it. Then, with a loud growl, he took off, the engine furious as he rushed out of the petrol station.

*****

I hadn't seen the dark shape crouched on the front step when I'd come home. I was tired, my eyes heavy. The need for sleep, even just for a couple of hours, was weighing heavy on my mind and my lids and my reactions. I wouldn't have got out of the car if I had realised. But it was too late as the metal gate that was hanging free from one hinge squawked loudly in the early morning silence, and suddenly the dark shape was on its feet and my heart had been consumed by my stomach.

"Emmie, baby," he spoke like a lover.

But he was no longer that.

"You been hard at work?"

I ignored him, walking straight towards the front door. There was no way I would make it inside without him. Invited or not, he'd be straight in behind me, and I didn't want to wake the neighbours, to draw attention. Turning the key in the lock, the door gave way just a little. Yet it wasn't my hand that pushed it open, but his. Reaching over the top of me, he nudged the door from its frame as he slipped a hand into the small of my back and pushed me inside the house through the opening.

As the door clunked back into place, I half turned. Not really to face, more to glance over my shoulder as to where he was while I formulated a plan, one that would more than likely fail. The dog barked from the utility room. Deep and threatening. She'd been his, originally. And she had as much love left for him as I did.

"I need some money, Emmie."

He stood over the top of me again. I could smell the stale stench of cigarettes on his breath, mingling with the sickly sweet scent of alcohol. He wasn't drunk, though. Far from it.

"I don't have any."

"We both know that is a lie."

"Gaz…"

"You've been working at Ernie's. He'll have paid cash in hand, and I need summit to give to Trev."

"Gaz. I've nothing left till payday. This is for the kids. To feed our kids. It's not even going to get us through the next week. Please."

The despair had hit me hard in the stomach, desperation dragging any inch of self-respect right from me.

"Please…"

But his fist hit harder than despair, snapping my head sideways, the skin popping almost audibly and the whimper escaping from me sounding more pitiful than a beaten dog.

"Give me that money, bitch."

He pushed me aside, grabbing my bag from my shoulder and rifling inside. The envelope crinkled under his hands. Blood dribbled down from my lip, from the spot where heat radiated, stinging harder with every beat of my heart. Gaz tucked the notes into his back pocket. Then he smiled, reaching out for me, grabbing at the collar of my t-shirt and dragging me back to him.

"Dinna say I dinna leave you with nuffin." His fist tightened against the material, his breath hot across my cheek.

I turned my face away, the trickle of blood oozing irritatingly from the cut in my lip. For a moment, I thought he might try to kiss me, but whatever seemed to go through his head, it wasn't that. Then, with a shove that sent me staggering backwards against the kitchen table, he let go, pushing the white envelope into my hands and strode out of the house.

I watched the faint light of morning creep through the space where the door was left open, breathing slowly, containing myself until I knew he wasn't coming back, and then I raced across, slamming the door back into the frame.

Blood pooled onto the back of my hand from where I wiped at my mouth, and my fingers trembled on the envelope as I thumbed through what was left. Twenty pounds. Barely enough to feed the kids for more than three days and nowhere enough to feed me as well. My heart beat frantically in my chest, the heavy drumbeat of panic welling inside of me and the opposing march of dread, and despair and tiredness. My knees buckled, and I folded, sinking onto the floor and letting my exhausted head drop into my arms. I was too tired to cry. Too exhausted to be angry. I would just sleep. For now, I would just sleep.

Behind me, in the utility room, the dog barked. It was quieter than before, not now a warning. There wasn't enough for her to eat either. I rubbed my mouth against my arms and closed my eyes.

Chapter Four

Indie

“The garage’s been done over,” Sicknote’s voice trembled down the phone. “It’s pretty bad.”

“Fuck.”

“Me an’ Tony disturbed them. Took off in a van and a bike. Some sort of racer.”

“I’d seen some. Not long ago. Be right there.”

Emmie watched me with interest, keen blue-green eyes fixed on my face.

“Gotta go. Nice seeing you again, Emmie.”

“You too, Indie.” My name rolled off her tongue like silk and for a moment I just stood there watching her.

She looked so different in decent clothes, even though all she wore was a plain white top which hugged her petite body and blue jeans. They were far more flattering than the hospital uniform which she'd worn today. She'd looked tired when I'd initially approached the window. But who wouldn't be in the middle of the night when they'd already completed one long shift before this one? I had a good idea why I was seeing her here tonight and I didn't like that. Not at all. Yet, right now, I had to take care of business. My business.

The Harley roared underneath me as I forced it out into the night. I wasn't wearing my colours. We'd all been cautious over the last few weeks after my father mandated we move to security level one, meaning no one rode alone with their cut on their back. A lot of the younger club members hadn't even known what security one was, or the significance of it, or whether it was really that necessary. But those of us who'd been around a while knew it was the first step towards being at war. And with each day, we were getting closer.

My garage was at the back of an industrial estate, just off Newcastle's Scotswood Road. And this time in the morning the entire estate was still asleep, except for the squalling tone of the alarm I could hear even over the deep tones of the Harley. The carnage was clear the minute I turned the corner. The big roller shutter over the entrance to the work floor and pit was bent and mangled. But the metal was good, and despite the battering it had clearly taken, it had yielded little.

The shutter was bent inwards, a huge dent in the middle, rammed at a decent speed by something heavy. The prospects hung around in front, the headlights of their car casting shadows that hung in the crevices of damaged metal.

"Sorry, Indie. It's a right state," Tony Cannelloni whined in some attempt at sympathy. Misplaced sympathy.

"This isn't a state," my grumble deeper in the loaded silence. "It's a right fuck-on though."

"Reckon we can get it secured tonight?"

"Nah. But no one, not even me, will get in now it's bashed to fuck."

Not even to open up tomorrow. And that meant losing a tonne of work, work that lined the

Kings' war chest. And I guessed someone would know that.

"I wanna know who this was."

"It'll be the Notorious," Sicknote muttered.

"Maybe. But I need proof."

I glanced upwards, straining my eyes in the dark at the camera that hung down onto the forecourt. The shadows clung tightly, so from this angle all I could see was a dark shape and a red dot. Surely, whoever had hit the garage would have also scanned the place for cameras. They were easily detectable.

Bright white lights illuminated the carpark like someone had just switched on floodlights. Behind me an engine purred, almost Harley like. But this was no Harley, despite the sound it tried to mimic.

"Fuck, Indie. They've made a right mess," Fury noted, stepping down out of the pimp-my-ride truck. "We know who they are?"

"It'll be The Notorious. My money's on it," Sicknote pushed.

"Probably," I agreed.

“So why don’t we just hit them straight back? Right now. They’ll not be expecting retaliation right this minute.”

Fury looked at me, quirked an eyebrow, then turned to the prospect.

“And who we’re gonna send to do the job, eh? You two? You looking to earn those patches quicker, Sicknote?”

“Nah…I just thought it would be a great idea.”

“Reckon you should just leave the military strategizing to the vets, mate,” Fury grinned and even in the dark, Sicknote’s cheeks coloured. “Although I want to see those camera feeds,” Fury continued.

I nodded, tipping my head, and he followed me towards the garage and round to the steel steps that led up the side of the building.

We crowded round the boxy monitor that sat on a shabby wooden desk, grainy images moving on screen. The cameras had picked up some movement, but they were old, long past replacing.

"Shit, Indie. These images are crap. We're replacing these cameras of yours next," Fury complained from the side of me.

"There!" Sicknote blurted, his forefinger just skimming past my nose as he pointed at the screen we were all looking at.

I turned and glared, and he quickly wrenched his arm back to his side, the Adam's apple of his scrawny throat bobbing with a tense gulp.

"Fucking idiot," I breathed, not quite under my breath.

We could all see the same images. The same low-res video output of a truck, a car and another singular spot of white from the headlight of a bike. It didn't take a clear image from my cameras to know that this was the same trio of vehicles I had seen pass me moments earlier. The CCTV images were too shit to get a clear look at the people who slunk about in the shadows, never mind the registration plates of the cars. And they'd made no attempt to conceal themselves, other than the balaclavas on their faces.

"Reckon you know who they are, Sicknote?" I taunted.

"It's difficult to tell."

"Uh-huh. You still wanna point the finger at the Notorious?"

Nothing. His lips thinned.

"Still could be them." Fury shrugged.

"But enough to go retaliate?"

"Who else would target the garage, Indie?" Fury pushed a hand through the long-dark hair that fell down to his shoulders.

"Probably is those fuckers. But if we get it wrong…"

"We could have done with the number plates." The prospects stood quietly behind us.

"They're probably cloned or summit. Pity my cameras are shit."

"Aye, mate," Fury slapped me on my back. "Guess you should have paid me for the decent ones I've been putting up everywhere the last few weeks."

Fury and his fucking cameras. He got a boatload of the things. Fell off the back of a wagon, he told the club. But he was selling them to anyone who stood still long enough and members' businesses were resembling something from Big Brother.

Cameras.

"Wait." Three heads turned towards me. "These fuckers passed me earlier."

"Yeah. You said, Indie," Fury shot me his best exasperated look.

"No. They passed me and then passed the petrol station on High Road. Bet they have cameras there."

"Yeah. But how we gonna get our hands on those images?"

"Think I might just know someone."

*****

It was mid-afternoon by the time I made it back to the hospital. The garage shutters had taken some effort to straighten out, even just to get the place open. And then I'd had to turn away customers as the fucking things hadn't rolled up high enough to let a car pass under. I suppose I should be thankful the heavy metal had done its job, and despite the number of times the truck rammed it, it had never fully yielded.

I'd left the prospects and Magnet watching over the company who were fixing the problem. Sure, they could probably be trusted. They knew who we were, after all. But I didn't want them wandering around the garage, sticking noses into places they shouldn't, or even getting too familiar with how secure, or not, everything inside was.

Visiting time was manic. Cars raced around the carpark, desperately trying to find a space, and it was like the whole of Gateshead and Newcastle combined had descended to visit their sister-in-law's cousin, twice removed. I tucked the bike between a car and the wall, on the white chevrons at the end of the row of parking spaces and hoped it was still in one piece when I made it back.

The ward my father was on was busy, family milling about, a buzz of voices competing against the beep of machines and the incessant yammering of the call buttons from bedsides. We'd made sure my father had a room right at the far end. I would have paid cash to make it happen, but the twins had sorted it without the need to hand any of our money over.

Slipping inside, the room was quiet, the buzz of activity outside not penetrating the tranquillity of the space. The only noise was the wheeze from my father, and the whoosh of a drip forcing fluid into his body. Ste was asleep. His skin was greyer than usual, and the rattle of his chest as ominous as ever. But it was the shape in the chair beside him that my eyes caught next.

She was curled up in the hospital-issue blue PVC covered seat, her knees folded up under her as she leaned to the left, her head in her arms. A lock of apricot fell from the bun on her head and the same apricot freckles dusted her cheeks and her nose. I'd moved closer without realising, my legs moving, but my mind had wandered ahead moments ago. Her chest rose and fell steadily under the manky blue smock-style shirt, but it rode up slightly, so that I could see the curve of her arse, the dark trousers pulled tight around her.

Emmie sat up suddenly, looking around wildly. First at me, and then at Ste, and then back to me, her eyes widening and her teeth reaching for her bottom lip. And on that bottom lip was a break in the skin. A red blotch that hadn't been there when I saw her last night. The skin around the cut was swollen and red, and mottled with cream from the make-up she was wearing to cover it.

She jumped to her feet, swaying for a moment from the body that was not ready to wake up just yet.

“Indie. I’m so sorry! I didn’t mean to fall asleep. I…I just sat down for a moment beside Mr Carter…Ste.”

She was terrified. Of what exactly, I wasn’t sure. But she wasn’t the one who should be terrified. That was the one who had done that to her lip. Because their face was going to look far fucking worse when I found out who it was. And I would find out.

Chapter Five

Emmie

The man with the greying hair stood over the top of me and for a moment I couldn't focus, but I knew who it was. He had a certain presence. Something commanding about him, although he always spoke quietly, in that low, vibrating rumble of his. Shit. I was asleep. Asleep at work. Shit. I sprang upright, my legs not quite keeping up, and darkness rushed at my eyes, stealing my sight for a split second, even though it felt longer. A hand touched my elbow, steadying me.

"Indie. I'm so sorry! I didn't mean to fall asleep. I…I just sat down for a moment beside Mr Carter…Ste."

His eyes scanned my face, stopping at the left-hand side of my lip, at the place where heat still collected, radiating from the spot where the skin was broken.

"Emmie," his voice was slow, as if he was having to think about the words he used. "What happened to your lip?"

"Err…nothing, really. I mean…it was just the dog."

"Didn't think a dog punched people."

His eyes moved to mine, and he'd stepped closer, so now I was looking up at him. Indie was so much taller from this angle. From closer up. Taller and wider. And imposing.

"That's not what it was."

A hand moved towards me, and I jumped backwards instinctively.

"Shit," he cursed softly.

"I…I need to get back to work. I shouldn't have been here. If they knew that I'd been asleep… I'm so sorry. That really shouldn't have happened."

My words were coming out in a gibberish rush, any sort of control I'd normally have, gone suddenly. And still Indie continued to watch me, a frown creating a ridge between his eyebrows. I understood why he'd be pissed off. I was supposed to be caring for his father, not sleeping on the job. And that feeling of guilt and dread seeped into me, not least because if I lost this job, I wasn't sure how I'd keep the roof over our heads. I was already struggling, week to week. Day to day.

"Emmie," he said again, moving to block the way when I tried to get round him. And for a moment, I wanted to cower, unsure of what he would do to me. "Emmie," his hand moved towards me, and I tried not to flinch.

His touch was gentle. Tentative. His forefinger pushing under my chin, tipping my head up and the pad of his thumb swiping gently under the swelling of the cut. Heat rushed to the spot from where he had disturbed the skin. And from the careful roughness of the pad of his thumb.

"Who did this to you?"

Indie's voice was gentle, but I didn't miss the command in his tone. Or how I knew there was no option of not telling him. And for a moment, I thought about the answer I could give. I was mugged. Attacked by a stranger. I walked into the door. I fell over. Those rich brown eyes never left mine, focussing somewhere deep inside of me, somewhere he could see what I was thinking.

"Tell me the truth, Spuggy."

"My ex."

That was all I could say. For a moment, I couldn't look at him. I didn't want to see the pity or the disgust on his face. But he gripped my chin again, and now I had to let him see me. His face was still, his lips pushed together, his expression almost blank. No hint of emotion. No sympathy, no anger, no disdain. He was perfectly stoic. And frighteningly calm.

Beside us, his father coughed, the sudden noise making me jump and Indie dropped his hand.

"Well now," Mr Carter croaked, his voice dry and raspy. "What's all this then?"

Now all words had disappeared, and I scurried away.

*****

“When are you coming for your kids, Emmie?” My mother’s voice crackled down the phone, the signal dropping in and out as I drove home.

“Ernie says I can do another shift.”

“You did one last night.”

“I know. I need the money, mam.”

“You’re working double shifts in the hospital. And now at Ernie’s too. How do you have no money?”

“I just don’t, mam.”

“It’s Gaz, isn’t it?”

I paused. A second too long.

“Jesus, Emmie. Why do you still have anything to do with him? You need to tell him where to go.”

I knew that. I’d tried. We were no longer together. But getting rid of him was easier said than done. More so when he was the father of my kids. And harder still when he knew he could waltz in and take whatever he wanted. There wasn’t a thing I could do to stop him. Not even the police had helped, going to them only making things worse. I should be thankful he at least didn't want to live with us anymore, that the kids couldn't see what he was doing.

"I just need to do another shift or two at the garage. Then I'll be ok till next payday."

Shrill voices shouted in the background, playful and happy. My heart swelled, then burst instantaneously.

"Nanna! Nanna! Can I have some sweets?"

It was Lily's little voice I could hear.

"Of course. They're in there."

My stomach fluttered, the deep ingrained flush of guilt. Guilt for the things I couldn't give them. For the lifestyle they missed out on when they were with me. For the second-hand clothes and second-hand toys I bought, so that they had something to wear and something to open on birthdays and Christmas. Luke was growing older, and whether he realised, he hadn't let on yet. But soon it would come. I'd already seen the occasional look of resentment he would shoot me.

"They can stay another night, Emmie," my mother said quietly, a note of resignation in her voice.

"Thanks, mam. Really. Thank you."

Another night and I'd be better able to cover the angry cut on my face.

"Was that him?" Ernie growled, his grey eyes darkening when I walked into the office at the back of the little shop on the forecourt.

I bit my lip, immediately regretting it, pain rushing to the battered skin.

"He wanted money," I shrugged, dropping my eyes, not wanting to see the reaction on his face.

"The money you earned last night?"

I nodded, keeping my eyes focussed on my feet.

"Jesus, Emmie. You need to go to the police."

"No. I can't. It won't make him stop. And not now he's in with Dekka's gang. It's like they've boosted his ego tenfold."

"You can't live like this, Emmie. You really can't."

"I know."

I did. I really did. And at times, I'd run through my options. *All* my options.

"Look. Keep the doors locked from as soon as you can tonight, and if you need to take off early, just lock-up and go. And if you need me, ring me."

It was kind to offer to get mixed up in my problems, but, a little taller than me, and somewhere in his sixties, I didn't think he'd be much of a deterrent. I smiled anyway.

"Thanks, Ernie."

He responded, his face full of kindness and his eyes full of pity.

The garage had bustled till around 9pm. People rushing from work to fill up cars for the next morning, mothers panic buying nappies after realising at the last minute there were none left for little Tommy to go to bed in. The evening rush quieted as quickly as it had begun, darkness engulfing the courtyard from the threat of winter creeping in. I checked the cameras inside and out. No one. Time to lock those doors.

Teetering, dangerously, I balanced on a box that sagged in the middle, threatening to lose its integrity and crumple to the ground. The lock slid in, and I stepped down, the box giving up just as I transferred my weight to the floor. And in front of me, a shape moved in the shadows, advancing at the doors. I didn't recognise him at first. The forecourt lights illuminated his hair, the peppery grey, swept to the side. Yet, instead of the bike leathers, he wore blue jeans over thick-soled sandy boots and a grey hoodie, pulled snugly up to his neck.

"Hey, Emmie," Indie half-shouted through the glass door barring his way. "Can I come in?"

I nodded wordlessly, turning the lock on the second door and sliding it back. I'd never seen him so casual. He'd always worn black jeans or leather trousers and the leather bike jacket. And I'd not heard the roar of his bike. Indie stepped inside, passing me and scanning the shop. The grey hoodie made him look wider, the sleeves clinging to the profile of his arms, and the denim jeans hugged his arse tight, not giving much as they travelled down his legs. Like my eyes. Shit.

I looked away, but already I could feel the flush on my cheeks, the hot tickle of embarrassment. He turned, his eyes pinning me for a moment, before softening into that rich brown.

"You need bread or something?" I croaked, my voice shattering the silence between us.

"Bread? Oh. No. Actually, it's you I need."

Blood rushed to my cheeks again, heat now prickling at my neck. Indie tipped his head, watching me, curiously, I was sure. His face stayed calm, the same tranquil expression I'd seen from him earlier, yet the longer I stared the more I thought there was a crinkle pulling at the corner of his eyes, a hint of amusement. And my skin flushed again.

"What do you need?"

"Your cameras."

"Cameras?" I sounded like an echo.

"Yeah. Just need to look at last night. Don't need a copy."

"Why would you need to look at cameras?"

"My garage got done over last night. Men in a truck and a bike. Saw them passing here just before I stopped to fill up. Reckon your cameras will have caught the registration plates."

He glanced around above him, as if searching for the cameras inside.

"Yeah. We can have a look. This way," I tipped my head towards the back of the shop.

Indie waited, and so did I, wondering what he was waiting for.

He broke into a smile.

"After you, Emmie," he waved his hand in front of him, waiting for me to move first.

I did move. I led the way to the back of the shop, listening to the firm footsteps behind me. Behind the doors marked private, sat a couple of screens, playing to themselves unmonitored images. Sitting down in front of one, I paused the live feed, pulling up the file icon and looking for the folder with the previous night's recordings.

"What time was it?" I asked, scrolling through the earlier footage.

"12.45 ish. I think."

His voice grumbled over the top of me, low and deep. The images on the screen rushed past my eyes, too quickly to focus on anything, the clock in the corner ticking by. He smelt clean, like freshly washed clothes, but also a hint of aftershave. Not offensive or strong. But light, almost floral, but not quite.

"There," he pointed at the screen, but I wasn't quick enough to slow it down, stopping the footage and scrambling to find the rewind setting.

The screen rolled backwards, picking up speed until it was way past the point Indie wanted to view. His hand covered mine, warm and rough, colourful tattoos dancing over his knuckles.

"Let me, Emmie," he muttered, stepping in a little closer, his clothes brushing mine.

I let go of the mouse, sliding my hand from under his and then sat and watched him control the screen far better than I could have managed. The footage slowed to a normal pace, and out on the road we watched a truck rush past, followed a few feet behind by a motorbike. And then, seconds later, the big bike of Indie's came into view, sailing proudly down the road before pulling into the forecourt.

Indie re-wound the footage, waiting for the vehicles to just pass, then paused the recording.

"Can this thing zoom in?" He pointed across me at the screen, but all I saw was the arm that had come across my body, and all I could smell was him, the light scent filling my nostrils.

"Emmie?"

"Err… yes. I think it does… can I?" Our hands met on the mouse, his fingers tangling with mine, just for a few moments before I pulled away.

Indie dropped his hand to the table, leaning his weight onto it, his arm touching mine. My cheeks burned, the heat spilling down my neck and onto my chest, and suddenly I was unbearably hot.

"Where would the zoom be, Emmie?" I could hear the hint of a smile in his voice, his usual gruff tone lightening.

"It's…it's just here."

I moved the mouse to the icons at the bottom of the screen, pressing one, the screen transforming suddenly as the image pulled closer until it was as large as I could get it. A movement on the other camera to my left caught my eye. People in the shop. I hadn't closed the doors.

"Shit!" The words slipped out unchecked.

"Emmie?"

"Be right back. I've some customers at the front."

"No problem," his words grumbled low from behind me.

Voices filled the shop. Harsh and cackling, rough words and strong accents, and suddenly I was nervous, a swell of apprehension starting in the pit of my stomach. They loitered round the front, rifling through the offers at the till.

"Where you been, Emmie? You've customers to serve." That voice. The one that instilled the deepest feeling of dread and fear every time I heard him.

Gaz turned to look at me, cool blue eyes filled with malice.

“Think you’ve got some money for me, babe.”

Chapter Six

Indie

I glanced over at the live feed camera, six frames displayed on the screen. I couldn't see what she had seen. Everywhere looked quiet. Empty. The screen beside it was paused, the image grainy where I had zoomed in too much, the registration plates of the vehicles I'd been watching for barely recognisable. But there would be enough there for Sicknote to get something from, I was sure.

The screen to my left flickered again. The four little squares changing, picking up different areas of the shop now. One of the empty squares now filled with bodies. Four men. And Emmie. And I didn't like that. For a while I stared, watching the figures. Emmie's back was straight, her legs locked, tension holding her still. But her hand fiddled with her trousers, picking at something I couldn't see.

Silently, I pushed through the doors from the back office to muted voices. Thick Geordie accents. But it was more than that. There was a roughness to them. Harsh and mean. I stayed an aisle away, listening, edging closer.

"Think you've got some money for me, babe."

The sound of his voice sent my teeth clenching together. He was familiar with her, but not friendly.

"Gaz," Emmie wavered. "I gave you everything I had last night."

"Nah. I let you keep some. Couldn't have my kids going hungry now, could I? But since you're in here earning another load from Ernie, I reckon I'll take my cut right now."

"Last time I checked, her wages were nothing to do with you."

Heads turned, eyes now on me. Yet when I glanced over the top of the four fuckwits stood before me, I saw her face. Eyes wide with fear. Genuine fear. Not anxiety or nervousness. This went deeper. Emmie was terrified of these men. Of the one she called Gaz. Her lips trembled, her eyes darting from them to me, and then back again. The fear on her face changing now, as she glanced at me, a begging in her eyes. And I didn't think she was begging me to save her. But myself. Emmie's teeth raked at her bottom lip, at the blob of broken flesh.

He had done that to her. He had hurt her. He had damaged that beautiful face.

"Fuck off, Grandad," the tall wiry one spat, cool blue eyes turned on me.

My fingers tensed, balling into fists. But it wasn't the insult that fired me up. It was looking at the man who had beaten Emmie and not being able to break his face because of it.

"The shop is closed, lads. Time to go home. It's past your bedtime."

The others chuckled. Gaz sneered.

"Look. Mate. If you don't want your nose broken, I'd leave now."

"Please, Indie. Please just go," Emmie's voice was shrill in the overly charged atmosphere.

A darkness flashed across the cool-blue eyes staring at me. A hardness.

"You know him, Emmie? A customer?"

"No. Not really, Gaz," her voice was faint.

The man stepped forward, three strides, with so much swagger he looked drunk, until he was looking up at me. He was only a few inches shorter, but enough that he had to tilt his head up to look me in the eye.

"You got your eyes on my wife, have you?"

"I'm not your wife anymore."

"Really? Cos last I looked you've never filed for divorce," he shot the remark over his shoulder, his eyes returning to me in an instant, watching my every move. And he should. Because there was nothing more I would have liked right now than to ram my forehead down onto the bridge of his nose.

"And I'd never sign those divorce papers. *Indie*. Emmie is mine. And always will be. Isn't that right, Emmie?"

Emmie said nothing, her eyes dropping to her feet, my stomach dropping at the same time. The heavy weight of disappointment, for a moment overwhelming.

"Isn't that right, Emmie?" Gaz barked, but his eyes never left mine, inching forwards right into any personal space I had left.

Fuck it. I slammed my head forward into the bridge of his nose as his howl filled the garage and his friends stood glancing at each other wildly. Gaz bent over, his hands coming to his face, blood gushing through his fingers and dripping onto his white, knock-off designer jumper.

"Don't fucking think about it, lads," I warned as the other three edged closer, each trying to decide who might make the first move. "Just get this fuckwit out of this shop."

The three men ushered Gaz towards the door, blood dropping onto the shop floor with every step he took.

"Oh, and Gaz?" I called, half-turning, watching as he pivoted back towards me, his hands cradling his splattered nose. "You ever touch Emmie again and it'll be more than your nose I'll break."

"You'll be fucking sorry," he spluttered, the flow of blood muddling up the sounds spilling from his mouth.

I watched them go, my eyes never leaving them till they were halfway across the forecourt. Then I turned back to Emmie, to the young woman stood in front of me with her arms wrapped round herself and tears in her eyes. Her teeth chewed at her bottom lip.

"You ok, Spuggy?"

"Indie." Her voice was a whisper. "You don't know what you've done."

"What do you mean?" I stepped closer, and she stepped backwards.

"You've made him angry."

"He'll not be back." I was confident. "He'd be stupid to come back."

She shook her head, tossing it from side to side, murmuring something I couldn't quite make-out. I edged a step closer, slowly, so that I didn't frighten her. But she was too busy, lost in whatever thoughts she was battling with to notice. She jabbered something else, something unintelligible, rubbing at her arms like she was cold. And now I was right in front of her, close enough to brush my fingers under her chin, making her jump this time and retreating.

"Shush Emmie. It's ok. They've gone now."

She lifted her eyes to mine, sparkling, full of tears that seemed unable to fall. Held in place by fear and worry. The sea green was as intense as I'd ever seen them, and this close, under the yellowing overhead lights, freckles dusted gently over her nose, the same apricot colour of her hair. The cut on her lip had reopened, a tiny prick of blood gathering at the break in her skin, fresh and wet.

"You don't know him, Indie. You don't know me. You don't know anything," she whimpered.

"Emmie, it's ok. He'll not be back. I promise." I'd make sure of that.

She shook her head again, pulling her face from my grip.

"No, no, no. He will be back. He always comes back. It doesn't matter what I do. Nothing can stop him. I can't stop him."

My stomach lurched, a sudden knot tightening in my chest. The pain of her words.

"The police?"

"I've tried. I tried to get a restraining order. But he kept coming, still. And each time it gets worse."

"The beatings?" I swallowed, not ready for her to give me an answer. Not sure I could cope with hearing it.

"Yes. And now you'll have made him angry. But it'll be me he takes it out on. He'll make sure the kids are in bed, or not home, and then he'll come round. And…"

She didn't finish the sentence, just stared at me, tears filling her eyes, one escaping and dripping down the side of her face.

"I can't stop him, Indie. I've tried. Believe me, I've tried. But no one can stop him."

"And you're still married to him?"

"He doesn't live with us anymore. But that doesn't stop him from coming round. Normally when he wants money. He said if I ever tried to divorce him, he'd beat me in front of the kids. They can't see that, Indie. They just can't. They don't know. It would kill me if they did. If they saw."

Her voice hiccupped, the tear that had been threatening in the corner of her eye, falling down her face. Her chest heaving as she tried with every effort to keep herself from crying. And suddenly my heart broke into a million tiny pieces.

"Emmie. I'm so sorry."

I pulled her towards me, a gentle nudge, and at first there was resistance, just a tiny bit. But then her head touched my chest, gingerly at first, and then heavier, her shoulders shuddering with each sob as she buried her face into my hoodie.

We stood there like that for what seemed like forever. And I just held her, my arms wrapped around her body, until the sobs slowed, giving way to an erratic breathing. Her hair tickled my chin, wisps of light ginger sticking up from the messy bun on the top of her head, the smell of coconut drifting up my nose. I closed my eyes, inhaling a big gulp of air, feeling her against me. And now suddenly I was lonely. Demon had Ciara. My dad had Tori. And me, I had no one. Not even a pet.

I rested my chin on the top of her head, keeping my eyes closed for just a little longer, letting my imagination loose. Imagining that this was more than comforting a young woman in distress. Imagining that I meant something to her, that I had the right to wrap my arms around her. Imagining that someone might hold me like that, when my time of distress arrived from where it lurked in the shadows.

Chapter Seven

Emmie

"I'm so sorry you got caught up in all of that," my words muffled against his chest, where my face rested against the hardness of pecs.

His whole body was hard against me, not the softness of flesh like I'd expected. But under that grey hoodie he was solid, a frame now hinting at so much more.

"Emmie," he whispered from over the top of me, the sigh he let out catching the strands of my hair and sending a shiver down my spine.

What the hell was I doing stood in this man's embrace? I'd only met him days before whilst caring for his dying father, and now I was wrapped in his arms. Where I could just stay for a little more. Where, for the first time in years, I felt safe. Even if that was synthetic. Fleeting. Because when Gaz licked his wounds, he'd be back, and it wouldn't be Indie he'd be coming for.

"Come on, Spuggy," Indie said, as if answering me. "It'll be ok. I'll make sure he doesn't come back."

I pulled away, out of his arms, ripping myself from him. "And how are you going to do that? Even the police couldn't help me. Neither could the Courts and their restraining orders and injunctions. Nothing stops him!"

My words were sharp. Even I could hear how they cut through this moment of comfort. Indie frowned. A sudden sadness in his eyes. But it wasn't pity.

"I can stop him, Emmie. I promise you; I can stop him."

I tilted my head, as if looking at him sideways was going to solve the mystery of Indie.

"How?"

"I just will, Emmie. That's all you need to know."

"Unless you're some sort of mafioso. Unless you can make him an offer he can't refuse, then I doubt it."

There was a tick in his jaw as he clamped his teeth together. I'd hurt his feelings, I could tell. He wanted to be a white knight for this weak little girl. He wanted to save somebody. But he couldn't save me.

"Oh, God." I squeezed my eyes shut at my own pathetic whimper.

Indie trying to help had just lit a bomb under this whole thing. I tried to hold on to the panic welling in me, building in my stomach, a fuse burning. Oh God. I couldn't keep Gaz out. He'd forced his way into my house on so many occasions I'd lost count. These days I just let him in. It caused less damage, to my home at least.

"Oh, God." The words slipped out again.

Indie moved. And I jumped, fear taking hold again. He winced in response, as if my movement hurt him. But he didn't stop. His arm reaching for me, his hand cupping my face, his palm warm against my cheek. Much too warm. And now everywhere else was warm, too. A fiery tingle of something ignited on my nerve ends.

"Little spuggy," his voice was a whisper, his thumb tracing a line over my cheekbone. "I can help you. If you let me?"

Let him? I didn't know what he was asking. He'll help me report it to the police? Indie read the confusion on my face.

"I can make him go away, Emmie. If you want me to?"

A prick of pain erupted on my lip. At the cut in my flesh, constantly pulled and irritated every time I chewed on it.

"I don't know what you're asking, Indie?"

"I'm asking you to let me help you?"

"The police…"

"I'm not talking about the police." His hand moved back, fingers grazing my scalp, moving my hair, gentle. But in his deep brown eyes was something fierce. Not quite terrifying. Not as terrifying as the thought of Gaz and what he might do next.

"Then what?"

"Just let me help you. I can't bear the thought of you feeling there's nothing you can do."

That was sweet. The nicest thing someone had said to me for a while. For years, even.

"And what would you do, Indie? To help me?"

"Tonight, I'll keep you safe. Let me come home with you." I opened my mouth to complain, or in surprise, or shock, but the thumb that had stroked my cheek now placed on my mouth. A tiny bit of pressure and the silencing look of Indie's eyes on mine. "No, Spuggy. I don't mean like that. I'll watch the house for you. I'll make sure he doesn't bother you."

His thumb moved, his fingers stroking back a loose strand of my hair and pushing it behind my ear.

"What? You mean you'll sit outside? All night? What about sleeping?"

"I don't need sleep, Emmie. I'll be fine. But you need to sleep. Desperately. I'll follow you home. We'll check your house is secure and then I'll watch it. I'll make sure he can't hurt you."

But what would happen the next day? And the day after that? Yet I didn't care. I'd worry about that later. The offer of sleep was more valuable than anything else. I so desperately needed it. And I needed to see my kids without a face full of bruises. Fingers stroked my righthand side. *My* fingers. Moving almost unconsciously over my ribs. Tentatively massaging a memory of pain. Indie watched me. A frown on his face. A storm gathering in those perfect brown eyes.

I nodded, fighting the need to wince.

I'd only just met this man. The man more years my senior than I really wanted to think about. Yet here I was, agreeing to letting him follow me home. To camp outside my house. And now I hoped he really wasn't a serial killer. But then, even that couldn't be more frightening than the thought of Gaz turning up on my doorstep.

I nodded again, my lip smarting from where my teeth gripped it.

*****

The forecourt was laced in shadows, dark and fearsome, but quiet. There'd been no customers for hours, the entire town asleep. Behind me the clock ticked incessantly, counting down to home time, cruelly slow. My eyes drooped, the heavy lids barely able to stay up, and the pounding in my head had taken on the marching beat of the clock.

Outside, two vehicles were parked. My battered, aging car and Indie's dark van. He was inside somewhere. Asleep, I assumed, because I didn't know how anyone could stay awake most of the night just watching someone else. And I could barely stay awake myself. It had been days now of snatching a couple of hours' sleep wherever I could, and sometimes where I shouldn't. I hadn't meant to fall asleep at work today, much less be caught napping. I'd sat down with Ste for a minute. We'd been talking, a distraction from the wracking cough that was gripping his chest these days and the distress from it. He'd held my hand as he'd drifted off, and I'd drifted off alongside him.

And now I was so, so tired. To where the thought of trying to keep my eyes open as I drove home was nearly as frightening as what might wait there for me. The tap on the window made me jump, and for a moment I couldn't focus on the greying hair of the man stood watching me.

"Ready to go home, Spuggy?" his voice was low in the silence of the night, as I slid the window back.

The clock behind me was almost at 5am.

The wind rushed through the open window of the little car. It had been a gamble to even open it a crack, as I wasn't sure whether I would get it up again, but the danger of me falling asleep was far greater. And so, I drove on through deserted streets; the wind forced into the car, ruffling my hair. Occasionally, the lights from Indie's van dazzled me, reflecting off the rear-view mirror and temporarily blinding me. Yet there was some sort of comfort in having him right there behind.

Until I pulled into my street of uniform houses. Of painted pebble-dash and dirty brick, of the same doors and same white canopies that hung over the top of them, the only difference the numbers that were screwed onto the front. I hesitated as I pulled the battered car alongside the pavement, examining every shadow for movement, movement that wasn't the silhouetted thrash of tree branches in an early morning breeze, or the sudden flicker of orange glow from the streetlights that waved in the short gusts.

There was nothing in the shadows, no one hiding in the darkness. Yet still I sat outside my house, staring at the dark unwelcoming windows, the faint sound of a dog barking inside. I needed to get out. To move one leg from the car. One step at a time. But I sat, fear spiralling around in my stomach like a trapped fly. No where to go, nowhere to get out, no stopping, only ricocheting. I shot upright suddenly, the scream stopping in my throat, eyes searching the sound of the noise and not seeing anything.

"You ok, Spuggy?" The voice was muffled. Indie's voice. The man who had stayed all night watching me work. Who had followed me here to keep me safe and was now going to watch my house all night long. Or at least for a few scant hours so I could get some sleep.

My heart slowed. The sudden thundering against my ribs de-escalating. But all I could do was nod. And swallow the thick wedge of nervousness stuck in my throat. The door cranked open, damaged metal complaining loudly, and a hand held out. For a moment I stared at it, not understanding. Then I slipped mine into his, feeling a gentle tug as he helped me to my feet, closing the door behind me with a clunk.

The streetlight cast gold across his face; the light leaving shadows where it bounded over his facial features. Over the strong jaw and the cleft in his chin. His eyes were too dark to see clearly. Shadowed orbs gazing down on me, silvery stubble covering his face, illuminating gently in the glow, which caught the sweep of thick greying hair over his head.

"Ready?" Indie asked, snapping my eyes from where they studied every inch of his face in the shadows.

"Ready?" I was confused.

"For bed?"

I swallowed, nervousness hitting my stomach hard, erupting into a flutter of something inside of me.

"I'll check your house is secure, Emmie." Was that the hint of a smirk on his face?

"Oh. I…yes…bed. To sleep. Erm…" I pointed to the door, cringing at the sudden loss of words.

"After you, Spuggy."

I nodded, a sudden pang of fear making bile rise to my throat, hesitating for a moment.

"It's ok, Emmie. I'm right here." His words drifted across my ear, soft and wispy, and warming.

My feet felt like someone had poured concrete in my shoes, because it took every ounce of effort I had left to take each step towards my front door. My eyes scanning everything for anything out of place. And yet, he was right behind me. With each stride, I could feel him at my back. So close I was almost warm. Pushing the key in the lock, I gave the door a little nudge, a tiny push to check it resisted me, and when it did, I pushed it again, shoving the wood from the frame.

"Just a sec, Emmie." His voice came from over the top of me again. "Let me check, first."

Indie moved past me, his body squeezing against mine as he moved through the gap. Touching me. Sliding against me. I closed my eyes and bit my lip, a prick of pain at the cut, but even that didn't dull these feelings. I was tired. Much too tired.

Chapter Eight

Indie

She stood on the doorstep behind me, and I could feel those worried eyes on me, watching me, not sure what she should do next. I felt along the wall as I moved, flicking on light switches, bathing the little house in a warm white glow. I passed through the rooms. The immaculately tidy living room, with worn settees, sagging at one end where someone always sat. A crop of toys lay on the floor. Mismatched dolls sat around a table, enjoying a wordless tea party on broken chairs, the toy table itself sloping to one side where a leg was bent out at an angle. The living room was secure, no sign of anything unusual.

I wandered to the kitchen, the frantic bark of a dog becoming louder. The kitchen was as tidy, but the front of a drawer was missing and another hanging off to one side, half exposing a load of tea towels. The kitchen table was nearly as battered as the one in our chapel and not one of the wooden chairs that surrounded it matched another. I walked past the fridge, my hand loitering on the door. My stomach tightened, a mix of guilt and curiosity battling for dominance.

"Is everything ok, Indie?" Her voice was soft, close, and I turned, seeing her there in the kitchen behind me.

She looked shattered. Eyelids drooping over the sea green of her eyes. I glanced around once more, content that everything looked as it should. No abnormal drafts. Nothing out of place. The dog barked from behind the door again.

"I need to let Daisy out." Her words stolen by a yawn she covered with her hand.

"I'll sort her out. Back door through there?" I pointed towards the sound of the dog.

"Uh-huh." She plonked herself at a seat at the table, her eyes closing a little more.

"Ok, be right back."

I pushed through the door at the far side of the kitchen, quickly snapping on the light and holding my hand out towards the snout and big jaws of the brindle Staffordshire Bull Terrier that raced towards me, to greet me or savage me, I wasn't sure. Her tail stilled, held out behind her as she carefully sniffed the back of my hand.

"That's it, girl." I lowered my voice, drawing out the words slowly.

Her tail bobbed left and right slightly, the cold damp nose exploring my skin. Then she gave my hand a nudge, dropping her head underneath it, and I rubbed my thumb gently between her eyes, my fingers scrubbing behind her ears. The dog held my gaze, the eyes that had challenged initially now relaxing.

"You ready for wee wees, girl?"

She turned, her claws pattering away from me on the worn laminate floor under our feet. A key sat in the lock. Really secure, Emmie, really secure. I turned it anyway, tugging the door from its swollen frame and watching as the black and brown dog ran out into the shadows. Somewhere in the dark there was a rustle, a movement of grass and leaves. The dog, probably, but I still stared into the darkness, straining my ears in the silence. Watching and listening. And it was the dog who bounded out into the light. No one else. I closed the door behind her, turning the key and locking out the morning approaching from the east.

The little house was quiet. Peaceful. But not as peaceful as the little sparrow with the apricot hair asleep at the kitchen table. Her head rested on her hand, her eyes closed, her lips pinched together. The bottom lip was fleshy, spoilt by the angry red cut, and her top lip didn't quite match. Thinner, it had a tiny scar over the left part of her cupid's bow, and my stomach knotted as I imagined how she could have got it.

Emmie sat propped against her hand, her chest rising and falling gently, the soft gasps of breath just whooshing from a little parting between her lips. I padded across, sliding my arm between her back and the chair. She murmured, so tired she could barely communicate and for a second her eyes flittered open, her head rolling sideways against my shoulder. I scooped another arm under her knees, lifting her effortlessly from the hard wooden chair, pulling her into my chest. She was so light. So tiny in my arms. She muttered again, something unintelligible, against my chest.

Following the corridor, I clutched her sleepy body against me to the foot of the stairs. The first step creaked loudly, and her head rocked against me, her words coming out on a breath.

“Indie,” she murmured.

“It’s ok. I won’t drop you.”

“Hmmm.”

Each stair creaked as I climbed the narrow staircase, carefully climbing to the floor above and nudging each door with my foot. I didn’t have to go far to the second door, which opened inwards to a double bed, almost lost under a hundred scatter cushions. Propping Emmie onto her feet, I swiped the cushions to one side, pulling the duvet back and then helping her under the covers. For a while I stood over the top of her, watching the wisps of the lightest ginger hair spill from her bun over the white pillowcase. I wanted to touch her face and wipe the strands away, to slide my thumb across those prominent cheekbones, down to those feminine scarred lips. But instead, I pulled the duvet back over her, tucking it snugly around her body.

"Goodnight, little Spuggy," I whispered, closing the door softly into place.

*****

The early morning had been quiet. Hardly a stitch of movement from the rows of council houses that lined the street. I'd gazed up and down the long lines of mismatched wooden fencing, slats missing and gates hanging off. Gardens overgrown or crammed full of kid's toys and trampolines so that there was barely space to turn around. Emmie's garden was bare of furniture, the grass screaming to be cut and the weeds raiding the gaps between the broken flagstones of the path.

Inside had been clean and ordered, with almost military style discipline. But her furniture was a mix of styles, and the sofa worn with age and arses. I'd bet if I'd opened that fridge or her cupboards, they would be sparse. She lived hand to mouth, more days missing hers than her kids. I knew her enough to realise that. And that thought made my stomach heavy with irrational worry for a woman I'd barely met. And that fucker of an ex, or whatever he was, wasn't coming anywhere near her again.

I untangled my phone from my pocket, pressing a number and waiting as the phone purred rhythmically.

"This better be fucking good, mate," a voice growled, just a moment before I was going to end the incessant ringing in my ear.

"Fury. Good morning to you, too."

"If it's morning, it's never fucking good."

"Still asleep, huh?"

"Indie, it's 6.30 fucking am. But for your information, I'm balls deep in a stunner right now, so this better be quick!"

"Really? You stopped rutting just to answer my call? I'm honoured."

"It was the only way you would stop."

"Anyway, balls deep? Couple of inches ain't that deep, mate," I taunted.

Someone moaned in the background, light.

"Reckon you can get on with it, Indie, so that I can get on with it?"

"Dunno. Might be enjoying living vicariously through you."

"You going down Twins' territory now, Indie? Time you got yourself a good fuck, mate."

The voice in the background moaned again.

"Aye, aye. I'll get to the point. I want info on someone."

"Who?" Fury's voice was suddenly breathless.

"Don't you fucking cum while I'm talking to you, ya prick!"

"Then fucking get on with it!"

"He's called Gaz. Gary."

"Surname would help."

"Dunno. Possibly Mills?"

"Gonna need more than that."

I sighed, frustrated.

"He's either the husband, or ex-husband of Emmie Mills."

"And what is she to you?" I could hear the smile on Fury's face. Fucker.

"My Da's nurse."

"Uh, huh? And you want info on her bloke because…"

"Ex bloke," I'd answered too quickly and now I knew he was smirking at me while fucking whatever flavour of the week he was with. "I dunno whether they are still married. But he's bad news. And if he's bad news for her, he's probably bad news for us."

"Or you, you mean?"

"Fuck off, Fury, and find me summit."

The moans in the background grew louder, Fury breathing heavier.

"No. Problem. Mate," he rasped. "Gotta. Go. Think I'm gonna…"

I shut the call off and stared up at the windows of Emmie's house. My mind duelling with other thoughts. Thoughts of light apricot hair wrapped around my fist, of those asymmetrical lips on mine, sea-green eyes looking up at me as she lay underneath me. Fuck Fury.

My phone rang in my hand, the vibration making me jolt upright from where I was slumped watching the little house.

“Yeah?” I answered the line of numbers on the screen.

“Mr Carter?” the voice was formal.

“Yeah?”

“It’s Jenny from the hospital.”

My stomach dropped like a hole had opened underneath the car and sucked me through it, dropping into oblivion.

“Your father has taken a turn for the worst overnight. We thought you might want to come see him.”

“Thank you,” the words stuttered over a suddenly dry throat.

I ended the call so I could dial another number. And this one didn’t leave me waiting.

“Indie?”

“Tony. Need you to take over a watch for me. I’ll text you the address. Need you here yesterday.”

*****

Machines beeped around us. A multitude of different chimes, in different rhythms, at different intervals. Incessant. Urgent. Filling my head full of fuzz, like I was in the room, but I wasn’t. Like I was watching the TV, or a movie, or in a nightmare with no ability to wake up.

He was lying almost flat, a squashed pillow giving his head the tiniest of support. Not that you could see much of his head, or his face. A tube protruded from his throat, attached to a machine that breathed for him. Big, loud, painful breaths. It was worse than hearing the constant wheezing of his chest these last few weeks.

A hand placed on my shoulder. Light and reassuring. But there could be no reassurance here. No comfort in watching my father die. I glanced down at the mobile phone in my hand, to where I clutched it like someone was trying to prise it out of my fingers. My knuckles were turning a creamy white from where the blood drained from them.

"He's stable now, Mr Carter."

I nodded, not taking my eyes off the phone. Where the fuck was Demon? He needed to be here. Dad would want him here. I needed him here. To share the burden. To have someone with me while I watched my father die. I couldn't do this one alone.

Chapter Nine

Emmie

Daylight assaulted my eyelids. Bright and warm. My arms and legs were heavy, stiff from an exhausted sleep. I must have stayed in the same position all night, barely moving, barely rolling over. And clearly too tired to put my pyjamas on. The jeans felt almost stuck to my legs, contributing to the stiffness and the inability to move much, pinning me in that same position all night.

But I'd fallen asleep at the table. I remembered now. I'd watched Indie take the dog out and then I'd just close my eyes. Indie. Shit!

The room swam, the creams and beige of soft furnishings, curtains and wallpaper peppered with mould spores from failing windows and poor maintenance, span in front of me. I launched myself out of bed, the tightness of jeans over weary legs sending me crashing painfully to one knee, the threadbare carpet offering little cushioning as I flailed around like a drunken moose.

But at the window I slowed, suddenly anxious to peek out of the middle of the curtains and into the street, nervousness sitting heavy in my stomach. I pulled at the middle, teasing them apart just a little. Just enough to allow an eyeball to peek out. And that enormous weight of nervousness dropped, morphing to disappointment in freefall. Indie's van was gone. The only vehicles in the street were a few old cars, less battered than mine but equally past their best, and a slate grey four-wheel drive I didn't recognise. Odd.

I let the curtains slip back into place and climbed back into bed, wriggling out of my jeans and sliding between the warm comfort of the sheets. My mind wandered off to dark places, contradictory against the brightness of mid-morning light. I hadn't seen my kids in days, working every available shift I could get my hands on, just to make sure I could put some food on the table, for them at least. Today was a day off, time to rest, to pick my babies up from school, to see their smiles and hear tales of maths, and timetables and who had fallen out with who.

My phone buzzed from the side table, and I glanced at the number, recognising the digits lit up from the green display. For a moment, I placed it upside down, listening to the rumble of the device against the wood. It was my day off. The first in a long time. And I was exhausted. Physically and mentally. But I was also broke. On the bare bones of my arse, and that phone call meant money. Turning the phone back over, I swiped across the display and placed it against my ear.

"Hey, Emmie. Any chance you could come in? Sarah and Beth called in sick and we're below quota."

"Sure," I stifled the sigh.

It was a full shift. It meant money. Money straight into my bank account, which meant it was harder for Gaz to get his hands on. Gaz. My stomach lurched, and I stroked at my lip, at the scabbing skin. A shift meant he couldn't get to me for a few hours.

"Oh, and Emmie?"

"Yeah?"

“Just to let you know, Ste Carter has taken a turn for the worse. He’s in a bad way. We’re not sure he’ll pull through this time.”

Silence.

“I just thought I would let you know in advance. I know you’re quite fond of him.”

*****

Straining on my toes, I peeked in through the little square window set high in the door. Even from outside the room, I could hear the machines beeping, an orchestra of noise, badly paced. Sounds I’d heard for years. The signals of doom, of pain yet to come. And I was used to every one of those beeps and shrieks, each variation of noise telling me something else. But today felt different, and I wasn’t sure it was because of the strange connection I had made with the dying man in that room, or whether it was because of the son I’d only just met days before.

Tentatively, I nudged the door open, carefully pushing through. Indie’s eyes were trained on the floor, a mop of thick grey hair flopping over one side. My feet squeaked on the floor tiles, and his head snapped up, his gaze meeting mine and then turning away again. Not wanting me to see the streaks of tears down his face, or the red eyes from hours of crying. The man who had been so stoic, so calm and composed, and now I could see how vulnerable he was in this moment, how hard these emotions were to him. The man who should always be in control. I knew. I'd seen this countless times. But this time it wrenched on my heart, like Indie himself was tugging on it.

Right now, I knew I was interrupting a real private moment, as he watched his father die before his very eyes, wasting away each second, the machine making noises in the background, each shrill sound making him flinch. Each sound dragging him closer to the inevitable. And maybe the sounds were some sort of comfort. With each beep, there was still life, however weak. However hopeless.

I'd moved across the room without realising. The sound of the soft padding of my feet on the vinyl floor tiles, barely registering against the cacophony of the machines. And soon I was right in front of him, dropping to my haunches, tilting his chin up to look at me, just as he had done last night. He let me lead his face to mine, the stubble on his chin from unshaved skin prickling against the side of my finger. I pushed his face up till those brown eyes pierced mine, digging deep into my soul. And deep in his, I could see his pain, of the need to be a man, to not be seen crying, to not be beaten by his emotions.

"It's ok," I whispered. "It's ok to cry, Indie. It's normal. Completely normal."

His eyes misted over again, a fresh set of tears rushing forwards and he tried to move his head from my fingers. But I gripped his chin, my thumb resting in the cleft in the middle, keeping his gaze on me. I wriggled closer, scooting between his legs, the warmth from jean-clad thighs radiating against mine and for a moment I needed to bite my lip, to still thoughts that were not welcome right now.

"I'm here for you, Indie." I had no idea why I needed to say that. I was his father's nurse. I could offer him comfort, but I wanted to offer him more. Much more. "No one will know how you feel. I'll keep your secret. I'll keep you safe."

But I didn't know how I could do that. How I could help him through this other than just be present? Give him that shoulder to cry on, that person to talk to. Because I saw no one else here supporting him. Helping him. Comforting him. And somewhere deep down inside me, an ember of heat rose to my stomach, fuzzy and warm. No one but me. I would help him through this.

Then I did something stupid. I wrapped my arms around him, pulling his face into my chest, pulling him against the thin shirt of my uniform, feeling the heat of his breath against me, and the gentle soaking of his tears through the fabric of my shirt. Holding him to me, I felt his body shake with gentle sobs, into my arms, into my heart. And then he moved, his arms suddenly consuming me, pulling me closer to him with a strength I had underestimated. And it was warm, and comforting and protective. So, I closed my eyes and selfishly enjoyed it. Enjoyed the comfort, the feeling of his arms around me.

We stayed like that for what seemed like minutes. Time ticking away as I sat quietly on my haunches, his face buried against my chest. The muscles in my legs burned hot, a tiny tremor starting in my toes as my limbs begged for release, starved of oxygen from the position they had held for so long.

And then suddenly he tore away from me, pushing up and onto his feet. He didn't utter a word. Or a sound. Nothing. But he strode across the room, plucking the black leather jacket from the coat stand in the corner and then silently left, uttering none so much as one syllable. And still I stayed, my weight on my haunches, glancing around at the room, bewilderment taking away any other thought. Behind me, machines beeped, softly menacing against the whooshing sound of the breathing apparatus forcing oxygen into the old man's lungs.

Chapter Ten

Indie

The room had suddenly closed in. The incessant beeping of alarms, screaming at me, terrorising me. For a moment she'd stopped all of that, halted it. Her arms had provided the comfort I didn't know I needed. The comfort I hadn't realised I'd craved. She was warm, her heart beating against me as I wrapped myself around her, feeling the rhythmical vibration against my chest. It was like it was her heart keeping me alive, stopping me from tipping over into the darkness, holding back the despair that was trying so hard to break my walls each time I stepped into this fucking awful room.

Maybe it was the room, the feel of death hanging around, waiting for his moment to take my father's life from him. To waltz him away into the underworld. And I could feel it too. Icy fingers around my throat, around my heart, squeezing ever tighter. Forcing the air from my lungs. From my body. Stopping the flow of blood. Stopping the beat of my heart. And then the room had shrunk again, the walls sliding towards me; the light sucked away till only grey and black shadows moved.

I needed to get out of there. To get away from the darkness. From the shrieks of the machines, because when they stopped that hideous sound, it was all over. And I wasn't ready for that. I wasn't ready for any of this shit. For Death to do his thing. For my father to breathe his last. For me to lead the motorcycle club I'd grown up in. To lead men into war again. Towards death. Towards everlasting torment.

My heart was racing, frantic against my ribcage. And I could feel the ragged pull of oxygen through my lungs, the back of my throat burning. I needed to get out of there. I needed air. I should explain. But I couldn't. Any words that I tried to get out were strangled by Death's steely grip on my throat. I had to go.

Pushing up onto legs that felt like they weren't a part of me, I stepped around her, ignoring the surprise in her eyes. And I didn't look back. Only at the door. At my escape. At the fresh air and silence that waited for me outside. I staggered forwards, yanking at the handle, a blue-clad member of staff on the other side almost falling in the room on top of me. And they looked even more surprised than Emmie as I barrelled through them.

*****

There was a buzz in the pub across the road from the hospital. Nurses drinking after a long shift. Visitors drowning their sorrows in a pint of beer or glass of wine. Just like me. I glanced around, my vision not as sharp, the clock on the wall behind the bartender no longer legible.

No one had talked to me. Not since the first few punters who had tried to make conversation and given up or backed away when I sipped, disinterestedly, on the drink I'd clutched in my hand. I barely felt the liquor on the edge of my tongue, the whisky having burnt my taste buds away, and all I could feel was that enveloping warmth every time I took a swig from the glass.

The bartender had piled the last two with ice, despite me murmuring something unintelligible about not wanting any. I'd scowled, but he'd pushed the thick chunks into the glass anyway, and now they melted, watering down the liquor and I guessed that had been his intention. But I didn't stop. Because right now I was numb. I couldn't feel anything. No pain. No sorrow. No dread. No anxiety. But the loneliness remained. And I needed much more alcohol to dumb that one down. Because that had lived with me for decades. Like a parasite feeding on my every energy, nothing I did made it go away.

The Kings had never filled that hole, no matter how hard I'd tried. But it wasn't my club, even if I was Vice President. It was my dad's, and soon it would go to the grave with him. Unless I had the energy to fight what might be inevitable, anyway.

I slid the phone out of my pocket, closing one eye as I tried to read the display and the tangle of text. I think it said that Magnet had some intelligence on who'd hit my place a couple of days ago, despite the number plate not giving us any clues. But I couldn't read the message properly, the words moving in front of me, coming apart and rejoining, running away from me every time I tried to focus.

Fuck. I needed another drink.

"Anuffer," I signalled to the bartender. He'd been joined by another now, unless I was seeing double. No, I wasn't seeing double. The other turned, and they seemed to discuss me, sending the heckles rising on the back of my neck. "Hey, Jo. James. Jonny. Whoever the fuck you are. A man could die of furst over here."

He shook his head at me or at his mate. I wasn't sure. But he walked across anyway.

"I'm sorry, mate. It's time to go home."

"What you shtalking about?" I held the glass towards him.

"You've had enough. I'm sorry we're not serving you anymore."

"Ssshut up. There's nuffing wrong with me."

I stood up off the bar stool, my head suddenly spinning, knocking me off balance and tipping me sideways. Scrambling for the bar top, my hands slipping on the smooth surface and now time slowed, as I slid sideways, towards the floor. Fuck.

But the floor didn't come, something stopping me, firm hands holding me and a tiny squeak coming from my side. I swayed, and stopped, my legs suddenly able to support my weight again, helping me straighten up and then lowering me back onto the seat. The grip on my arm and my side didn't loosen.

"You with him?" The bartender asked someone beside me.

"I am now."

"He needs to go home."

"I know. I'll sort him out. But I need a pint of water for him first."

I recognised the voice, light and gentle, sending the same energised tingles through me, diluting the alcohol in my veins with the purest of sounds. Emmie. Turning, I searched for her in the shadows, peering out from the liquor clouding my eyes, until I could make out her delicate face.

The pint glass slid towards me, filled with clear fluid. I wasn't fucking drinking that. I pushed it back again, but suddenly her hand was on top of mine, gently controlling.

"No, Indie. I need you to drink this. All of this."

"It's fucking water, Spuggy. Won't do me no good."

"You won't be saying that in the morning. Drink up. I need to get you home."

"You don't know where I live."

"You can show me."

I grinned, stupidly. And she shook her head.

"He not got someone who can pick him up?" The bartender asked from across the bar.

I grinned at him, too. What the fuck was I doing?

"It's ok," Emmie's gentle voice came again, the only thing I could really focus on. "I got this. Just give me a hand out to my car?"

The walk from the pub seemed to take an age. My legs were heavy, like they were filled with concrete, or lead, or some other heavy shit, each step almost dragging across the paving slabs. Arms gripped me gently from one side and forcibly from the other. And then at Emmie's car I was pushed and pulled, bundled into the seat beside her.

"You going to be ok getting him out at the other end?" The bartender's voice was grating on me now. Too low, gravelly, and I didn't like the way he spoke to my girl. Like there was an intent. Yes. Intent. He wanted her. But she was mine. Definitely mine.

Darkness swam in front of my eyes. I think Emmie answered, but I couldn't remember. My brain was swimming now, unable to keep up with the conversation on the street outside. I should be angry. I knew I should be angry, but I couldn't remember why. And then the engine started. A low, irritating purr. And now my head was whirring, and I closed my eyes, because with each streak of light I felt more and more sick.

*****

"That strange man has my unicorn!"

The voice was shrill. Infantile. And it ricocheted around my brain like some sort of torture device.

"Nanna! Nanna! He's got Mr Morris. I want Mr Morris back."

That whine was enough to pierce my ears. In fact, if I wiped at them now, they'd be bleeding. I was sure of it.

"Is he alive?"

A boy's voice now, cautious. Almost scared, but curiosity had got the better of him. And yet I still couldn't peel my eyelids from my eyeballs. Either my brain wasn't functioning, or my lids were just plain stuck. My mouth was dry too. Painfully and nauseatingly dry.

"Emmie? Why is there a strange man on your couch?"

Her voice was older. There was a hint of familiarity, but it was different enough that I didn't recognise it.

"He's cuddling Mr Morris!"

Who the fuck was Mr Morris?

"It's fine, Lily," and now I heard her voice, calming the anxiety that was building in my gut. "I'll get Mr Morris for you."

"More to the point, Emmie, who is he?"

There was a pause. Just a slight one, but it held in the air, stark and outrageous.

“This is Indie, Mam.”

“And Indie is who?”

I squeezed my eyes tight, the movement dislodging the eyelids that seemed to have become welded to my eyeballs, probably through dehydration. It seemed they were as dry as my mouth.

“He…err.. just needed a place to stay.”

“Uh-huh?”

Bodies moved in my blurry sight. A voluptuous woman, and two kids, one taller and the other skinnier.

“Well, here are your kids. Just in case you forgot you had any.”

“Nanna! Nanna! Don’t go.” The little girl wailed as the plump woman moved from my sight.

I tried to move my head, to follow the bundle of shadows, but the slightest movement sent me spinning out of control again. I clutched at the pink unicorn which had spent the night in my arms.

"I want Mr Morris!"

My head hurt.

Chapter Eleven

Emmie

Lily and Luke stood watching the man lying on my couch, inspecting him from the safety of a few feet back like he was some sort of unidentified object. Indie attempted a smile. But his brow furrowed, and all he managed was a grimace, sending Lily retreating to the kitchen.

"Mam! Mam! He's got my unicorn. I want my unicorn back."

"I'll get it in a minute. Let me just finish up here."

Breaking the eggs into the pan, I fished out a stray piece of eggshell that had come loose onto the gooey egg white. I glanced over my shoulder, watching Luke stare at Indie and Indie look back at him uncomfortably.

“Lily?” I asked the little girl standing in the middle of the kitchen floor, torn between the safety I offered her and rescuing her unicorn from the clutches of the hungover man on my couch. “Take this to Indie.”

Her eyes widened, like I’d asked her to walk into a cage of lions, but she nodded, dragging the pint glass of water from the kitchen bench and walking apprehensively into the lounge.

“Thank you,” he croaked, and she scuttled away to the safety of my legs.

Luke stared at the man before him, who had now pushed himself up into a sitting position and was sipping carefully on the water. Indie glanced at the little boy scrutinising him, his gaze shifting from the glass in a shaky hand to the disdainful stare of the nine-year-old.

“Kids. Indie. Breakfast’s ready,” I called from the kitchen, as I slid an egg on to a plate.

Luke didn’t move, standing like a sentry in the living room. Indie pushed up onto his feet, clutching the now empty pint glass, and took a tentative step forward, as if he wasn’t sure whether he would topple over again. And Luke watched, keeping his distance but never moving, not until Indie had passed through the doorway into the kitchen, lowering himself from one seat to another. Luke brought up the rear, watching Indie's every slow, laboured movement. And then beside me, Lily moved suddenly, darting into the lounge and rescuing her pink unicorn from where Indie had left him unattended on the couch. She scooped him up into her arms, holding him tight to her chest and whispering something to him I couldn't hear, and then she wrinkled her nose.

"Eurghh. Mr Morris stinks!"

I caught Indie's eye, the sudden look of embarrassment.

"What of?" I called back, piling the just-popped toast onto a plate.

"Aftershave. Stinky aftershave."

I smiled, a sudden warmth invading me, wrapping itself around me, and for the first time in weeks I felt relaxed. Too relaxed. I had an angry ex who would stop at nothing to make sure I stayed in the living hell that he'd created for me, and a bank account that proudly showed me ‘zero’ every time I peeked into it to see what I could squeeze out for food. But for a few short minutes, I was happy, and I hadn’t felt like that for years.

The table was almost silent. The only sounds the soft movement of jaws as the kids and Indie chewed quietly, a slight ding of a fork or a knife on a plate. There was a static, none of us speaking, all of us watching each other. And I watched indie. Intently. His skin showed the full range of colours, greys and greens, a flush of pink and a retreat to pale. He chased a little slice of sausage around the plate, slowly chewing and swallowing like his throat was constricted. And he’d worried the egg the entire time, not quite wanting to eat it.

Luke watched him too. For an entirely different reason. His eyes fixed on his every laboured movement and his face more stoic than Indie’s, but occasionally his lips twitched in the corners, a frown forming. It was the darkening of the eyes that took that tiny smidge of happiness away. The resemblance to his father, the tiny warning signs I usually got before a beating was forthcoming. Luke couldn’t help it. He was a carbon copy of his dad, almost a direct imitation.

“Indie? You want a coffee?” I asked, trying to spare him the glare of an almost ten-year-old boy.

“Aye, lass. That’ll be great.” He answered, his voice still a little shaky.

I moved from the table, turning my back on my two kids and the man I’d brought home last night. A man I barely knew. I must have been mad. But there was something safe about Indie. Or I’d just completely lost the plot.

“Hi guys,” I heard from the table, the voice soft and more gentle than the exterior that was attached to it. “I’ve not had the chance to introduce myself this morning. I’m a friend of your mam’s.”

Both kids glanced at me, then back at the strange man sitting across the table from them. Neither knowing what to say to the man they’d never met till this morning. The man they walked in on cuddling a pink fluffy unicorn and sleeping off last night’s liquor fest on their sofa. The man they didn’t know was a better man than the one who brought them into this world.

I stifled a sigh, watching the cold interaction. Watching Indie try to make conversation with kids staring him down across the table. And whilst they sat there scrutinising him, I didn't need years, or months, or even weeks to know he was a good man. I'd spent enough time with an abusive monster to know otherwise. Yet, here I was living in a fantasy, because no amount of Indie trying to protect me would save me from Gary. Gaz didn't want me. But no one else could have me either. That didn't mean I couldn't enjoy it, just for a few hours. Some hint at what normality could look like, feel like. Life was cruel, showing me what I couldn't have, tempting me, then taking it all away again the moment he left this house.

Still, Luke and Lily sat across from him, not answering, the three of them glancing nervously at each other, not really knowing what to say.

"This is Luke, my oldest," I said eventually. "He's nine, nearly 10. And this is Lily. She's six going on 16."

Indie smiled at her, and Lily's face melted, breaking into that big, beautiful grin of hers. Then she turned to Luke, expecting him to smile too, but getting nothing; her big brother sitting staring, disapproval etched on his face.

"What are you doing here?" Luke's voice was accusatory.

"Well," I started.

"I drank too much," Indie interrupted. "So, your mam helped me out last night. She gave me a place to put my head down for the night. I'm sorry I cuddled your unicorn, Lily. But Mr Morris was really good company."

Lily giggled, light and beautiful, and Luke scowled even more.

"I don't even know where I left my bike," Indie muttered to no one in particular.

Luke sniggered. "You have a bicycle?"

"No. A motorbike." I watched Luke's eyes light up, replaced quickly by the scowl he'd worn all morning. "It's at the hospital somewhere. I just don't know where, or whether it'll still be there this morning."

"I could drive you over for it?" I asked.

Indie shook his head. “Thank you. Really. I’ll get someone to drop me over for it. You’ve done way more than you should have done for me last night. I would have left me to sleep it off on the bar top.”

“Maybe get it later?” I prompted, feeling responsible for this man’s wellbeing. “You’ll still be way over the limit.”

He looked at me, his eyes fixing on my face, a small smile pulling in the corner of his mouth, and something sad in his eyes despite the smile. I tugged my gaze from his, suddenly self-conscious, glancing around the room and catching the curiosity on my children’s faces. They watched us intently, Lily grinning from ear to ear, revelling in a burst of happiness around the kitchen table and Luke looking tense, unable to process what was going on in front of them. It was probably the first time they’d seen their mother and another man have a conversation that didn’t involve some sort of sarcasm and degradation. In fact, I don’t remember the last time a man made me feel so comfortable in his presence. That happiness filled me momentarily, before a bitter taste chased it away, realisation that this, whatever it was, could never go any further. The scab on my lip was crusting over. The swelling had gone down, but the memory of pain was still there. And it was only the sting of my fingers moving over the tightness of the scab that made me realise I was touching the spot.

Indie stood up from the table, sliding his plate from where he'd been sitting in front of it and then collecting up the empty plates from in front of Lily and Luke. I held out my hands as he brought them to the sink.

"I've got it Indie, thanks," I muttered, waiting for him to drop the plates in my arms.

But he ignored me, instead edging to the sink and dropping them under the soapy water, nudging me gently to move over.

"I got this, Spuggy."

I watched as he pulled a plate out of the soapy water and cleaned it, placing it on the draining board. Eventually I turned, plucking the clean crockery from where he'd left them, rubbing them dry with a tea towel. And for a few moments, we worked in silence, his arm brushing against mine, his presence enveloping me. With his eyes focused on the plate he was gently washing; I sneaked a glance at him. Light grey stubble now covered his jaw, and strands of thick greying hair out of place from a drunken sofa slumber.

"Emmie," he said, turning towards me, and I jumped, my heart bounding in my chest.

It was a reaction I'd never get over, one that would always be with me, probably for the rest of my life. Indie noticed my nervousness, his jaw tightening as if he disapproved, making my stomach feel like I'd thrown it over a cliff. I smiled weakly, feeling the heaviness of his disapproval, a twinge of fear worrying about what might come next.

His tone softened further. "Would you mind if I took a shower? Freshen up before I move off this morning? I might feel a little less like a rave victim."

"Of course. I'll show you where the bathroom is."

Stairs creaked behind me, the combined weight of us making the old wooden steps complain. The staircase seemed so narrow right with Indie following me closely, the sound of his steps and the gentle tickle of his breath on the back of my neck, pressurising the small space. The same pressure I felt in my stomach. But it wasn't dread this time, or fear, or anxiety, but something I'd not felt for years. I shook my head, stemming the stream of unhelpful thoughts filling my brain. Unhelpful. Misplaced.

Water hammered the tiles in the bathroom, echoing loudly around the sparsely furnished upstairs rooms. I paced the floor, a new flood of anxiety coming over me, a conflict of emotions and a heavy dread. And I couldn't pick either out from the other. Instead, I peeled back the curtains, making a tiny gap, my eyes scouring the street below. The same cars parked on the roadside, battered and well used, apart from the four-wheel drive with the tinted windows. It was too new for this street, for the people who lived hand to mouth, just like me.

I swallowed, forcing back the thick feeling of nausea grabbing at my throat. It was difficult to see from this angle, through the tiny space I'd made in the curtains, peering at the car, trying to see through the tinted glass at the occupants inside.

"Emmie?" His voice grumbled from behind me unexpectedly, and I jolted, nearly tearing down the curtain in shock. "I'm so sorry, Emmie," he said, more softly this time. "I didn't mean to frighten you."

Indie stood in my bedroom, clutching a pink unicorn towel around his waist, his body half covered in colourful tattoos, winding down his arms and across the hardened pecs of his chest. They stopped just in line with the end of his sternum, leaving his stomach bare, the ripples of a six-pack untouched by the ink. The sudden intrusion of his nakedness had stolen any words, or any sounds I could make, my eyes darting over his body, unable to stay in one place long enough to process any of what I was seeing. Muscle, skin and tattoos. That was what I was seeing.

My cheeks grew warm, an irritating heat to my skin. I didn't know what to say as I stood there staring at a half-naked man wrapped in a unicorn towel.

"I just need another towel. This one's a bit small," he said, the hint of a grin on his face.

I couldn't speak. I couldn't look anywhere but at him. At the mass of muscle in front of me. At the reds, and the blues, and the green snaking up his arms, covering, or rather complementing, the muscle of his biceps. Oh God. I'd never expected that was underneath the black T-shirt and the blue jeans I was used to seeing him in. Or the black leather bike jacket. I'd never even caught a hint that all those muscles would be hiding under his clothes. Now I didn't know where to look. Well, not quite true. I knew exactly where to look; and I stopped looking there. And thank God the unicorn towel of Lily's was enough to cover up most of his bottom half, because my eyes wandered everywhere.

"Emmie? Do you have a bigger towel?"

Indie's voice broke my thoughts, making me flinch, the heat of embarrassment licking at the base of my neck.

"I… err… yeah. I'll find you one, just a minute."

But now the only way to get that towel was to squeeze past him in the doorway. The doorway he seemed to fill with his almost naked presence. And as I slid past him, holding my breath, he seemed even wider. His damp skin brushed my hand, the fresh soap smell radiating off his warm body. I held tighter to my breath, in case he could hear my rapid breathing as I passed, or the flutter of my heart.

I moved to the top of the stairs, to the airing cupboard where I kept the towels, pulling off a big white fluffy one from the top of the pile. When I turned around, he was behind me again, all muscles and tattoos, and a white fluffy towel I pushed against his chest. Indie retreated to the bathroom, clutching the pink unicorn towel around his waist and the white towel against his torso. I watched him go, the unicorn horn on the back of the pink towel waggling at me as he walked away.

The next time I saw him he was fully clothed, the jeans back on from the night before, and the black long-sleeved top covering up the tattoos I hadn't known he'd had. The towels in his hands were bundled up, clutched under his arm as he walked towards where I stood in my bedroom, peering out through the crack in the curtains.

"Do you have a washing basket?" He asked, signalling to the towels in his hands.

"Here, I'll take them."

I held my hands out, waiting for them to be put into my arms. Instead, he dropped them on the bed behind me, stepping closer. He reached up, his arm moving too quickly, and I started, squeezing my eyes shut. But the arm that reached out didn't cause pain, but sat gently around my shoulders, nudging me towards him. My breath stopped in my throat, my body tensing, and I wasn't sure whether it was from the shock of him touching me, or the electrified pressure now building in the pit of my stomach.

"Thank you, Spuggy," his voice was low, inviting.

I glanced up at him, at the rich brown eyes staring down upon me, grasping for reasons he would thank me. And then he ducked his head, placing a gentle kiss on the top of mine. I closed my eyes, savouring that moment, feeling his lips lingering against my hair. A million electrified tingles cascading from the root to the tip, reminding me of everything I really wanted and everything I didn't have. Pulling away, I let my gaze fall back to the window, moving the curtains again and glancing back down into the street, back to the car. The car that had been parked in my street since the altercation Indie'd had with Gaz in the garage. And now a new sensation filled my stomach. Fear.

"Emmie, what's wrong?" Indie asked, right behind me.

I could have lied to him right then, made something up, but what I knew of him was that he could see more of me than I realised.

"That car out there in the street. With the tinted windows."

"Uh, huh?"

"It's been there two days now. Since you had that run in with Gaz. They're watching me. I know it."

And now that I acknowledged that fear, panic welled in my stomach, slithering up my throat, wrapping its fingers round my neck.

"It's ok, Emmie. That's just one of my guys."

"One of your guys?" The words threatened to choke me, panic squeezing ever tighter.

What the hell did he mean, one of his guys?

"Who are you?" I whispered.

Chapter Twelve

Indie

Those beautiful blue-green eyes widened, panic contorting her pretty face, her mouth dropping open in a silent ‘o’.

“One of my guys from the bike club,” I added quickly, but the words didn’t soothe her and she stood there frozen to the spot, like a terrified bunny caught in headlights. “My motorcycle club. It’s just Tony Cannelloni. I had him watch you when I couldn’t.”

“You sent a guy to watch me?” She choked out eventually.

“Yes. I promised you he wouldn’t get near you. But when they called me to the hospital, I needed to put someone else on you.”

“And when you say motorcycle club…”

"It's not what you think," I interrupted, cutting off the words about to escape from her mouth. And that was the first lie I told her. "We're a group of men who share a love of bikes.

"An MC?"

"Yes. But we're not like you think." Or we wouldn't be. Not when I got the chance to clean the club up, and it looked like that opportunity would come around soon. "We love to ride bikes and get together at weekends. We have rules and regulations. Things we should and shouldn't do. And ways to behave and ways not to behave. But that doesn't make us something bad."

Not always. We often did bad things, but for the right reasons. No one would ever understand that until they were in the moment with a choice to make. But I didn't need to tell her all that, not unless I wanted to frighten her away from me even more. When the war was over, and we established territories once again, maybe I could move it away from where my father had taken it to. And maybe one day we could be a regular club with no more fighting, and just enjoy our love for bikes. Be a brotherhood without having to lay our lives and our livelihoods on the line.

Yet, even though I said those words to myself, even though I tried to convince myself it was all possible, somewhere deep down, even I didn't believe it.

"I couldn't watch you twenty-four hours a day, Spuggy. So, I made sure someone I trusted watched you."

Again, a half-truth. The prospects had never really proved themselves to me, but if they failed, they would never be patched in, and so I knew Tony Cannelloni would not fail me.

Emmie sighed from beside me.

"No amount of watching me and my house will stop him coming. And he nearly never comes alone. He's always with someone. One man will never stop him."

But I wasn't one man. I was the Vice President of the Northern Kings MC, one of the oldest and most feared MCs in the north east of England. I shook my head, chasing away my own thoughts, thoughts that were growing darker and darker.

"That's because he's a coward, Emmie. Any man who beats a woman, any man who feels the need to travel in pairs to abuse his wife…"

"Ex-wife."

"I thought you were still married."

Emmie bit her lip and then flinched.

"Any man who abuses his ex is a coward. A bully. But when you out bully the bully, they run away with their tail between their legs."

Her eyes filled with tears, the Mediterranean green now looking like polished glass.

"No matter what I've done, Indie. No matter how I've tried to stop him. It's never worked. When I've gone to the police, or tried to defend myself, nothing. He always comes back. He always will. He'll never leave me alone. He doesn't want me, but he won't let anyone else have me."

I reached out for her again, pushing my hand around the back of her head, my fingers entangling into the hair that fell loose around her shoulders. I'd never seen it like that. It was always tied up in that messy bun on top of her head, with those apricot strands that fell around her face, providing the most incredible frame for incredible features.

And now it was my turn to sigh. To feel that sense of foreboding, dull anxiety niggly at my nerve ends. Wondering whether she could feel what I could feel? Whether she was drawn to me like I was to her? How could she? She was at least 10 years younger than me. That dusting of freckles across her nose, those Mediterranean eyes, every part of her a siren call to my brain, bewitching me with some sort of sorcery. And I knew that no matter what I did, there was no way I was going to shake it off.

"Emmie, pass me your phone," she jumped again, my words suddenly filling the quiet space between us.

She was just like a little bird, my sparrow, my spuggy. Ready to fly away at the first signs of danger, twitching, on edge constantly, knowing that a predator was just around the corner. She looked up at me questioningly.

"Let me give you my number," I urged, watching a shadow of doubt cross her face.

Slowly, she pulled her phone from her back pocket, squeezing her thumb against the side until the display lit up, and then handed it to me. Moving across the screen, I hit the numbers and then deleted about the same amount I'd typed in, my fingers clumsy against the petite display. And then I handed it back to her.

"Anytime you need me, Emmie. Ring me. Day or night. If you need anything, anything at all, I want you to ring me."

Her eyes searched mine, presumably looking for sincerity, and I hoped she found it. Because if there was something I was sure of, in amongst these last few weeks of instability and uncertainty, it was the need to protect her. And that urge was overwhelming and preoccupying. And suddenly I wanted to kiss her right then, to taste those precious lips, and that innocent smile. I needed to get gone before I went too far.

*****

We had the best attendance ever in church that night. The upstairs room in my pub was packed. Every member of the club who should have been there was there. But that was what war did to you.

No one missed these meetings now. Everyone eager for each tiny sliver of news, any tidbit that would tip us off to the Bloody Hand's next move, and every member wanted the reassurance that the club had their back.

So far, we'd only had to deal with minor hits. Low-level break-ins, minor criminal damage and a few windows put out. Nothing the Police would be interested in and barely enough to get this biker spat on their radar. The attempt on my garage a few nights back was the biggest issue we had faced. Despite all of this, it was still a threat, a pattern of events that had always led to something in the past. I glanced around the table at the tense faces. The furrowed brow of Fury, Magnet's jaw ticking, the only hint of tension in the luckiest man alive, and the Twins' comedic antics unusually quiet, some brothers feeling the threat of a biker war for the very first time. Most of the younger members had only seen a few spats during their membership, because we'd extinguished the proper threat years before. But now they were reeling and nervous, and that in itself was dangerous.

Demon sat across from me, pensive. If he was tense, he wasn't showing it, which was unusual for him. But maybe it was just the addition of Ciara in his life, the only person to tame his temper. And I couldn't say I wasn't jealous. That I'd watched him change, watch him evolve with his girl by his side. And suddenly he didn't depend on the club anymore. Maybe that was what I needed, a distraction? A beautiful distraction of light bronze hair and blue-green eyes.

"Indie!" Fury's voice pulled me from the inside of my head.

"Sorry, what?"

"How's Ste?"

"He's still alive," I shrugged, wishing I was following the path of my own fantasy and not being forced to update the club about how their president was doing. "The chest infection isn't clearing. It's not looking good."

The men at the table all reacted. A curt nod of acknowledgement from Big Red, a faint smile from Magnet, his face full of sympathy and his own pain, and the rest glanced at each other, their eyes diverted from me, as if looking at me and acknowledging my words was too much to bear. They should be on the fucking end of watching it all play out. Of hearing the incessant bleeping of those fucking machines, and not knowing whether the next alarm was going to signal the death of your own father, even though you knew it was coming.

"What news about the garage?" I asked the room, changing the subject, my head throbbing under the effort of being the leader they wanted in my father's absence.

Magnet glanced at Fury, a wordless exchange between them.

"Come on then, let's have it," I prompted.

"Seems we've got a street gang on our asses now as well," Fury started. "The break-in at your place? We couldn't get anything from the plates of the truck and bike. Fakes. Our contact couldn't trace them anywhere. And that same truck and the bike were seen down the street from where they'd put Beanz' windows out the night before."

"Seems the fuckers are thick, too. They got out at Beanz's place and yours and we could pick them up on camera," Magnet continued excitedly. "More than one of them had the same tattoo. A playing card on their necks below their ears. An ace."

"What the fuck do they want with us?" I asked the room, the blank faces and shrugs in reply, answering my question.

I nipped the bridge of my nose, closing my eyes, thinking. But all I could see behind my eyes was a swirl of shadows, of hate and fatigue. All we needed now was a street gang on our tails. Another thing to be looking over our shoulders for. And I had no idea why they'd be targeting us. Did the stupid fuckers not know who we were and what we could do?

"They're called the Aces," Magnet continued. I rolled my eyes.

"Never heard of them," Demon grunted from across the side of the table.

"They're small fry," Magnet continued. "They were the ones that hit up the cutting house a few months back."

"And why the fuck have we not dealt with them before now, then?"

My tiredness was pouring into the cracks in my persona. No one answered, instead each person round the table glancing at one another, hoping someone would offer themselves up as tribute for my wrath.

"Think we were too busy dealing with Demon's shit, Indie. They hit us just before Demon laid out the Notorious President," Fury answered, and I watched Demon shoot him a look.

"And then we got caught up with burying the bodies of the Polish mafia," Magnet added, pushing Demon further under the bus.

"Fuck's sake. This is the last thing we need. A biker war, the Mafia after our arses and some annoying fucking street gang giving us grief."

"I don't know what beef they've got was us, but don't think it'll take us long just to extinguish them, if that's what you want to do Indie?" Big Red offered.

The question was for me, the future of the club right now in my hands. As Vice President, it was down to me to make that call. But I wasn't a cold-blooded murderer, not like my father. Yet I was no saint. There was still blood on my hands. The many bodies I'd disposed of over the years were testament to that.

"Why don't we send the prospects with some of the younger members?" Fury suggested. "Rough them up a bit. Introduce them to who they're dealing with?"

But sending the prospects meant pulling Tony from his sentry duty and I didn't want to leave Emmie unwatched.

I shook my head. "No. Demon will do it."

Demon flashed me a look across the table, and I shrugged in response, inviting any challenge that he had. But he said nothing.

"I want them taught a lesson," I spoke directly to Demon. "I want them to know who the Kings are. I want them to get the full feel of what we do, and the only person for that job is Demon. Magnet, Fury, Bill and Ben," I turned towards the Twins now. "You provide back-up. Demon do your thing, break some bones, smash some skulls, but don't kill anyone. The last thing we need is the police on our arses as well."

Fury tensed, something suddenly serious on his face, catching my eye, an instruction I understood without him saying anything. I dismissed the meeting, beckoning to Fury to stay, and we watched everyone else trudge out.

"What is it?" I asked, wondering what the next bit of good news was going to be.

"Something you ought to know," he said when the room settled into silence.

I could feel the apprehension spilling off him, unease clear on his face.

"Fuck's sake, spit it out, Fury."

"Emmie's ex."

"What about him?" I asked, now suddenly interested in what Fury had to say.

"He runs with the aces, Indie. You still want that instruction you just gave to stand?"

Now that order I gave was no longer just business. And now I wanted that bastard to know I was part of them. Part of one of the biggest MCs in the north of England that they'd just tried to fuck over. And I wanted to take the buffer off Demon and let him go all out. But it was Emmie's ex, and the father of her children. And I wasn't sure how easy that would sit with her if she knew I'd had him murdered. I thought for a moment, pondering over my options. But it wouldn't take a murder. When I'd broke his nose the other night in the garage, he and his mates had fled like a bunch of pussies. And that seemed to be the extent of the Aces. I didn't think Demon would even need to break any bones to get the point across.

"No. We're not changing tack. Fury, tell Demon. Make sure the message is put across. But don't kill anyone and definitely no one that looks like Emmie's ex."

Chapter Thirteen

Emmie

"Hey," Ste croaked.

"How're you feeling today?" I asked, moving round to his bedside.

"Like death warmed up here."

The twinkle in his eyes was there still, not as bright, not with as much energy, but it was still there. But that energy didn't quite reach his voice. Ste had stabilised over the last two days, the antibiotics finally winning over the stubborn infection that had ravaged his body, weak from the cancer. His skin was greyer than I had ever seen it, like a living corpse, and his eyes had sunken into his face, dark bags of skin sagging underneath. Cheekbones jutted out at an angle, more prominent than ever before, and if it hadn't been for the white goatee covering his chin, he would have looked almost skeletal.

I'd seen this so often. Patients ready to be taken, their bodies ready to give over to death but fighting out the last few moments as they clung to life. Ste's body had brought one more fight, the last stand in defiance of the disease, waking in the early hours of one morning when I was on the night shift. The old man was confused at first and then almost disappointed when he realised the sterility of a hospital still surrounded him, connected to tubes and wires, and still in pain. But despite all that, there was a smile for me when he came to, when we'd removed the intubation that had by now scarred his lungs even more.

I'd worked nights the last four or five days, Lily and Luke at my mother's and Gaz nowhere to be seen. Yet the peace was unsettling, wondering when he would be back, knowing that this wasn't forever and that this would never last.

Morning was breaking over the east, a red-orange glow splitting the darkness in two, the nights growing longer day by day. And every night a different car sat outside my house, another member of Indie's bike club keeping an eye on me. The twenty-four-hour vigil continuing, someone always nearby, never moving far from my doorstep, following me into work and waiting for me. They never approached, never spoke, made no connection with me whatsoever. I always knew they were there watching, and despite the weirdness of it all, I felt oddly calm and protected. With no Gaz to continue to take my money off me nearly every payday, my bank account looked the healthiest it had ever been in the last few months and years. There was food in my fridge, and hot water when I needed it. But there was no Indie.

I'd not seen or heard from him over the last few days, a continual period on nights not helping. Each day led to new disappointment, each day when I didn't see him at work, or watching me from outside my house.

This morning was colder and darker, autumn fighting winter but losing every day. The darkness felt overwhelming today, a tiredness creeping through my bones from continued night shifts and time spent without my kids. And for the first time, there was no car parked in the street, no one watching over me. Disappointment dealt me a heavy blow, a blunt force trauma, and a sudden pang of nausea. Maybe they'd just been busy? Maybe they'd all had something else to do and just tonight they couldn't be here? It was such a treacherous emotion, hope. Always there to cheer you up and then deflate you in a second. Unrealistic. Unwelcome. Uncertain.

Stepping out of the car into the fading night, I twisted the key in the lock, the electric central locking no longer working. I checked my surroundings, the hostility of the darkness making me feel vulnerable, agitating my nerve endings. I stared left and then right, searching in the shadows, watching for movement, for shadows moving in shadows. Everyone was sleeping except for me.

The garden gate was open when I got to it, the first sign of something not right. I always shut my gate. Always. I swallowed, pulling myself together, searching for the rational in my irrational. Someone might have pushed something through the letterbox, junk mail or something, and then left the gate open. A flicker of movement at the door caught my eye, shadows resonating against each other, worry expanding within me again.

I took a step back, ready to bolt, my brain lagging.

"Emmie, it's okay. It's just me."

The voice was low, but in the rising panic that filled my head, I couldn't think. I stepped backwards again, clutching my bag against me, waiting for the first blow to come, for that punishment I knew he would deal out at the first chance he got. And now, without them watching, he had that chance.

"Emmie, Spuggy, it's me. It's Indie. It's okay."

My heart drummed against my chest, the frantic rhythm not slowing. Even now, he'd identified himself. Yet as the panic faded, and the fog that filled my brain cleared, I could make him out in the shadows. He stepped closer, the dull streetlight just lighting him enough to show the leather trousers pulled tight round his legs and the black jacket with a leather waistcoat over the top. It was just Indie. Dressed head to toe in leather, tall and captivating, my eyes scanning over him, not taking anything in, but seeing everything, from the way the arms of the jacket pulled tight over the biceps, to the way the leather gathered at his groin.

"What are you doing here?" I asked when my ability to speak returned.

"Just thought I'd call in to see you."

"At 4 o'clock in the morning?"

"Yeah, well, I guess I'd catch you after you finish work."

"How do you know I finish work at this time?"

Indie looked over my shoulder pointedly into the empty street.

"I have had people watching you 24/7, remember? Realised you were on night shift this week when I didn't see you at the hospital and then my guys said you weren't coming home till the early hours. I can go?"

No. I didn't want that, no matter how stalkery that all sounded right now. I'd never been one to make good decisions. I cocked my head, stepping forward and pushing my key into the lock, and nudging the bottom of the swollen door with my foot.

The light inside the hallway snapped on, spilling out over the step outside, lighting up Indie's features as I turned slightly, just inside the doorway. His greying hair was brushed to the side as usual, a couple of strands at the front knocked out of place. The cleft on his chin was visible again, his face almost freshly shaved, as fresh as the smell of him. The light caught on something in his hands, something I'd not seen in the shadows. He smiled at me with a lopsided grin, but with the hint of nervousness on his face, and then shrugged, pushing the bunch of flowers towards me.

"I don't know if you like flowers, but anyway, I just wanted to say thank you for looking after me the other night."

He shrugged again, as if he was expecting some sort of rejection. The bunch of flowers suspended between us. I stared at them, at the mix of pinks and whites, of lilies and chrysanthemums. And roses. The same mix and colours as Gaz used to buy for me. After he'd struck me for the first time. After he split my lip for the first time. After he blacked my eye for the first time. Then the flowers stopped coming, but the beatings didn't. And there were no flowers the first time he broke my nose, or after he knocked me unconscious, or when he split my lip open the second and third times.

Indie winced, sensing my reluctance, and I sensed his disappointment.

"Sorry, I didn't mean to offend you."

"You didn't, Indie. I'm just not used to flowers as a nice gesture, that's all."

He cocked his head sideways, and I could see the question poised on his lips. A question I didn't want to answer.

"Thank you. They're lovely," I whispered, the words sticking in my throat. "Come in."

He followed behind me, forcing the swollen door back into its frame, locking us out of the fading shadows, dawn breaking over the east. I moved to the sink, rummaging underneath for a worn vase.

"What you did for me the other night, Emmie. I really appreciate it. I couldn't have let any of the club see me like that."

His voice came from behind me.

"Why?" I asked, turning tentatively, because every time I was this close to him, something happened to me.

"Because it's just not what we do."

"Again, why?"

"Because of my rank."

"Rank. I thought it was a bike club? That sounds more like the army."

His face flickered, a flash of darkness crossing his eyes.

"Vice President," he answered. "And with my father on his death bed, right now I'm more or less the president."

I stared at him, not following.

"I don't get why that means you can't show emotion when your own father's dying?"

Those words were so much harsher than I'd intended, tiredness and confusion a stubborn cocktail. Indie frowned slightly, a battle going on behind his brown eyes. But instead of answering my question, he stepped forward, pushing his hand behind my head, his fingers entangling into my hair and the next thing I knew, his lips were over mine. Moving against me, softly at first, a tentative flick of his tongue teasing at my flesh. And for a moment, I froze, unable to really process what was going on. Or why he would suddenly kiss me.

His lips were careful, moving against me slowly and gently, waiting for me. Waiting for me to pull away or join in. I should pull away. Make a sensible choice for once in my life. But why change a habit now? And so, I parted my lips, feeling the tip of his tongue stroke across mine, and his hand tighten against the back of my head. I kissed him back. Slowly, to match his pace. Tentatively, to match his caution. Waiting.

He stepped in closer, a little nudge backwards, jamming my back against the edge of the sink. I exhaled, my mouth opening just that bit more, and his tongue immediately stole the space. And now the kiss was urgent. Strong lips plucking mine, his tongue pushing in and out of my mouth as mine struggled to keep up with him. His other hand cupped my head, pulling me closer. No means to escape. But I didn't want to escape. I wanted more.

More of the surging heat rushing my body, filling every part of me from my toes to my finger ends. A pulsing, sudden need. A feeling that was only a faint memory, flooding my brain like a flashback.

I closed my eyes, relishing. My own hands snaking around his waist, feeling for the edge of the leather jacket and sneaking my fingertips underneath. His lips still moved against me, the movement of his tongue bringing my insides to boiling point, and I pushed my hands under his jacket a little more. His stomach was hard underneath, as I knew it would be after I'd seen what I had the other morning. He stilled suddenly, his tongue drawing back, but his lips still touching mine.

"Steady little Spuggy," he warned, breathing against my mouth, stilling my hands that were peeling up his t-shirt, working my way towards his bare flesh. "Don't make me lose control, please?" He rasped, sucking against my bottom lip and making my legs instantly jelly.

And now suddenly I wanted to see what losing control looked like.

He kissed me again, more gently now. The sudden rush of fervour gone. Just a little nibble along my bottom lip. But the ember burning deep in my stomach ignited in a fury of flames and a sudden explosion of heat wracked my core. The groan fell from my lips before I'd even known there was one to stop and I pushed my hands fully under his t-shirt, feeling the warmth of his skin and the resistance of muscle underneath.

There was a growl, a rich vibration against my mouth and he stepped in further, pushing himself against me, the edge of the sink biting into my back. But I didn't care. Didn't care that I barely knew the man devouring me in my kitchen, a new sensation building between my legs. I could feel the bulge of him against me now. Pushed into my leg, as his lips pulled down my neck, the stubble of his chin scratching and his lips soothing, red-hot tingles pulsing down my skin with every tiny movement.

And then he stopped, his lips poised against my throat, the tip of his tongue just there on my skin but not moving. And between my legs I pulsed, hot and heavy. Then he peeled away from my neck, his lips dragging against mine momentarily, as I waited, my mouth poised open, waiting for him. He didn't kiss me again, instead holding my head to his, his forehead pushed to mine, his breaths coming in heavy gasps.

Chapter Fourteen

Indie

I stopped then, as suddenly as I started, pulling myself from where my lips wanted to suck on the gentle skin of her neck until she sank to her knees. Gripping her head, desperately trying to regain control, I rested my forehead against hers. Her fingernails scratched at my stomach, sending a burning, furious need straight to my dick that was jammed painfully against my leather bike trousers. And suddenly her fingers relaxed, unsure of what to do next, her breathing coming in sharp bursts like she'd been running a race. I wanted to trail over the softness of her throat, to where her pulse thumped against her skin and back to those pink lips that were swollen from where I'd pulled and plucked and sucked. I wanted to devour her, needed to devour her. But I was scared to hurt her, and worried I'd scare her.

So instead, I stopped, ignoring the fire licking at my belly, the tension in my balls, and the need to spin her around and fuck her against the sink. And my stomach still sparked, just like it had the first time I'd set eyes on her mere weeks ago.

I stepped back slightly, gazing into her eyes. Darkened eyes, like the Mediterranean during a storm. My thumb felt over her cheek, still cupping her head, strands of apricot brushing the backs of my hands. I trailed it across her tight skin, tracing a line over her freckles like I was joining the dots. She gazed back at me, the storm in her eyes showing no sign of settling, and my thumb brushed over her lips, pushing down over the flesh of the bottom. She moved her mouth, raking her teeth over the tip of my thumb, grazing the skin until there was a tiny prick of pain. Delicious pain. And now I had to think about something else. About anything else, to stop me picking up from where I left off.

Emmie's breath had barely slowed, still inconsistent, ragged. I knew what I was doing to her right now. And I knew where I could take this to.

Where I wanted to take it to. But I wouldn't do that. Instead, I stood enjoying the electric charge between our bodies. I closed my eyes again, dropping my forehead back to hers, listening to her breathe, waiting for the ability to regain control.

And eventually stepping back, I put some space between us, before the control I had just regained left me again.

"What's wrong?" Emmie asked, her voice weak, uncertain.

"I'm sorry, Emmie."

She just stared, not understanding. Fuck. I know how it looked. I wasn't trying to be an arse, in fact, that was exactly what I was trying to avoid.

"I didn't mean to be so forward. I didn't mean to take advantage of you. I'm so much older…"

"I'm an adult, Indie. Not a kid. I know you're older than me. Is that what bothers you?"

"No. Yes. Well, sort of."

She stood watching me, her arms cradled around herself.

“I don’t mind,” she whispered, her eyes dropping to her feet.

“Don’t mind?”

“Your age, Indie. An age gap doesn’t bother me.”

But maybe it bothered me. That I might take advantage of her inexperience.

“Does it worry you?” she asked again, her eyes tracking up my body, pausing a moment at my groin, where my hard-on still fought against the tight leather. And now I could see the hurt on her face.

I stepped back towards her, not missing the sudden flinch that she tried to hide. Cupping her face again, I tilted her head up, forcing her eyes to meet mine. Because I needed to see the reaction when I told her my age. When I made her realise how much older I was than her. And how we shouldn’t be doing this, even though it was all I had thought about since the moment I had met her.

“Emmie, I’m forty-eight.”

Her eyes didn’t flicker. Not once.

“And I’m twenty-nine, Indie. I’m not a kid.”

“That’s a nineteen-year age-gap, Spuggy.”

She shrugged; her eyes still fixed on mine. Her beautiful lips were still pink where I’d ravished her mouth, pulling the blood to the surface.

“That means nothing to me.”

“Why?”

“Because I like you.”

Her teeth moved over her bottom lip, raking at the flesh nervously. Squeezing my eyes shut, I inhaled, stealing a few seconds to slow things down. Slow the millions of thoughts racing through my brain, ricocheting off the shell that was my skull and bouncing back again, only to collide with each other and rebound.

“That isn’t always a reason to continue, Emmie. You’re so young. You have your whole life ahead of you.”

She sighed, her eyes dropping back to her feet. But when she looked up at me again, the stormy darkness had cleared and those Mediterranean jewels shone. But it wasn’t because of the twinkle of happiness, but the gloss of tears, the exact opposite.

“Spuggy? What’s wrong? What did I say?”

“Those words,” she whispered. “People say that to me all the time. But they just don’t understand.”

“Then make me understand.”

I moved my hands around her waist, picking her up, almost throwing her up in the air. She was so light. I propped her on the bench, my eyes meeting hers. Eye to eye, no excuse not to look at me. She bit that lip again, trying to still the little waver of emotion.

“Make me understand, Emmie,” I prodded.

“I met him when I was fifteen. He was older, only a couple of years.”

“How many?”

“He was nineteen. And he was the first boy to notice me. To like the colour of my hair and the freckles on my face. He didn’t seem to care I didn’t have the boobs that the other girls in my year did, or the hips, or that I was six stone wet through. I thought he just liked me.

"He seemed so gentle. So attentive. He was there to pick me up from school, took me out. Even bought my alcohol for me."

"Course he did, Spuggy. You were underage."

"But I loved the attention. I always thought I was ugly. And he was the first boy to tell me I wasn't," she paused, unable to look away and those Mediterranean greens stared straight into me. "The only man who ever has, even if that all changed later on. We waited, you know, to do it."

"He waited till you were sixteen, huh?"

Emmie nodded.

"And things were great for a while. Even though my mam hated him. Guess she saw what I couldn't. She tried to make me break up with him. Kept telling me I 'had my whole life ahead of me'. And when eventually I didn't stop seeing him, she kicked me out. She told me I couldn't live under her roof if I didn't follow her rules, and one of those was to stop seeing Gaz."

I edged forward, her knees now just brushing my thighs, trying to ignore the increasing closeness. Emmie paused, watching me closely.

"Go on," I urged.

"So, we got a flat. It was tiny. A one-bedroom thing. But it was ours. Or at least for a while. I don't know when it happened. I can't point to when it all changed. It must have been happening gradually, but suddenly I was at home doing all the housework, cooking all the meals, my entire wage going on the rent and the food. I'd got sick one day. Sick of him going straight out with his mates after work, coming home drunk and doing it all over again the next day. So, I confronted him."

She paused, taking a breath, and so did I, preparing myself because I had a pretty good idea where this was all headed. And I wasn't going to like it.

"It was a stupid thing to do. I'd waited a couple of days. Trying to find a time when he'd come straight home without going to the pub first, but there hadn't been one. So, this one night, I just came out with it. He said nothing. Not a thing, just stood and stared at me for what felt like minutes. And then, suddenly, he struck me. It was a slap. Nothing much. But it stung, the shock probably hurting more."

I could feel the pain in those words in my stomach. A deep, rumbling anger. A resonating despair.

"That was it for a while. He brought me flowers the next day. Came straight home from work. Think he might even have washed the dishes. And I remember the slap had been worth it. Because he'd changed. Had done something about it. But then, just a few weeks after, he was late home again. I said nothing this time. Not a thing. But he was ready to pick a fight. And I tried to avoid it. I really did. He didn't hit me this time. It was just a push. But I tripped over a shoe on the floor and fell pretty heavily. He was so sorry. And the next day he brought me flowers.

"There were a few more bunches of flowers after that," she mumbled, and I knew what she was telling me. "Then eventually they stopped. And then suddenly I was pregnant. I was nineteen. I had my whole life ahead of me. And now I was carrying his child. Things got better for a while. He seemed to have changed. He was excited. Excited to be a daddy. We got this house from the council and suddenly we were grown-ups.

“His excitement didn’t last long. I was seven months pregnant when he gave me a black eye. I can’t even remember what it was for. I hid it from the midwife. Cancelled an appointment, waiting for it to fade. But it was still there the next week, green and yellow, like mould, and I didn’t have enough make-up to cover it. There wasn’t money left in the budget for me to buy make-up.”

I was listening. But it was so fucking hard. Each word she spoke made me angrier and angrier, and the knife blade of emotion wedged in my gut turned a little more.

“When Luke was born, Gary improved. Just for a few months. Suddenly, he was the doting dad, desperate to show his son off. Show him off to his mates - gang mates, that is. By now he was running with a gang, dealing drugs and handling stolen goods. I wanted him to stop. But there was no way I was going to ask him to. Yet that didn’t stop him from hitting me. And soon he didn’t even wait for an excuse.”

I couldn’t bear anymore. I didn’t want to hear any more of this. I nudged at her legs, and she took the hint, opening them wider, allowing me to step inside them. I slid my hand around her jaw, gently, slowly, and this time she didn't flinch, only giving me a weak, sad smile.

"I'm so sorry you've been through all that, Spuggy. You're free of him now. I promise."

"Mmmm," was all she answered, and I could see the disbelief on her face.

Nothing I could say would make her believe that. But he'd been warned not to come anywhere near her again. And after the kicking Demon had given him, he would have to be suicidal to even try.

"Now, about that age-gap you were talking about," her voice almost sang in the atmosphere, and I knew this conversation hadn't finished. I knew there was more. But was happy to end it for now. Because if I heard any more this morning, I might just finish what we'd started on Gaz the other night. Only this time I wouldn't leave him with just a broken nose and some sore ribs.

Chapter Fifteen

Emmie

Indie's expression was as stoic as usual, even if his eyes hinted at something else. He'd listened intently, the vein in his neck becoming more and more prominent. I could have gone on all night, telling him the whole story. But I didn't want to talk anymore. I wanted him to kiss me. I wanted him to make me forget. Because when I was with him, I forgot, even for a moment, but it was enough.

He'd wriggled between my legs now, his thighs gently pushed inside of mine. His hand cupped around the back of my head. And now I willed him to kiss me again, to sate this feeling inside of me, of burning pressure. My eyes searched his, the deep rich brown, engulfed in kindness, even when his face was hard and serious.

“Spuggy,” he whispered, his fingers grazing the back of my head, a shiver erupting from the spot.

“Why do you call me that, Indie?”

“Spuggy?”

I nodded.

“It means sparrow. A little bird.”

“I know.”

“You remind me of a sparrow.”

“How?”

“The first day I saw you, watching you peck at your food. You were like a little bird. But you weren’t fragile, you were resilient and tenacious. I could see that by watching you. Like a sparrow. So now, you’re my Spuggy.”

I smiled, the warmth creeping over my skin, penetrating my layers and jolting me straight into my heart.

Indy grazed the back of my head with his fingers, the movement sending a shiver down my spine and an urge to close my eyes and just enjoy the closeness. The moment lasted just for a few seconds before it was washed away with that continual loneliness.

"I'm older, Emmie," he said, suddenly disturbing the gentle silence. "Much older."

The last sentence was a whisper, strained and reluctant.

"It's not a big deal. Not to me."

"But it is to me, little sparrow."

"Why?"

"I don't want to take advantage of you."

"And how would you do that?" My voice was breathy, betraying the intention behind my words.

His eyes focused on mine just for a moment. Intense brown eyes. Indie's jaw clenched, a fleeting moment that he lost his usual control, before it was firmly replaced.

"I really could find many ways to take advantage of you."

Those words hit me like a steam train, sending my stomach clenching before spiralling out of control, and dropping deep down inside my body. He spread that pressurised tingle, morphing into a deep ache, and a deep need. The spark of pain at my lip distracted me for a moment, but that moment was gone too quickly and the heat in my stomach intensified. I needed to get off this bench.

Indie dropped his hand from my head, and I felt suddenly exposed, the chill of the autumn morning rushing to invade the space. I wanted to take it and put it back, my fingers brushing the back of his hand as it moved away from me. The tone of his eyes changed, and even though I stared into them, I couldn't work out exactly what I had just seen. Then his eyes dropped to the floor, hidden from my gaze.

"I should go," he said, his voice strained.

Disappointment hit harder than I had expected, stalling my heart for a fraction of a second, my chest tightening as though I were on the edge of a panic attack. And now this felt like rejection, that he didn't want to be here with me. I dropped my eyes to the floor, both of us now studying the ageing laminate.

Fingers smoothed under my chin, tipping my face.

"I don't mean to push you away," Indie's voice was careful, gentle, but raspy. "But I need to know you're comfortable with this."

"Because you're not?" I whispered, unsure whether I wanted the answer. Or whether I could cope with it if he even gave it.

Indie pursed his lips, and the next drop of dread hit my stomach. His hands moved, and desperately I tried to diffuse the little spark of fear that the sudden movement ignited, my nails digging into the kitchen bench beneath me. His fingers were rough against my cheeks, hands full of years of hard work.

"No, Spuggy. Because someone has taken advantage of you nearly your whole life. And I want you to know, despite our age differences, I would never do that to you."

"I know that."

"You don't little sparrow. You can't know that just because I told you. I need to show you."

"Then show me," the strangled whisper sounded desperate, and an embarrassed heat rose to my cheeks. "I've a day off tomorrow."

For a moment, no one moved. Indie's hands stayed on my cheeks, his deep brown eyes boring into mine as we now stared silently at each other. Maybe I'd been too forward. Too desperate. But then the intensity in his eyes cleared, and his mouth flickered, a thin smile appearing.

"In that case, Spuggy," he said, "I'll see you tomorrow."

The kiss on my forehead was light and chaste. And it was the most meaningful thing. He stepped away from me, smiling gently, and then turned, leaving me alone in the kitchen, the door thumping into place. The spot on my forehead was hot, reminding me where his lips had been.

*****

"Mam! Mam! You're burning my toast!" Luke shouted, his voice filled with annoyance.

"Shit." I winced, glancing round to see if either of the kids had heard me.

Luke sat scowling as I plucked the blackened toast from the toaster and tossed it in the bin, where it bounced off the side and dropped to the floor.

"God's sake."

Daisy bounded forwards, reaching the cremated bread before I could get it, grabbing both slices and dashing off to the lounge where she was probably now spluttering burnt crumbs all over my carpet. I stood at the bench, pinching the bridge of my nose, and mentally counting to ten.

"What's wrong, mam?" Lily's little voice pierced the tiredness engulfing my system and shorting my fuse.

"Just burnt the toast, baby," I paused, looking at the concern on her sweet little face. She was getting older. Not so oblivious to the way I behaved, or the feelings I gave off. She frowned. "It's nothing, I'm just tired."

"Can we stay home with you today?"

"I'm not staying here all day," Luke chipped in. "This house is boring."

I ignored him. Ignored the guilt that inflamed in my stomach.

"No baby. It's a school day."

"I don't want to go to school," Lily whined. "I want to stay here with you, Mammy. I miss you."

It had been days since I'd seen them properly, with a pattern of night shifts this week and twilight shifts the week previous. My mother had dropped the kids off at 6.30 this morning, all dressed and ready for school before she herself went off to work. And now, as I stood watching Lily slurp the remnants of milk out of her bowl and Luke finish another round of toast as if he hadn't eaten for weeks, that threat of guilt from earlier hit me again. Only this time, it had doubled.

Daisy's tail knocked at my legs painfully, just happy to be in our company, all of us together. It had been a long time. A long time since I could let them have second and thirds at breakfast, not knowing where the next pound was going to come from. I was far from rich these last two weeks, but at least I was keeping what I'd earned. If it kept up, I might afford some new toys for them at Christmas, rather than the ones I bought from a charity shop.

And there it was again, the spear of dread. Punishing me for every hopeful thought. For every thought that wasn't worry and despair, reminding me that hope wasn't a good emotion, just raised expectations before cruelly cutting you back down.

I glanced at the clock on the dashboard of the car, the display showing we were ahead of time, but that time we'd made, was quickly going to be used up as I scanned the streets for a parking place closer to the school gates. The morning rain had misted a thin coating on the pavements, my headlights reflecting on the slippy sheen. And it seemed everyone had taken their car to the school, ditching walking for staying dry.

"You've parked miles away," Luke complained.

"There was nowhere else."

I turned the engine off, stepping out into the thin drizzle as the morning cleared.

"Drive to the gates, Mam. I'll get out there."

"I can't get near the gates, Luke. Just get out of the car, please."

Luke folded his hands across his chest, light blue eyes staring at me defiantly, and for a moment he was so much like his father I forgot who I was looking at.

"J…just get out." I stammered, a sudden pang of fear rushing at me, making me doubt myself.

When I looked back at the boy in the car, the man I thought I saw staring at me had dissolved, the boy's eyes searching mine, confusion replacing his earlier stubbornness. I shook my head. "Just get out," I whispered.

A little hand pushed into mine, warm against my palm, the same light-blue eyes looking up at me. She smiled happily.

"You haven't taken us to school for ages, Mammy," her little voice brightened up the dull morning.

Luke skulked along beside us, dragging his feet, each step scuffing another layer of leather off the toes, each stride another step closer to needing a new pair of shoes. I stood at the back of the yard, well away from the other parents, watching the kids form a line, standing patiently till the doors opened and they were ushered inside in the same formation. And then, as soon as the big glass doors had consumed them, I left, keeping my eyes fixed on the ground, leaving chances of small talk to a minimum. Ignoring the creep of loneliness and the acknowledgement of no friends. Ignoring, at least for a few hours, that Gary had taken everything away from me.

I pulled up behind the big black and chrome bike; the engine vibrating so much I thought I could feel it through my car tyres. Indie turned slightly, watching me from over his shoulder. His bike jacket was different today, something adorning the leather. Another leather vest with an embroidered motif on the back. I couldn't make it out at first. But as he straightened up and the deep purr of the bike stopped, I could see it more clearly. Three crowned skulls, their mouths hanging open in a hideous laugh. The words the Northern Kings MC, Newcastle Upon Tyne, written on the back.

Chapter Sixteen

Indie

I watched the little silver car roll to a stop on the curbside. The engine skipped a beat, not keeping the continuous purr, more of a sore throat and a cough. The exhaust rattled side to side; I didn't need to look at it to know half of it was dropping off. The little silver piece of scrap came to an absolute stop, the travel of the handbrake clicking up four notches too far.

I let the bike settle to the left, just in front of Emmie's car, watching it over my shoulder. It was still early after a night of little sleep. A night I'd spent twisting and turning, wondering whether pursuing her, this, was the right thing. Finally, I settled on being selfish, that this, her, was what I wanted.

"Thought we'd get breakfast," I said to her, patting the seat behind me.

She looked at my hand, then looked back at me.

"I don't have a helmet," she answered.

"Figured you wouldn't. Came prepared."

I moved my leg over the bike, sliding the visor off the handlebar where I'd hung it, before moving to the pannier and pulling out a black leather bike jacket. Holding the jacket, I waited for her to slide an arm in. The leather was stiff, not worn in years, and the zip stuck just over her navel.

"Indie, I think I'm too fat for this."

"Bollocks, are you fat." I nipped the edges of the jacket together, holding it in one hand and pulling at the zip with another, trying not to think about where my hands were, or it was gonna be one uncomfortable ride through Northumberland.

Climbing back onto the bike, I beckoned her with my head.

"I don't know about this, Indie," she said, her voice muffled behind the visor of the helmet she wore.

"I promise I'm not gonna let you fall off."

She stood a little longer, contemplating the bike, and then slowly she slid her leg over. Emmie wobbled instantly, panicking, grabbing at me. I pulled her arms around my waist and moved the bike off the kickstand, slowly centering it. Then, tapping the side of her leg, I turned the engine on, the bike fired up beneath us. Emmie's arms tightened around me, pulling herself into my back, and before she could change her mind, I glided forward.

The bike roared, the wind battered the visor of my helmet, a chilly morning doing all it could before the autumn sun kicked its ass back to the shadows. Emmie had hugged me for the last hour, her arms wrapped firmly around me, tightening up every time we took a sharper corner, or every time I opened the throttle, driving the bike past the cagers going painfully slow in front of us.

It was nice to have someone behind me, my back almost warm through the leathers as her body snuggled against mine. I could have gone for miles.

Just kept riding, till we could go no further north. Just like my cousin had done those years before. Rode north and north again with his woman on the back. The ultimate freedom. No club. No patch. No responsibility. Just the wind rushing his skin and a good woman with him. I'd been jealous then, the embers still dying now. But maybe with Emmie, I was one step closer to doing all that.

And I could leave the club behind. Leave someone else to deal with what was to come, deal with the wolf at our door. Because I didn't think I had the stomach for it. Not that I ever had, just the ability to shut out the bad bits. To compartmentalise so well that no one could get to those bits. Not even me. Yet with that, all sense of happiness had wicked away. All sense of meaning. And I just moved from year to year, from one birthday to the next with meaningless indirection.

Until now.

I should grieve more than I was. I should let myself be consumed by it all. Like I had those first days after his diagnosis. When he was back and forwards to hospital. When I wasn't sure if this was the end. Just a few months ago, I'd wanted to give in to that overwhelming darkness. To the muddy depths that pulled me deeper. Until Emmie. And now I wanted to wake up the next day.

I stroked over the hand that curled around my body, feeling her fingers relax slightly over the top of my leathers. I should just keep riding. But I'd promised her breakfast. So, I turned off the road that would have taken me to Scotland and rode out towards the sea.

The tide was just going out, still swamping the land with water as we stopped at the end of the road, looking out towards the horizon. Emmie's arms relaxed from around me, tightening instantly as the bike lurched to the side. Pushing my visor up, I patted her hand.

"It's ok, Spuggy. I won't let you fall." And I meant that in so many more ways than the literal.

The bike rested against the stand, the engine rumbling underneath us, and even though I loved the sound of its voice, I turned it off.

"Holy Island?" Emmie shouted through her visor.

Carefully, I peeled her arms from around me, sliding off the bike in front of her. She wobbled a moment, not sure what to hold on to, the tilt of the bike pushing her curbside. I reached towards her, sliding her visor up.

“Yes,” I answered. “I can hear you better with this up. But yes, we’re going to Holy Island for breakfast.”

“But the sea?”

“Tide’s moving out. We’ll be able to cross in a few minutes.”

“Is it safe?”

“To cross?”

Emmie nodded.

“Yes. As long as the tide’s going out and not coming in. When it comes in, it comes in quick. See those masts over there?”

She nodded again.

“That’s the only thing that will save you if you get stuck in the tide.”

Emmie followed my hand to the dark sticks in the distance that rose into the sky, and the little hut that sat on the top. There was no part of me that wanted to spend ten hours in a wooden hut in the North Sea waiting for the tide to go back out. But I'd known people who had done it after trying to play 'Billy big balls' and race the sea.

As we stood watching, the tide drew further and further back, eventually exposing the road that led to the little island.

"Hop on, Spuggy. Time for breakfast." I swung my leg over the bike, turning and patting the space on the leather behind me.

"Is it safe yet?" she asked nervously, her eyes fixed on the sea, the first rays of sunlight reflecting off its surface.

"It will clear the causeway in a few minutes. By the time we reach the middle, there'll only be puddles left."

She bit her lip, as if steeling herself, then slotted the visor down, shielding her face, and climbed on behind me.

The bike roared to life, a small row of cars now waiting behind us, and I led the procession over the road, moving carefully over wet sand and puddles, keeping the wheels out of the crops of seaweed which hadn't retreated with the tide. Remnants of the sea flanked the road, gradually sinking away, a reminder that we were crossing on its terms. I never rushed the ride to Holy Island, not unless the tide was fast approaching. Being granted permission by the sea to approach was a grand gesture, one that I acknowledged every time. There was nothing so beautiful as nature and nothing as cruel. Not even my father. I shook the thought from my mind, shooing the darkness away just for a little while. My ray of sunshine was at my back, and although I couldn't see her, I could feel her warmth against my body, even with leather against leather.

The causeway disappeared, the sand covered tarmac clearing to normal road, still wet from the morning's rain, sand and Marram grass replacing the water, easing us up onto the island itself, welcoming and safe. On either side of us the scenery transformed, the thick reedy grasses softening till eventually it morphed into fields of luscious green, nourished by sea air, and sea minerals.

The road wound on. We passed two carparks, ignoring the restricted access signs and the 'residents only' orders, filtering through a street of houses and taking the first left we came to. It was hard to get lost on the island. With so few houses and fewer streets, you could redirect yourself in no time. The little road of six or seven properties ended, and I turned right, the heavy rumble of the big bike echoing loudly off the thick brick walls on either side of the narrow lane and as we pulled up alongside a small crop of weathered stone cottages, every curtain at every window twitched, save for the very cottage right at the very end.

Nearly every other house was a guest house or air BnB on the island now. Very few true residents left. But at a tiny door, at the furthest end of the street, a two bedroomed cottage stood, the only one not offering rooms to rent. I stopped the bike, killing the engine and helping Emmie move from the seat, the bike leaning left, safe on the kickstand.

The door opened before we got there, the tall woman bounding out, her arms outstretched and the widest of grins on her face.

"Indie. My boy!" she bellowed, her messy dungarees hanging from one strap, blue and pink paint smudged on her cheek.

Then she turned, her face quieting, her eyes moving over the petite leather clad frame in front of me. Her smiled faded, a quiet satisfaction replacing the elation of before.

"Emmie, this is my Ma. Ma, Emmie."

Her smile widened, not as animated but warmth radiating from her, and she held out a paint-stained hand towards her.

Chapter Seventeen

Emmie

I didn't need to be introduced to the woman who bounded out the door. Her hair was grey. All different shades, streaks of white, black, dark grey, all melded together. A thick strand fell from her ponytail, swinging past the gentlest light-brown eyes I had ever seen. Her hair and the wrinkles on her skin aged her, but the light in her eyes and the energy she radiated did not.

The revelation that we were standing on his mother's doorstep took me as much by surprise as seeing me did to her. Yet her smile quickly returned, warm and welcoming, and any misgivings about the situation I might have had didn't even get the time to properly form.

"Emmie, this is my Ma. Ma, Emmie."

She held out a hand, splashes of pink and blue, of white and yellow all over her skin. Her finger ends a blur of colours. I stared for a moment, wondering whether I was about to become the same colour as whatever she had been painting. Tentatively, I placed my palm in hers.

"Grace," she introduced herself, and even her voice was colourful. A merge of accents all rolled into one, and not one I could pick out independently. "Come in. I assume you'll be wanting breakfast?"

"Whey aye. Does a bear…"

"Dinna finish that sentence lad if you don't want a clip round the back of ye heed."

The Geordie accent rolled to the fore, dominating the hodge podge of tones I'd heard earlier. And Indie grinned back, his face suddenly boyish, as if all his worries had evaporated out into the surrounding air. And I couldn't help feel the same.

I followed them through the house, my eyes scanning left and right, unable to concentrate on any of the pictures I walked past, each frame almost touching as they took up every space on the walls of the narrow hallway. The cottage opened up at the back to a cosy lounge with wood crackling in the log burner on the far wall. There was only one small sofa, the flowery covered settee pushed back against the wall, making space for the manky dust sheet that almost entirely covered the carpet underneath it, and the easel and table of paints that was set out in the middle of it. The curtains were drawn back, an enormous expanse of window looking out across the island and the little castle that sat on a mound of rock at the very end. Lindisfarne Castle. Even in the distance, the castle atop the rock was breathtaking. And the painting on the easel that stood in front of the windows was just like staring out of the thin paned glass just a few steps away.

"That's incredible," I breathed.

"Fantastic view, isn't it?" Grace answered, taking a cloth and wiping her hands.

"No. I mean the painting." It was one of the most amazing things I had ever seen. But the sky was bluer, and the mound of rock more coloured, with patches of green, and the gentle hue of pinks and purples, of flowers growing into the rock face.

"Why thank you, lass." her voice was like rumbling velvet, gentle, but deep for a woman, and maybe this time I detected a hint of Scottish or Gaelic. "I like this one, Indie," she turned away from me, and then she let out a low chuckle as she walked away through a little door on the other side of the room.

We could just see Lindisfarne Castle from the little kitchen table. Just. If I wriggled a little closer to Indie and peeped over his mother's shoulder, I could just see the castle jutted out on the rock.

"I like a girl who appreciates a good view," Grace broke through my thoughts as I sat staring out through the cottage windows. She tipped the teapot, sloshing the dark brown liquid into the chintzy cup, a drop or two spilling out onto the saucer underneath.

The crockery was an eclectic mix, no one piece matching another, so that the table was a mass of colours, patterns and textures. There was no tablecloth, only placemats on the round oak and the seats were as random as the cups and saucers, different shapes and styles, as if any attempt to comply with order was intentionally thwarted. I fished around the pot of sugar cubes, trying to pick out one just the right size that looked like it would deliver a teaspoon of sweetness to tame the overly strong tea. Beside me, Indie turned a saucer round in front of him, inspecting the pattern with a frown before depositing his unmatched cup back on top of it.

"Indie hates this house and everything in it," Grace said, her voice full of amusement.

"Not everything, Ma. I just don't know why you can't have something that is part of a set."

"Belonging to a set doesn't protect you, Indie." She picked up her own cup, holding it up in front of her eyes, thumbing over the rim, to where there was a huge chunk missing. "This one was part of a set once, and now it's the only one left, tired and used, and broken." She put the cup back on a saucer with a chink, the smile she had worn since we had arrived, gone.

Indie shook his head, and I glanced between them, confused.

"How's your father?" she asked suddenly, a new smile plastered back on her face, but it lacked conviction.

“Still alive,” Indie grunted, his eyes suddenly seeking something on the plate in front of him.

“Stubborn bastard.” Grace shook her head, rising to her feet and sliding the plate out from underneath her.

I stood too, knocking the little wooden chair so that it landed backwards on the floor, the flowery cushioned pad slipping and now hanging from the only string that attached it to the back. Picking up my plate, I tipped the fallen chair upright.

“Leave the dishes, pet. Indie will sort them,” Grace ordered, and I watched him nod, getting to his feet immediately and stacking what was left of the dishes on top of each other before dropping them into the sink.

“He’s well trained, my lad.” Grace winked at me. “Got good manners, despite that stupid emblem he wears on his back.”

*****

Fresh sea air rushed at us from every side as we walked, our backs to the castle on the mound. The narrow streets of elderly houses were crammed full of people, even mid-week.

“It’s a beautiful place,” I said out loud, gazing at the thick stone walls of the properties we passed, every one different from the last.

“It’s even better when the bulk of the tourists have gone home and it’s just the island, its residents and the sea,” he slid an arm around behind me, hugging it around my hips and pulling me in closer, a funny combination of safety and excitement crossing my skin.

“Your mam been here long?”

Indie nodded. “It was her favourite place when I was a kid. We used to come often. She would ride behind my dad and me behind my Uncle Ade.”

“I don’t think I’ve met him?”

“Ade?”

I nodded this time.

“Be difficult. He’s dead.”

“Shit. Sorry.”

“Don’t be. Was a long time ago. My father is the only one left of three brothers. Ade was killed first and then Si, about eleven years ago.

“When my parents split up, she got a hefty chunk of money out of him as part of the divorce. Rightly really, he treated her like shit. Always another woman in the background he was fucking about with. Anyway, she moved out here. She sells her paintings to the tourists and the coffee shops and just does her thing. Never met anyone else. I don’t think there was anyone else for her. Only my dad, and he was an arsehole to her.”

I bit my lip, unable to ignore the venom in Indie’s voice.

“She doesn’t like the bike club either, huh?”

“No. She blames the Kings for half of his behaviour, for how they treated women back then, as a sexual convenience.”

“And are they still like that?”

Indie stopped, turning me into him, pushing his finger under my chin so that he held my gaze prisoner with his.

“No, Spuggy. Not inherently. We…I have worked hard to clean the image up the last few years. I can’t speak for all the guys in the club, hell the twins just love to share.”

“Twins? Share?”

“Trust me, you’ll understand when you meet them,” he rolled those rich brown eyes, sunlight suddenly breaking from behind a cloud, and his face shone, the light glinting off the grey in his hair, making it more silver than ever before, God-like. A God dressed head to toe in black leather.

“I don’t share, Emmie. And I don’t cheat.”

I went to smile in response, but the movement stopped, his lips pressing against mine, a careful kiss, tentative and gentle, the tip of his tongue gently dipping between my lips, teasing and stroking. And under the leather jacket, my body fired up, every millimetre of my being coming alive. I pressed back against him, pushing harder against his mouth, my fingers grazing his neck, the roughness of shaven skin under the flesh of my fingertips. Teasing my fingernails up the back of his neck, I moved over the short, cropped hair until my hands were lost in the thick tufts, pulling our faces together.

And now his lips moved faster, his tongue more determined, probing and stroking against mine, his hand snaking under the leather jacket he’d made me wear. Pulling back slightly, I traced my tongue over his bottom lip, smooth and fleshy, and then I sucked on it, pulling the blood just under the surface where I could taste the tiny hint of metal. Then I nipped at the spot with enough force to hear him wince, and his arms wrap round me tighter, pulling my body into his.

"Careful, Spuggy. Anymore of that and I'll fuck you on the altar in those ruins over there for the entire tourist population to see."

My stomach tightened, my pussy pulsing suddenly, any common sense and preservation I had left, leaving me immediately.

"Yes please," I whispered. "Fuck me anywhere you want."

Indie made a noise. A low vibration that I felt through my mouth and across my tongue, down through my stomach and all the way to the place I wanted him the most.

"One day, little sparrow. One day, I'll sacrifice your pussy to whatever God might hear your cries. But right now, we've an hour's ride home and you have kids to pick up. And whilst I fear the wrath of no God, I can't really say the same about the wrath of your kids."

He smiled at me, warm and rich, his brown eyes lit with an expression I'd never seen on him before. And then he bent forward, placing a kiss on my forehead, warm and soft.

We'd not been on the road long, crossing the causeway and leaving the beautiful sultry island of Lindisfarne behind us. Indie had shifted his weight from side to side, only slightly, but enough that the bike felt like it was making the tiniest alterations underneath us. And then suddenly another bike pulled up alongside, another sitting just behind him, just behind our right flank. The surrounding air was filled with an orchestra of angry growls, of multiple bikes, all vibrating loudly at slightly different times, so it felt like an angry mob of lions chasing us down the road.

The lead rider moved his hand, two gloved fingers pointing at us and then up ahead, before moving them in a sort of wave and now we were moving away, towards a wide layby on the side of the road.

Chapter Eighteen

Indie

We'd not been long off the causeway and on the main road before I saw the tiny flecks of a group of bikes coming up behind me. They rode two abreast, the usual bike club formation, and they were riding fast. My eyes flicked from the road to my mirrors, watching the black dots become forms on bikes, and then those bikes themselves take shape. Familiar shapes. Harleys. And then they were right behind us.

I twisted sideways, trying to move away from Emmie so that my colours were more obvious, but she was clinging too snugly behind me, so that every movement I made, she did too. The bikers sat on my tail, an attempt to pressurise and intimidate, and then broke formation, driving up my right flank.

I caught the side of their patch, of the Nordic runes, and tip of a horned helmet. I knew who they were, but they couldn't make me out. I shifted again, trying to move my back enough that they'd catch enough of my cut that they could see who I was. The lead rider pointed two fingers at me and then the side of the road, moving his hand up and down, signalling for us to pull over.

There was a layby just coming up, wide enough to fit us all in. Me and six of the Valhalla's Vandals. The bike slowed, the engine growling loudly, six others around and behind me, amplifying the sound. I cut my engine, but the bikes surrounding me didn't follow suit. A sign of hostility, of power. Control.

Emmie hugged me tighter, her arms rigid with tension and her head moving from side to side over my back. Patting her hand, I wriggled from her grasp, dragging my leg carefully over the bike and turning my back to show my patch as I took off my helmet. Behind me the engines of the Harleys turned off, a quietness descending around us, a sign these riders had suddenly recognised my colours. When I turned back to them, the first two riders were removing their helmets. A mark of respect between aligned clubs.

"Indie. We didn't see your patch, mate."

"Ya alright, mate," I answered, holding out an arm that was met with a firm clasp from the man standing in front of me, with the shaved head and long dark beard that was greying around the edges. "What ya doing pulling random riders over anyway, Snatch?"

"Tomahawk has had us checking out riders all month."

"Why?"

"He's paranoid, mate. Thinks everyone riding a Harley is the Bloody Hand or one of their new little mates, The Aces."

"The Aces?"

"Aye. Some dodgy little street gang that is running around after the Hand."

"Didn't think they were bikers?"

"You heard of them, then?"

"Aye. Been testing some of our shit the last few weeks. But they aint got bikes, mate."

"Not yet. But there's reports of a load of bike thefts up north. And there's definitely been a few unmarked riders up and down this way. Tomahawk reckons The Hand will be challenging us first."

"Why you? Why not the inner-city clubs?"

"Because we're more isolated. Won't be able to get the backup as quick. It's easier to take us out if they launch an all-out offensive."

The man behind Snatch nodded in agreement.

"I don't reckon we're anywhere near that, mate," I added. "Tomahawk has always been a paranoid fucker. And no one else in the coalition is reporting anything."

"Apart from you guys."

"Just from this street gang, though. We had a run in with them a few months back too. Checked them out but couldn't find owt that would put them in bed with The Hand. I cannit even see why the Hand would be interested in them."

"They're just soldiers. Someone easy and game to send in to create some problems, get folks' back up, to put the cracks in the coalition."

And that resonated with me. Snatch was talking all kinds of sense. Of a reality that I knew was already here, that I was trying to ignore. But despite Tomahawk's paranoia, he was probably right. What better way to infiltrate our interclub relationships than to send out such a small threat that we all took it for granted? We'd certainly done that while we were preoccupied with other things, while I was distracted by my father. And with Emmie. I hadn't seen the Aces testing us. And what messages had I sent back? Barely nothing. A beating here, a broken nose there, and mostly because I wanted Emmie's arsehole ex warned to stay away from her.

Not one of those messages was the show of power we had really needed. A means for them to be scared.

Fuck.

"Tell Tomahawk we'll talk at the rally," I said, signalling this conversation with the Vandals was over as I pulled my helmet back over my head. "Looks like we have a church meeting tonight."

*****

“I didn’t have you down as a churchgoer,” Emmie commented, handing me back the black helmet.”

“Huh?” I was confused, the ride home and thoughts milling through my brain, not helping to grasp what she was saying.

“Church. You said to those bikers back there you had a church meeting tonight.”

I chuckled, the sensation dislodging the weight of worry that had sat on my shoulders all the way home and I reached forward and kissed her forehead, savouring the taste of her skin, of the slight saltiness that had gathered under the helmet, despite the coolness of the breeze that had threatened us on the ride back.

“What?” she asked, her eyes even more beautiful when she wasn’t sure.

“Thank you for just being you, Emmie,” I whispered to the top of her head as I pulled her in against me. “Church just means a meeting of the bike club, Spuggy. It’s just what we call it.”

"So, no prayers, then?"

"Nope. But we don't mind a sacrifice occasionally."

"Don't think that's very religious."

"Just depends which one you're talking about." I shrugged, watching the creep of a frown cross her face. "Anyway, don't you have kids to collect?"

Emmie stepped back, glancing at her watch, that little frown teasing at her lips again.

"Guess it's that time again," she mumbled and then she looked up at me, the sea-green of her eyes twinkling. "I enjoyed today, Indie. Thank you. I've not been on a date, in, well, nearly in forever."

"A date, huh? Is that what that was?" She chewed on her lip, looking suddenly uncertain and now I felt guilty, knowing my words had made her doubt herself. "Today can be whatever you want it to be, Spuggy, as long as there are more days like today. More dates, or whatever you want to call them."

She smiled faintly, but still with that hint of vulnerability. And that pained me to see that even with our closeness growing, that she was still so unsure. Whereas I was never as sure of someone in my life.

*****

"Got pulled over by the Vandals today." I opened the meeting, my eyes scanning the faces that sat around the table. "Just south of Holy Island."

"What were you doing that far north, anyway?" Demon asked, not worried about showing his dissatisfaction at being called to church at short notice.

"That doesn't matter. What does is that they were doing spot checks of unidentified riders."

"How come they couldn't identify you?" Magnet sat across from me. "Thought we'd stood down security level one?"

"My cut was covered."

"How?" Magnet continued, looking as confused as the majority around the table and totally missing the importance.

“Might want to ask him, by who?” Demon teased, leaning back in the wooden seat, and folding his arms across his chest, a challenge on his face.

I sighed. “Emmie was on the back. They couldn’t see my colours.”

“Emmie?” Cade repeated like an unwanted echo, glancing at his brother. The carbon copy sat beside him.

“Yes, Emmie. I took her out for the day, ok. The Vandals pulled me over. Wasn’t till I got off that they could see who I was.”

“Emmie is the lass he’s had the prospects watching these last few weeks,” Demon added, clearly finding my discomfort entertaining. “And the ex of the man whose ribs I broke, a week or two ago.”

“Hope she’s a good fuck then,” Caleb answered, the response more to his brother than to me. “Cos I still have a car he hasn’t fixed yet, and it sounds rough as fuck.”

“Enough. You’re all missing the point.”

“Doesn’t sound like Indie’s lass is, though.”

The room erupted into laughter, and I might have been slightly amused if any of the jibes had been even remotely justified.

"Look. The Vandals are worried." I tried to restore order in the room.

"They're always fucking worried," Demon complained. "Tomahawk spends too much time smoking wacky backy, he's always fucking paranoid some ones coming for him."

"He was right about the Bloody Hand being back though," Fury reminded my brother, shooting him a look that told him to 'shut the fuck up and listen.'

"The Vandals have been under attack, too. Low-level shit like we've been seeing. Break-ins, criminal damage. According to Snatch it's the Aces."

"That gang we've just dealt with?" Fury asked, looking at me and then glancing at Magnet and Demon.

"Aye. Snatch and Tomahawk reckon they're prospecting for the Bloody Hand."

"But they've got no bikes, mate. The Hand will want them on Harleys, not the fucking scramblers we saw in that CCTV footage."

"Maybe not?" Reap's voice came from the far end of the table, deep and rumbling. "What a better way to distract us by taking up our time chasing a street gang. Anyone checked on the Notorious lately? Know what they're up to?"

The room fell into a vibration of murmurs, heads turning to each other, mulling over the words that Reap had spoken.

"We've not had eyes on the Notorious for weeks. Indie's had us watching his lass instead." Demon was enjoying throwing me under that bus tonight.

But he was right. I'd pulled our attention away from our biggest threat. And that wasn't the Bloody Hand, or the Aces. The Notorious would be the first to challenge us, long before the Bloody Hand made their first move, and I'd lost sight of all of that.

I nodded. Not at anyone in particular, but an acknowledgement of the decision I'd made.

"Magnet, get the prospects watching the Notorious. I want to know their every movement. Cade and Caleb, I want to know what businesses they are running and what they are bringing in cash wise. If they're building an army, or the finance for one, then I want to know about it. Everyone else, I want you increasing your presence. We ride in our cuts. Make sure people know we are here. That this is our town. Not the Bloody Hand's, not the Notorious' and not a fucking street gang."

The men cleared out. Everyone but Fury. The fucker was making a habit of this. I didn't look up, but I could feel him there, just over my shoulder.

"What now?"

"You know it's only a matter of time, don't you?" He mumbled.

"For what? My dad dying or the Bloody Hand starting a war."

"Both. But on the subject of war, we need to look up and look out more. Because if we don't, they'll come at us from all corners. They're already winding up the other clubs, making us look at other people. How long before the first MC signs out of the coalition, Indie? And when that happens, we weaken, and we have more people to watch from over our shoulders."

I said nothing. And Fury said nothing more. But the silence between us said a lot. I closed my eyes, tired and dry, and put my head into my hands.

Chapter Nineteen

Emmie

The street outside was quiet, darkness rolling in, bringing a thick mist with it. I pulled the curtains shut, casting out the formidability of night and the thick spookiness the creeping mist was bringing. Lily lay on the sofa, half asleep, her little eyes sagging as she tried to watch the end of the film. Luke was already upstairs, the drone of his computer filling the gaps between the warble of an animated character on the television downstairs.

"Come on, baby," I said, scooping the little girl up into my arms and wobbling up the stairs, taking care not to bounce her head on the banister as I lurched off balance to one side.

"Mammy, can I sleep in your bed tonight?"

"What's wrong with yours?"

"I like yours better."

"Ok, Princess." I kissed the top of her head, disturbing a strand of brown hair that fell across her face.

The double bed was huge for her little frame, and she looked swamped under the covers as I tucked her in.

"Are you coming to bed now?" Lily asked, barely able to keep her eyes open.

"Soon, baby. Once I've tidied up."

Tidied up, washed the dishes, folded the clothes and put the dog out. Everything I hadn't done today because I was out with Indie instead. Indie. My stomach warmed. A sensation filling me. Something I hadn't felt for such a long time. Not since Gary. And look how that had ended. I shook the thought from my mind, ignoring the voice of doom that had woken in the back of my head.

Downstairs, Daisy whined, scratching at the utility room door and carving another cut into the rotting wooden frame. I opened the door; the dog rushing out and the cold night air rushing in. I could hear her bark. A half-hearted woof, a smell catching her nose or an animal moving in the night. Or even next door's cat, which liked to taunt her from a position on top of the fence.

But then the bark changed from conversational to meaningful and urgent. My heart seized, skipping a beat, the muscles in my chest tightening, the icy fingers of fear wrapping around my throat. There was someone out there.

"Daisy!" I hissed, pulling the back door open a few inches. "Daisy!"

The dog didn't return. The barking stopped, a slow, deep growl coming from the shadows in the garden. And then a voice, velvety and familiar.

"S'ok girl. S'ok."

"Indie?"

"Hey Spuggy."

"What the hell are you doing out there creeping around in the dark?"

"Came to see you. But you must have put the dog out at the same time. Thought she was going to take my arm off."

My heart leaped, not having caught up with the conversation, thumping against my chest like I'd just run a race. This man was going to send me to an early grave. For a moment, that thought meant little other than mere words. Yet there was a terrible truth behind them, because my choice in men had nearly done that. Now this one was the vice president of a motorcycle club, one well-known enough that when he got off his bike today, the riders that pulled us over went almost pale. And I was letting him into my home. I'd already let him into my heart, no matter how much I could try to fight it. Though I never had.

I beckoned for him to come in; the dog loping by his side. Then she stopped between the two of us and shook her whole body vigorously, rain droplets that had been sitting on her smooth coat firing at us. I shrieked, jumping backwards, away from the soggy dog who now sat at Indie's side, her tongue lolling out of her mouth. He reached down, his fingers scratching behind a floppy ear. And if she could have smiled, she would have.

"How was church?" I asked, watching his hand stroke over her head.

“Boring. But we got done what we needed to do.”

“And what was that?”

“Just some matters of business that couldn’t wait.”

“Because of that conversation with those bikers today?” I asked. I was pushing my luck, asking about club business.

“Pretty much.”

But he wasn’t going to tell me. And neither did I really have the confidence to ask. Sometimes it was better off not knowing. I’d learnt that much from Gaz. Ignorance could be bliss, sometimes.

Indie dropped his hand from the dog’s head, moving across the kitchen floor towards me, the old lino clacking under his heavy boots. He was still dressed head to toe in his leathers, his cut hanging over the black bike jacket and the leather trousers clinging to thick thighs. And here I was dressed in my pyjamas, a thin dressing gown covering the vest and shorts underneath.

His arm shot forward, fingers linking in the ties of the gown, tugging me towards him. I stumbled over my feet, a pitiful squeak leaving my mouth as he scooped an arm around my waist and pulled me into him. The leather was cool through the thin material, making my nipples tighten, pushing out through the layers of thin cotton and shiny silk. Indie dipped his head, saying nothing as his eyes scanned my body, resting on my chest for a moment longer than everywhere else. Then his voice purred, a deep vibrating rumble.

"Little sparrow. So nice to see you in the flesh, not hidden behind your uniform."

His fingers tilted my chin, in that gently commanding way that left me nowhere else to look. Then his lips pressed against mine, hot and hungry, his hand moving to the back of my head, keeping me pushed into him, giving me no room for escape. This kiss was hard, and meaningful, and far from the careful, controlled way he'd kissed me before. And now my stomach was aflame, and those flames touching somewhere deep inside me, a sudden pressure taunting me.

I gasped, as much for air as for him. He barely let me breathe, his lips crushing mine, his tongue hard and almost forceful, taking the kiss from me, one hand in the back of my hair, fingers grazing my scalp and the palm of his other hand wedged into the small of my back, pushing my body into him.

I thought I could feel him through the leather, a roughness against the most sensitive part of me. He walked me backwards, his lips and tongue never leaving mine, his stubble scratching my skin, a leather covered hard-on teasing against my stomach. Then he stopped for a moment, his hands grabbing my waist and picking me up and depositing me on the edge of the kitchen table, a sudden rush of cold bleeding through the thin material of my pyjamas.

Indie nudged my legs apart, stepping between them, the leather-clad erection now pressing against my pussy, driving a surge through me, an embarrassing squeak leaving me at the sudden roughness of his bike trousers. He smiled, knowing exactly what that had done to me, acknowledging the control he was taking from my body. From me. And right now, I wanted to give it all to him.

He kissed my mouth again, his tongue pulsing in and out, teasing and taking as I tried to keep up, but was left hopelessly behind. His hand wrapped around the back of my neck, the movement of the rough pads of his fingers sending an electrified shiver right the way down my spine. His lips pushed harder, taking more and more, his weight pushing down on me. He swiped the dressing gown off my shoulder with his free hand, the callouses on his palms scratching the warm skin underneath. His lips never leaving me, he tugged the other side down my arm.

And then he hesitated, taking his mouth from mine, yet his lips still lingered there, like he couldn't move far from me.

"Can I touch you, Emmie?" his voice was strained, struggling with control.

I faltered for a moment. I'd never been asked before whether that was what I'd wanted. And now I didn't really know how to answer. Indie took a step back, looking at me intensely.

"You can say stop, Spuggy. At any time. I won't ever force you to do something you don't want to do."

"I want to do this."

"Then tell me."

"Tell you what?"

"What do you want, little sparrow?"

He stood back, watching me. Never stepping towards me. Waiting for my response, for permission to continue. And I felt odd, unable to say the words he needed to hear. Because I'd never been asked like this. It had always been assumed that because I was in a relationship that this sort of thing was taken from me freely. And still he waited. Patiently. No pressure.

"I don't know how to say it, Indie."

"Say however you feel. In whichever way you need. I'm not touching you again until you tell me it's ok. And if it's not, then that's fine too."

I swallowed, buying time for those words to form, to have the confidence to tell him what I wanted. His eyes wandered over me, trying to stay away from my chest, where my nipples were standing out through my clothes, or between my legs where I could feel my pussy swollen and needy and probably leaking through my shorts.

"Indie. Kiss me again. And don't stop. I'll tell you if I need that. Make this feel natural."

He nodded, understanding on his face, and stepped back towards me, rough fingers swiping across my shoulders, scratching my skin in the most delicious way, and I arched my back.

"Gonna get rid of this top, Spuggy."

"Yes."

A rush of cool air hit my skin, my nipples hardening further, and I leaned back on the table, watching his eyes now focus on my breasts, at the nipples pointed towards him. He smiled. It was gentle, not smug, like he was quietly rewarding himself. Then he closed the space, his hands groping up my back, his lips finding mine again, and this time he sucked my bottom lip into his mouth, and insane pressure echoed deep in my groin. A hand moved from my back, stroking over my skin, rough skin scratching against mine, a thousand burning and confused tingles dashing over my flesh. A mix of signals that my body wasn't sure how to react to.

His fingers brushed over my bare breasts, gently feeling for my nipples and even the lightest touch sent me gasping, my head dropping back to expose my neck. He wasted no time, his lips and tongue filling that spot, sucking against the place where my pulse bounded uncontrolled. His fingers closed around my nipples, a tweak, and a pull against the hardened flesh, and I fell back onto my arms even further. Then his lips trailed from my neck, at first following the vein that throbbed with pulsing blood, teeth grazing over my collarbone, the contradiction of pain and pleasure, his mouth teasing me with a slow, tortuous descent towards my breasts.

His hands moved away, creating the space for his mouth, scooping around my back where he could pull me closer to him, supporting my weight as the gentle grating of stubble sent my eyes closing and my back arching. Soon he would have taken the ability to form words away. The ability for me to stop him or keep him going, a thick delirium descending on top of me.

His lips moved lower, tracing hot wet lines across my skin, and between his hot breath and the cool air, I felt like my flesh was on fire. I squirmed, pressure building between my legs, ready to explode, the need for some sort of release reaching a new high. I needed to scoot down the table to meet him. To feel the leather bulge pushing against me. Stubble scratched across my nipple, a sudden contradiction to the soft plucking of his lips and I whimpered, the sound invading the super-charged space echoing off the walls.

"Is that what you need, Spuggy?" he whispered, his lips poised above my nipple.

I arched my back, pushing myself towards him.

"Yes," I hissed.

He hesitated a moment, but I couldn't see what he was doing. My eyes tightly shut as I tried desperately to maintain control. And then suddenly his lips covered my nipple, gentle at first, testing the boundaries, waiting for me to tell him to stop. But I couldn't have uttered those words even if I'd wanted to, and his mouth closed around me. The flick of his tongue on the end sent my pussy pulsing and my stomach clenching, and my head rolling backwards like it might come clean off my neck. His tongue flicked and licked, chasing a flurry of tingles and convulsions through my body. Then he sucked hard, dragging my nipple into his mouth, kneading my breast with his other hand, punishing my flesh and my mind all at once.

A hand trailed down my stomach, pushing the thin cotton vest lower and lower, a finger teasing across the waistband of my shorts. A promise of more. I tried to say yes, to make sure he didn't stop, but all I heard were a garble of words, a mix of sounds. But he didn't stop, gently tugging my shorts down my legs, and nudging them off with his knee. And now I lay on the kitchen table naked. Spread open to him like a sacrifice, just like he'd threatened me earlier that day.

He moved from my nipple, pulling his chin down my tummy, scraping my hot flesh with the scratch of his five o'clock shadow, his brown eyes watching me watch him. And then he spoke, his fingers swirling over my skin the entire time.

"Can I taste you, Spuggy?"

"You mean…?" I croaked.

“Let me taste this sweet pussy,” he whispered, hot breath tickling my skin, his fingers brushing over the fine hair at my entrance.

“Indie. I…no one’s ever gone down there… not with their mouth.”

I was suddenly uncertain.

“Let me guess. You’ve been expected to do it, though?”

I nodded, biting my lip. Indie’s fingers curled into my flesh, his nails scratching.

“Then let me show you how it should be done, little sparrow.”

I pressed my teeth harder into my lip, only nodding my head, suddenly nervous.

His eyes darkened, a flash of something feral, and for a moment I was hesitant. But then he tugged his eyes from mine, dropping his head and I felt his face against me, between my legs. And then his tongue. A tentative tease at first, a gentle swipe through my folds, and I tensed.

"Relax, Spuggy," he murmured against my pussy lips, a sudden surge of deep vibrations filling me, and I squeaked.

And then another swipe. I could feel the flattening of his tongue against me, pushing as he licked, and stopping at the top, flicking the tip over my clit. I jumped, a surge of electric hitting me. He repeated. The heavy drag of his tongue, the little flick of the tip, the inside of my legs crawling with deep, resonating tingles. Then again, only after the flick, he covered my clit with his mouth, sucking gently.

"Shit!" The word slipped out, part gasp, part cry.

Indie hummed in approval, the vibration hitting me deep and I gasped again.

He licked again, finishing in the same flick, but this time he sucked harder, and my legs clamped around his head, trapping him there. Oh God. He stilled, giving me a few seconds for the moment to fade, and then his lips and mouth and tongue worked harder and faster, licking and sucking and then more pressure. The tip of his tongue pushing into me, exploring inside me, flicking and moving and thrusting in and out. My fingers buried into thick tufts of grey hair, something else taking over my body. My hips moved against him, in time with his tongue, rubbing against the rhythm I was creating.

Indie hummed again, a noise of encouragement, his lips and tongue moving faster against me, pulling, plucking, nipping, sucking, flicking, licking. My hips rotated, my pussy bucking against his face, my hands gripping his hair, the pressure building inside almost boiling.

"Oh, God!" It was my voice I could hear, an alien cry. "Oh shit. Indie. Fuck."

The words weren't making sense. But they tumbled from my lips with every thrust of my hips.

"Oh fuck. Oh fuck. Oh fuck!"

The sensation hit me like a steam train, and I pulled Indie's face into me, darkness pooling in front of me, a metallic taste trickling into my mouth from the teeth that had held onto my injured lip.

"Oh God!" I breathed, my thighs tensing, clamping around his head, as I rode his tongue and his face. "Shit!"

Chapter Twenty

Indie

Emmie lay back on the table, completely naked, her thighs still wrapped around me. I glanced up from the pussy I'd just been burying my face in for the last few minutes, watching as her stomach arched up towards the ceiling, the skin tightening over her tiny frame. The bottom of her ribs jutted out; the pink nipples of her little tits pointed upwards. Her chest was still heaving, her eyes still closed.

I got to my feet, my knees creaking from where I'd been kneeling between her legs. From here, I could see her better. The paleness of her skin, a slight darkening over her hips and around her belly button. Faint lines from where her skin had once been stretched. Her tits had lost a tiny bit of their fullness, but they were beautiful and petite. Just like her delicate nipples, a blush of pink in the middle, more prominent against the pale glow of her flesh.

Her apricot hair had come loose from the messy bun on the top of her head, strands criss-crossing her face, matching the colour of the freckles that dusted her button nose. She was incredible. And she was doing nothing to relieve the bulge in my pants. I closed my eyes for a second, chasing back the thoughts of my hand wrapped around that bun, guiding her mouth to my cock. Fuck.

Then suddenly she snapped her eyes open. Big, wide blue-green orbs looking back at me, almost shocked to see me standing over the top of her, watching her. She gasped, her hand clutching at her chest as she struggled to sit upright. And then she tipped herself forward, almost into a seated foetal position, her other hand grabbing at the dressing gown that lay underneath her. Dragging the shiny material across her body, she covered herself from my view.

"What's wrong, Emmie?" I tried to hide the disappointment in my voice.

"I…err."

"What is it, Spuggy?" I tipped her chin up, gazing into the Mediterranean sea, unable to fathom the reason for the sudden change.

Emmie tried to drop her eyes from mine, a colour fading from her flushed cheeks.

"Tell me." And now my voice was rough, commanding.

"I don't want you to see my body," she answered, straining to move her gaze from mine.

"I don't understand, Emmie. Why?"

"I…I just don't like it. It's disgusting."

"Again, Emmie. I don't get it."

"The stretch marks, the saggy skin. My boobs."

"Jesus, Emmie. There's absolutely nothing wrong with your body."

"There is Indie. I hate it. All of it."

"Well, I don't, darlin'. I love it all."

"I don't see how you can."

I dropped my hand from her face, taking a step back.

"Take it off."

"What?" Emmie asked, her blue-green eyes widening, a look of horror creeping across her face.

"Your dressing gown. Take it off."

"Indie…"

"Don't make me rip it off you." The words ended in a growl, and I closed my eyes for a moment, wondering whether I'd gone too far.

But slowly she pulled the dressing gown down, showing off the beautiful tits I'd just sucked.

"And the rest, Spuggy."

She bit her bottom lip, but I'd already seen the quiver start and again I wondered whether I was pushing her too far. But she opened the gown at her waist, her crossed legs hiding most of the pussy I'd just eaten.

I stepped forward, tracing my fingers down her neck, cupping my hands over her tits. They had a more tear drop shape, but they still sat in my hand nicely, the skin smooth, the nipples reacting to my touch. They still made me want to lick and kiss them and they still made my dick hard, painfully hard in the tautness of the leather bike trousers. Then I slid my hands further down her body, dragging the tips of my fingers across her stomach. There was a little bump, the slightest bulge in her thin stature, the evidence of her body bringing life. I traced the shadows of stripes that lay on the top of the skin, a slight unevenness to the touch, subtle marks left from pregnancy. It was all beautiful. She was beautiful.

"This," I whispered into the air between us. "All this. This is who you are, little Emmie. This is what I love about you. Just like your apricot hair and your little nose. Or the way those apricot freckles dash across your skin, making you look all sweet and innocent. And this body," I ran my hand down her side, tracing the slightly puckered lines down her left hip. Then I grabbed her hand and pulled it towards me. "This body makes me feel like this."

I pushed her hand into my groin, holding it against the raging hard-on in my trousers. The hard-on that could never be sated by looking at her beautiful body, or tasting her gorgeous skin, or sucking that juicy pussy. This hard-on could only be sated by being driven deep inside of her.

There was a creak above us. The soft thud of footsteps overhead and then the groan of stairs.

"Shit!" Emmie hissed, yanking her hand from where I held it on my erect, covered cock.

She pulled her dressing gown around her, scooping up the discarded vest and shorts and pushing them inside the silk.

"Mam?" the voice called.

I stepped back, making sure I covered her body from the voice now at the bottom of the stairs. Giving her time to get herself decent.

"Yes, Luke?"

"Is Dad here?"

"No. Why do you think that?"

"Oh, it's him," the boy's voice was now behind me. "Heard voices. Thought it must have been Dad. Thought I could hear shouting."

"No." Emmie answered much too sharply. "No one was shouting."

"Ok," Luke replied, clearly satisfied with the answers his mother had given.

He padded over to the sink, dragging a thick glass tumbler out of the cabinet above his head, before filling it with water and taking a noisy gulp.

"Indie was just going," Emmie disturbed the silence, flashing me a look.

I nodded, squeezing her hand, and making towards the front door.

"Make sure you lock this straight away behind me," I instructed.

Emmie smiled faintly, following me out. Pulling the door hard into the frame, I listened for a second. A bolt slid into place. Then a lock turned. And finally, I heard the jingle of a chain against the wood. Emmie, Luke and Lily were safely locked away for the night.

I grabbed at my crotch, adjusting myself so the erection sat in a more comfortable place. Didn't seem like this hard-on was getting sated tonight, either.

Chapter Twenty One

Emmie

Rain hammered the windows, waking me up before my alarm went off, and even under the thick duvet I was cold. I yanked the covers up around my chin, warding off the chill, hoping I could steal another thirty minute's sleep. I waited for the heaviness to take me back under just for a few minutes.

"Mammy! Mammy!" Lily's voice was overly shrill, ricocheting through my head, shattering any chance of that extra time under the covers.

"What, Lily?"

"I had a really great dream."

"So did I. Wanna know what it was?"

"Uh-huh."

“I got to stay in bed all day.”

“Mammy. Don’t be silly.”

“Sorry, baby. What was your dream about?”

Lily jumped on the bed, bouncing across me heavier than her three stone and a bit body should feel.

“I dreamt you married, Indie.”

“Really?”

“Uh-huh. And Daddy was there. And he was really annoyed about it.”

“That sounds about right. You hungry baby?”

“Uh-huh.”

“Let’s go get some breakfast then.”

Because I didn’t need either of those visuals in my brain. A contradiction of hope and dread. And no matter what Indie had said, I didn’t think Gaz would stay away for long.

The rain was relentless, bouncing off the pavements. Water ran down the street, the road resembling a river.

“Hurry up, Mam.” Luke complained as I stood looking out of the door and wondering whether there was any way to avoid being completely soaked. “I don’t want to be parked miles away again. I’ve got a hole in my shoe.”

“When did that happen?”

“Couple of weeks ago.”

“Why didn’t you tell me?”

“I didn’t want you to worry about having to buy new ones.”

The guilt was sickening, like I’d just been struck by a stomach bug, and my eyes prickled with the threatening heat of tears. Tears for the boy who hadn’t wanted to tell me he needed new shoes. I bit my lip hard. Hoping I could swap the pain in my heart for the pain in my face.

“Mam?” he urged, breaking through my self-pity.

“Wait here. I’ll get the doors open and then, when I wave, you two run across.”

I was soaked in seconds, the rain pounding on the top of my face, running down my hair and into my eyes as I dashed to the driver's door, ramming the key in the lock. There was a low dunk as the car lock slid open and mercifully the central locking worked, the rest of the locks clicking simultaneously. I ran around the car, yanking the doors open and waving at the kids, watching as they splashed down the garden path, barrelling towards me.

Lily giggled loudly, shrieking when she stepped in a puddle, water drenching her feet before we even got to school. Luke followed, holding his rucksack over his head, just making it to the passenger door before leaping in. I pushed the doors closed, scrubbing water from my eyes. And as my vision cleared, I noticed a car parked in the street. Just a few metres down the road. It was older than the usual cars that had kept a constant vigil over us the last couple of weeks, not as well cared for. But it sat on sentry duty as the rest had.

A big rain drop dripped down my face, pooling in the corner of my eye and almost blinding me, reminding me I was standing in the middle of a torrential shower with a coat that had lost its ability to repel water a long time ago. I climbed into the driver's seat, my clothes squelching with every little movement.

"Mammy I'm cold," Lily complained from behind me.

"Ok baby. I'll get the heating going."

I stuffed the key into the ignition, my hands trembling as I turned my wrist. The car spluttered. Nothing. I turned the key again, listening to the engine trying its best, but it sounded like an old man, coughing and choking before cutting out again.

"Mam, I think the car is dead," Luke said after I'd tried another five times, slapped the steering wheel twice and sworn at least once.

And still the rain hammered on the windscreen. I wanted to scream. And to cry.

"Ring Nanna," Luke said softly. "She'll come get us."

"Nanna's at work, Luke."

"What about Indie?" Lily asked. "He'll come help us Mammy."

I sighed, detaching my mobile from a soggy pocket and wiping the water from the screen.

*****

"I'd say it was fu…."

"Knackered," Indie interrupted the man poking around under the bonnet of my car.

"Aye that."

"Look, I'll get you and the kids to school. Fury will take your car to the garage, and we'll figure out what's wrong. Can't do much here stood out in the pi… in the rain," Indie corrected himself, glancing over the top of me to Luke and Lily.

"Do you mind?"

"Course I don't Spuggy."

Indie slid his arm through the car window, yanking the keys from the ignition and then tossing them at the big man he'd brought with him, with the dark hair piled on the top of his head in some kind of messy man-bun.

There was a swarm of activity at the schools' gates. Cars fighting for the next available space, parents rushing around under umbrellas, their heads bowed to the rain. Indie bumped up the curb, stopping directly in front of the gates.

"We're not supposed to park here," Luke pointed out.

"I know, mate. But just for today, we're gonna break the rules."

"I don't like breaking rules. You get consequences for breaking the rules," Lily added, folding her little arms across her chest and sticking out her chin in defiance.

"Normally you do. But today it's ok. Nobody's gonna tell you off today, Princess. In fact, I bet there's not a single teacher out on that yard."

Lily stared out the tinted van windows, and then, as if satisfied with what Indie had told her, she nodded her head and pulled her bag from beneath her feet.

"Be right back," I muttered, pulling open the van doors and ushering the kids out into the torrents of rain.

There were no neat queues of children this morning. Just an urgent hustle and a bulge of bodies as each parent pushed and prodded their kids through the doors. An umbrella speared me in the side of my face, glancing off the wet hoodie that was pulled over my head, restricting my peripheral vision and making me vulnerable to the attack from the spike of another umbrella on the other side. I pushed through the surge, nudging the kids through the doors out of the weather and then fought my way back out of the scrum.

"Jeez, Emmie, you're soaking, babes." Indie's hand squeezed my thigh. An affectionate touch, but all it did was make my insides simmer.

"I'll dry," I croaked, trying not to think of anything else. But under his grip, my nerves fired, acknowledging the touch on my leg, a reminder of how he'd left me last night and the same pressure built.

"Let's get you home and changed, Spuggy."

He moved his hand to the gear stick, selecting first and pulling away from the curb.

"But the car."

“Plenty of time for that. I’m not having you get pneumonia right in front of my eyes.”

“You know getting wet doesn’t cause pneumonia, don’t you?”

Indie shrugged, his eyes now on the road. “No matter. You’re going home and getting changed first. Besides, you’re making my seats wet.”

He turned his head halfway towards me, a smile across his face. He’d not shaved this morning, the stubble on his jaw more prominent, casting a silver sheen over his skin and making his jaw more angular. I clenched my legs together, ignoring what was eating at my insides, ignoring the tingles deep in my stomach, focussing on the road and the sound of the rain assaulting the windscreen as we drove through the storm.

Indie parked the van directly opposite the garden gate, knocking the van into gear and reaching for the ignition.

“Wait. We need to move to the other side of the street. Mr Jones from twenty-five won’t be able to get past if we stay here.”

Indie looked at me and then back at the road.

“There’s loads of space. I could get a bus through there.”

“Yeah, but Mr Jones will struggle. And then he’ll complain. And it’s not worth it.”

Indie shook his head. “We’ll only be a few minutes, Emmie. I’m not moving. Now out.” He nudged my thigh, and I bit down on my lip.

He waited for me on the pavement, rain pelting onto his leather jacket, dark splashes forming on already dark jeans. Reaching for me, he grabbed my hand, the van beeping behind us as he locked it, and then he jogged forward, pulling me with him, running up the path a little in front of me. His strides were long, covering the wet ground quickly, towing me behind him as I fell back, unable to keep up. At the door my hands trembled, wet and cold, the keys stuck in a soaking wet jeans pocket, my skin stuck on the wet denim. Eventually, I pulled them out, shoving the key into the lock and bounding through the front door out of the rain.

“I’ll just go change my top,” I called, my words muffled as the hoodie I’d peeled off got stuck over my head.

“The lot, Emmie.” Indie was right behind me, following me through the house.

“Just a dry top will do, the rest will be ok.”

I dumped the wet hoodie in front of the washing machine in the utility room, Daisy rushing out to meet me, her tail thrashing painfully across my cold, wet legs. I dug a clean jumper out of the dryer, still warm from where the machine hadn’t long finished its cycle. And then I turned.

“Oh no, little sparrow,” Indie’s voice was low, gravelly. “I want you completely changed.”

I’d heard the command in his voice but wasn’t prepared for the hands that scooped around my waist, picking me up suddenly.

“Indie!” I shrieked, looking down over his back, my head hanging towards the floor, my hands searching for something to grab hold of as he turned and walked out of the kitchen, and I dangled precariously over his shoulder.

Chapter Twenty Two

Indie

Her jeans were saturated, and no amount of clean, dry tops were going to solve that problem. The girl would catch her death if she left these clothes to dry by themselves.

"Indie!" she shrieked, as I launched her over my shoulder and made my way out of the kitchen and up the stairs.

"Put me down!" she squeaked again, hanging upside down, her hands scrabbling for purchase against the slick leather jacket until the only place she could hang onto were the pockets of my jeans.

I ignored her, bounding up the stairs, the sway of her body as she fought me, barely knocking me off balance. She was so light. A perfect weight to throw around. The layout of the little house now familiar to me, I moved straight to her room, dropping her on to her back at the bottom of her bed. She gasped audibly, a mix of shock and the telltale whimper of a sound I'd heard her make when I'd had my face buried in her pussy last night. And I like the way it sounded, more so when I towered above her, looking down on her little body spreadeagled on the bed.

"Get these wet clothes off," I instructed, my voice unusually gruff.

Her eyes widened lying on her back, staring at me.

"If you don't take them off, Spuggy, I'm gonna. So, start stripping."

Emmie's throat bobbed, her teeth raking her bottom lip, those blue-green eyes filled with uncertainty. But her fingers moved to the button of her jeans, quickly flicking it open, and lifting her arse off the bed, just high enough that she could push the soaked denim over her hips and down her thighs.

It was different seeing her in the daylight, knowing we were the only ones in the house. Her legs were slim, not nearly enough meat on them, but the skin was smooth underneath. Youthful skin of someone not quite thirty. The wet denim stuck at the widest part, and she struggled to move them any further down her legs. I grasped the top of them, pulling at them till, after a moment's resistance, I slid them off her legs.

And then she was there on the bed, just her knickers and a thin long-sleeved top that was itself wet over the collar and the caps of the shoulders. I stepped back towards her, cradling her back as I helped her sit up, gripping the bottom of the shirt with my other hand and whipping it off over her head.

Now I could see her. That pale flesh covering a small frame. Nipples poking through what was probably a white bra but was now a shade of grey, and the mint-coloured lace that covered her pussy with little pink flowers embroidered on the front. She was a mis-match of naivety. And it did everything for my dick.

Emmie crossed her arms over her chest, suddenly sub-consciously, watching me with uncertain eyes.

"I saw all of you last night, Spuggy."

"I know, but it's different this morning."

"Why's it different this morning?"

"Just, it's lighter. And the scars look worse in the daylight."

"These aren't scars, Emmie." I traced my fingertips over the stretch marks, feeling her shudder underneath my touch. "These are you. And I love them."

I nudged her legs open. The light turquoise lace knickers stretched over the little bulge of her pussy. I didn't bend down, but stood over the top of her, gently taking her wrists and peeling them off her chest, wrapping them round her back before pinning the pair of them with one hand. Her body tensed.

"Indie?" she asked, the uncertainty now lingering in her voice.

"Shush. It's ok, little sparrow. Trust me." And I knew that was a huge thing to ask of her. To ask her to trust that I wouldn't hurt her. That I would always stop if she asked me to.

I swiped one strap off her shoulder, and then the other, her body shuddering underneath me. Then

I flicked the catch behind her, the dull bra popping off to reveal the tits I knew she didn't like. But I liked them. I liked how they fit nicely into my hand. I cupped the right one, flicking my thumb over the perky nipple that had greeted me, watching as she squeezed her eyes shut, taking a sharp intake of breath. And I liked how the slightest touch over them made her flinch, how it moved her to the edge of control.

I let go of her then, peeling my own leather jacket off, catching her eyes glance over the black t-shirt underneath, then move to my arms, but never straying down my stomach or to my groin, as if she was purposefully staying away. The heavy jacket fell to the floor with a dunk. Underneath, my t-shirt was damp where the rain had soaked through the stitching. An excuse to take it off. Emmie's eyes widened, moving over the tattoos that covered my skin.

"They won't bite, ya know," I grinned. "You can touch them."

She nodded silently, chewing on her bottom lip. I grabbed her legs, pulling her right to the edge of the bed so that now she was looking up at me, her face just above my groin, and then I kneeled down, so we were almost eye to eye. She lifted her hand up, moving it towards me and then hesitating. Wrapping my fingers round her wrist, I guided her to me, holding her hand onto my chest. For a moment she didn't move, uncertain what to do next. But then she leant forwards, placing her other hand on me. They looked so petite against my inked skin and the bulging muscles of my chest. Her fingertips smoothed across me, gentle and tentative, tracing the lines and patterns. And then bumping over the knotted skin, the vibrant ink covered.

"There's a scar under here, Indie," she muttered.

"I was stabbed."

She snatched her hand away, looking up at me, alarm in her eyes.

"I was in the army, Spuggy. For years. War wounds."

Her eyes softened, the alarm dissolving to sympathy, and she reached forward again, her fingers back on my skin, moving over my collarbone and over my biceps.

“And here?” she whispered, her hands moving across a small round circle of puckered skin.

“Bullet wound.”

“Army,” she stated, more to herself.

I smiled faintly, and she took it as my answer. But that was a reminder of a different war. One she didn’t need to know about. Her fingers moved on, searching and feeling, tracing hot lines across my skin, each gentle movement resonating deeply inside of me and sending energised messages straight to my cock.

“You’ve so many scars,” she whispered.

“I’ve had a full life, Spuggy.”

“And you covered them with tattoos?”

“Uh-huh.”

“Why?”

“Because then I didn’t have to look at them every day. And I like tattoos. Win, win,” I shrugged.

She looked at me, the blue-green of her eyes darker than usual, her pupils wider.

“Tattoos, huh?”

"Don't even think about it, Spuggy. I love looking at you as you are."

"But I don't."

Cupping her face, I pushed my mouth against hers, silencing her with my tongue. Her lips obliged, parting for me to slip into her, moving with me as our tongues danced with each other and my hard-on strained painfully against the denim.

Emmie's hands moved back to my body, feeling over the muscles, tickling the hair on my chest and the strands that grew on my stomach, fingertips sinking lower till I could feel her just above the waistband of my jeans. Her finger bumped over the button, gripping it and then releasing it, as if she doubted what she was doing.

I pulled away from her, releasing her mouth.

"Just know, if you open that button, I'm commando. Didn't have time for pants when I got that distress call this morning."

Emmie giggled, light and tuneful. And God, how I loved that sound.

Her fingers moved back to the button, working over the fabric till there was a little pop and the release of pressure at my waist. Pushing away from her, rising to my feet, my groin now in line with her face. I stepped back a little, not wanting to present her with my hardened cock by whacking it on the end of her nose. Not today, at least. Toeing off my boots, I kicked them to the side, pushing the jeans down, my erection launching out like a thing possessed.

When I stood back up, she was staring, her eyes wide, a tinge of red on her cheeks, her lips slightly parted. And I had to concentrate hard not to grab a fistful of that apricot hair and pull her head to meet me. Instead, I reached for her hand, pulling it towards me and placing it over my shaft. She rested it there, not moving, the only sounds between us, our breaths increasing in pace. Squeezing her fingers closed round my cock, I guided her hand slowly up and down, watching the red brighten on her cheeks and her teeth bite down hard on her bottom lip.

Chapter Twenty Three

Emmie

The thing stared at me. The end bulging, the bulbous tip filled with blood, the whole thing jutting out from his body. I didn't know where to look or what to do with it. Other than stare. He took my hand, moving it to him, gently squeezing my fingers closed around him. And with his hand cupping mine, he moved it slowly up and down the shaft, moving me over him.

It was thicker and longer than I'd known, my fingers just joining round it, the foreskin tidily pulled back over that head. A ridge caught under my fingers, a vein protruding through the flesh, a bead of moisture right at the very tip. I moved my thumb over the top, smoothing that little bead of pre-cum over the satiny, smooth bulge of the head of his erection.

I'd never seen one look like this. Although I'd only ever seen one before. And it matched him, as if someone had sculpted both him and his penis from the same materials. The damn thing was as muscled as he was.

"Emmie," his voice rumbled from above me, his hand relaxing on mine, reaching forward so it gently wrapped around the back of my head.

I expected him to push my head towards his cock then or give an instruction that involved my face being even closer than it was. Instead, he tucked his thumb under my chin, tilting my head up.

"Emmie. I'd really like to fuck you right now."

Those words hit me square in the stomach, releasing a flood of heat which rushed out to every conceivable corner of me. I bit my lip, pulling his hand away from my face and scooted back up the bed, pulling him toward me as I backed up. He followed me, crawling up the bed on his hands and knees, the muscles in his arms bulging and flexing with each little movement until I couldn't go any further.

And now I was underneath him, the only thing between us the lacy thong. Indie dipped down towards me, leaning on his arms either side of my head, his body pressed gently against me, his lips tracing across my jaw, plucking at my skin, then grazing against me with his teeth. His flesh was hot against mine, the little bits of hair on his chest and his stomach tickling at my skin; and between my legs, and against the cotton that covered my pussy I could feel the head of that cock.

He trailed his mouth over my neck, moving over to my jugular vein and sucking against it so suddenly hard that I gasped. My back arched; my pussy rubbed against his throbbing hard on. He growled against me, an actual growl, against the spot where my heart rate was escalating, beating against his lips and tongue. Sliding his arm down my side, his fingers felt for something, and then he'd suddenly found it. Linking into the waistband of my knickers, he slid them down my legs. I kicked out of them and now there was nothing between us.

Indie sat up onto his haunches, scooting backwards, and then moved to the heap of his clothes that were at lying on the floor at the foot of the bed.

He rummaged around in the pile, grabbing something from a pocket before coming back to stand at the bottom of the bed with his erection in his hand.

"You sure you want this, little sparrow?"

He was already stroking the condom down on top of it, the rubber not taking anything away from that big bulbous head. I swallowed. Unable to find the words. Not knowing how to answer his question because I'd never really been asked like this before. So, I nodded, and watched the hint of a smile drift over his face. And now he crawled back towards me, yanking my ankles to pull my legs open to crawl in between. His hand moved in the space he'd created, fingers running over the spot between my legs, and I could feel the wetness he was spreading over me.

"I need you wetter than this, Spuggy," he mumbled, almost to himself.

His fingers swirled over my clit, a sudden pang of electric jolting through me and I cried out, my body trembling suddenly. And then those same fingers sank inside of me, pushing through my internal flesh.

"Shit!" I cursed, my body clamping down on him in response.

"That's it, Emmie," he encouraged. "Relax for me, baby. I'm not going to hurt you."

He moved slowly, tentatively, the whole time watching, testing my reactions. And those fingers swirled inside of me. Circling and massaging, heating me up from the inside out until I was wriggling underneath him. And then a different pressure, another finger slipping inside, opening me up and stretching me out. But now I was so wet they were moving freely, and quickly.

"Good girl, Emmie," Indie purred in my ear, bending over the top of me as he dragged his fingers out. And then I felt something against me. Much bigger than his fingertips, the pressure nothing like his fingers had caused. "Last chance to say no to me, Spuggy."

But even as he said it, I felt the first part of him slide inside.

"I want this, Indie." Those words didn't sound like me, the voice strained, alien, on the verge of losing control, and my stomach pulsed, like it had its own heartbeat.

He reached down, his lips crushing against me with a ferocity I'd never felt from him before, his tongue pushing into me, and then between my legs I felt more of him slide inside, inching carefully. Each little movement of his cock drove me hotter and hotter, like the slow burn of a firework fuse. Then the ignition hit the powder, and with a thrust he forced me open, hitting the top of my cervix, a sudden thrust I wasn't expecting. And I shouted out, arching my back, a mix of pain and pleasure jolting my system.

"I'm sorry, Spuggy," he breathed against my neck. "Did I hurt you?"

I shook my head. "You didn't." But the rest of that sentence was consumed, a flood of heat rushing through my body, the feeling of him inside me. Filling. Possessing. And it sent a shudder through me.

He stayed still, his cock inside my pussy, his hand wrapped around the side of my face, his forehead pushed against mine and his eyes closed. As if he was waiting for something. I moved under him.

"Emmie. Please. Don't move." He grunted.

"What's wrong?" Something wasn't right. Had I upset him? I tried to push up on my elbows.

"Emmie. Please." His voice sounded so strained.

"Indie. What's wrong? What have I done wrong?"

"Shush."

I stayed still, listening to him breathe, feeling his cock in me, a pressure rising but not daring to move to take care of it.

"Shush," he said again, although I'd not uttered a word. "You feel so fucking good. I just need you to stay still for me, Emmie. Or this is going to be over in an instant. I've wanted this since the moment I set eyes on you. And right now, you're about to blow my mind and my balls."

His lips met mine again. A soft kiss, tentative, plucking at my mouth. A distraction, for him at least. I kissed back, pushing my hands into the tufts of thick grey hair, pulling his face to mine, my tongue becoming urgent, pleading with him. Then he moved away from me, his mouth and lips nibbling over my chin, along my jaw, down my neck. And between my legs, his hips moved slowly. A painfully careful rhythm, his cock gliding through the tissues inside of me, dragging slowly through sensitive flesh. Untouched flesh. I can't remember the last time I had someone inside me. And whenever that was, the memory was not welcome.

He moved differently now. Longer thrusts but teasingly slow, stoking a flame from the smouldering embers inside me. The heat increasing with each long, careful stroke of his dick. I pulled my legs up, wrapping them around his waist, letting him sink deeper into me. A growl vibrated against my throat, a graze of teeth, and I whimpered, arching my back, meeting the next thrust of his cock.

"Ah fuck, Emmie." Indie's words tickled the flesh at my throat, his hips speeding up, the thrusts faster and heavier. "Fuck."

Indie moved hard, pushing his cock into me faster now, his lips and tongue working against me frantically, like a starved man at an all-you-can-eat feast. His hands came between us, the roughness of the pads of his fingers suddenly against my nipples making me flinch, my own hips rising into him.

"For fuck's sake Emmie."

"What?"

"You're going to make me come."

"Isn't that the whole point?" I panted, my whole-body tensing as he rolled a nipple between his fingers.

"Not this quick, little sparrow."

He dipped his head, sucking in the nipple on my other breast, his fingers still working the right, my body shuddering under him and I gasped loudly, trying not to make a noise, but failing miserably.

"I want to hear you, Emmie," Indie spoke against my nipple, cool air rushing to the spot he'd just taken his mouth from. "I want to hear every whimper, every cry, every word as you come undone, Spuggy."

He sucked it into his mouth again, flicking the end with his tongue, and I cried out.

"That's it, Spuggy. Let me hear you."

He pumped into me, much more roughly this time, and now that fuse inside me really was lit, heat licking at my flesh, at my stomach, climbing higher. Indie let go of the breast he was kneading, sliding that hand down between us. I felt him over my clit, his fingers searching. And then when he found it, he swirled, sending a shock of energy pulsing through me.

I arched into him, into the hand that worked me, unable to escape the pressure of his cock. And now this pressure was building. And building. And my cries were coming louder, my body reacting to him unrestrained. And he reacting to me, each sound from my mouth making him move those hips harder, each whimper and gasp, making his fingers swirl against my clit. And now I pushed my hips into him, feeling every thrust right up into the base of my stomach, my body pulsing right down to the end of my toes.

"Shit! Oh Shit!" And now I sounded possessed.

Indie grunted now, pumping and thrusting.

"I need you to come, Emmie. I need to feel me round you before I lose control and finish. Come on, baby."

He dipped his head into my neck, dragging his tongue up over that vein, grazing his teeth over the skin as he reached the middle. My toes curled, my stomach tensed, an entire load of butterflies taking off inside me all at once and the heat exploded, coursing through my veins and reaching every part of me. I might have gasped, I might have cried out, I might have just whimpered, maybe for a moment I stopped breathing all together, the intensity hitting me like such sweet punishment.

Indie grabbed at my neck with his lips, his hips bucking wildly, a series of guttural gasps against me as he sucked the skin of my neck into his mouth. And then he let go, with one last hard thrust, pushing his cock into me as far as it could go so that our bodies were almost perfectly aligned with each other.

And then for a moment he dropped his weight on top of me, squashing me almost into the mattress, breathing against my neck. I could feel his heart bounding in his chest, my own joining in and now there was a chaotic vibrating.

Chapter Twenty Four

Indie

I'd lost total and utter control, narrowly keeping from coming long enough to make sure she got hers first. And then when she did, as her body shuddered under everything I did to it, her eyes squeezing shut and her mouth dropping open, and she made those sounds. I could have listened to the noises she made forever, the most beautiful sounds as her pussy tensed around my cock, her eyes fixing on mine. And those cries. Like a siren call of a mermaid.

"Indie," her voice was faint, half a pant.

And she smelt so good. The heat of her body, the smell of exertion, and that earthy, salty smell of arousal. Sated arousal.

"Indie," she whispered.

I kissed her neck, gently plucking at the skin, the faintest taste of metal at the tip of my tongue.

"Indie."

She wriggled a moment, my dick slipping out.

"Indie, you're squashing me."

"Shit. Sorry, Spuggy." Fucking schoolboy error. And she was the cause.

I pushed up onto my elbows, taking my weight off her small frame, listening to the little whoosh of air as she exhaled. Her neck was marked, a purplish tinge forming where I'd sucked on it too hard. Fuck. She'd reduced me to a bumbling fucking teenager, not the forty-eight-year-old army vet, and to top it off, I'd nearly shot my load early as well.

"What's wrong?" she asked nervously, staring up at me while I chastised myself for my shit fucking performance.

"Nothing, Emmie. Other than me wishing we could stay right here all day." It wasn't really a lie. I needed at least another round to redeem myself. "Suppose we'd better go get this car sorted."

*****

“Where the fuck have you been?” Fury grumbled as he slid from under the car.

“We’re here now, man. Stop ya bitchin. You figured out what’s wrong with it yet?”

“What’s fucking wrong with it? Be quicker to figure out what’s right with it. When was the last time you had this thing serviced?” He turned to Emmie, who was standing awkwardly by my side, her green-blue eyes wide as saucers as the big man stood up in front of us.

“I d…dunno. Couple of years ago.”

“You know you’re supposed to service these cages at least once a year, don’t you?”

“I….”

“Fury, enough.” He looked at me, frustration clear on his face, one side of it streaked in oil, but recognising the tone of my voice and the command in it. “It’s ok, babe. He’s just in a one because your car’s leaked oil all over his pretty face.”

“I dunno how the fucking thing was still running. Spark plugs are the problem, but the timing belt is on its last fucking legs and the engine intake needs looking at."

"We got parts in?" I asked.

Fury shook his head. "Not to fit this model. Ordered them, though."

Emmie tugged on the sleeve of my top, turning away from the angry man with the dark hair piled up on the top of his head in his man-bun.

"Indie. I…I don't have the money to do this," she whispered. "We can just leave it. I can use the bus."

"Don't worry about it. I'll sort it."

"No…Indie…I,"

"Not another word from that pretty mouth of yours, Spuggy. Fury. ETA on those parts?"

Fury frowned. "Tomorrow at the earliest."

"Really?" I grumbled, knowing how much Emmie needed that car.

"Aye. Apparently another materials shortage. Although I reckon they're just lazy fuckers and don't want to fucking work."

I turned back to Emmie, watching her chew on her lip, her face strained.

"Don't worry, Spuggy. I'll be your chauffeur until the car's fixed."

"I dunno Indie. My shifts are all over the place these next few days. I don't want to inconvenience you."

"Babe, no part of you could ever inconvenience me. I'll sort it, I promise."

Fury rolled his eyes, mimicking sticking his fingers down his throat and fake gagging.

"And you can fuck off and get this car stripped. We'll do what we can till the parts get here."

Fury put one hand on his hips, lifting his forefinger in the air and swivelling it down the front of him like he was drawing a snake shape.

"Back to work, Princess," I grumbled, watching him flick his head and spin on his heel. And as he went to move away, I slapped his arse, the sound loud in the cavernous space of the garage.

"Harder, Daddy," he called over his shoulder.

When I turned to Emmie again, she was watching us wide-eyed.

"What?" I asked her, the grin not quite staying off my face.

"I…err…I'm not quite used to guys doing that to each other."

"What? Messing around?"

"Yeah. Like that, I mean. Gaz would have had a meltdown if another man touched his bum."

"Gaz sounds like he's not sure who he is, Spuggy. And Gaz has never been in the army. It's pretty normal banter. Means nothing other than we're mates." I pushed her elbow gently, turning her away from the knackered car that was starting to sit, piece by piece, in the garage. "Come on. Let's get a coffee while we point and laugh at Fury on the cameras."

"Are you not going to help him?"

"Nah. There's not much of the big stuff to do. Besides, gonna get some paperwork done whilst my hands are clean."

Fury didn't stop, sliding in and out on his board as he took off engine parts from underneath and from on top, and soon Emmie's car had both front wheels removed and half of the engine out on the concrete at the big man's feet. I should have rolled the car over one of the pits, but every spot was taken up with vehicles, waiting for something, as a national material shortage wracked the country.

"Was Fury in the army too?" Emmie asked suddenly, her lips making a tiny 'o' as she blew across the mug of coffee she held in her hands.

"Yeah. It's where we met. Why do you ask?"

"The tattoos. You both have tattoos."

"We just like tattoos, Spuggy. None of these are army issue. It's just the norm these days." I rolled my sleeves up and turned my arms over. "Besides, kinda helps when your brother's a tattoo artist."

"You've a brother?"

I nodded. "Half-brother." He still was, as far as I was concerned. Even if right now he didn't think so.

"I've never seen him at the hospital."

I felt the frown pull at my lips, a pang of guilt niggle at my heart, and that deep sense of anxiety that I recognised from each time I cooked up some excuse to tell my dad why Demon hadn't come to visit him.

"He and my dad fell out not so long ago. Dad said some things that upset him, and Demon hasn't forgiven him yet." Emmie's face softened, a look of sympathy, but understanding and I guessed she'd heard that all before.

"Ste doesn't seem like the type to upset people. He's always so lovely, your dad."

And for once, my beautiful observant girl couldn't be farther from reality.

"Demon, huh? Is that like a rider name?" She added, as if sensing a sudden tension.

"Yeah. He was always mischievous as a child. But he also had some hellish temper tantrums. Like he was born out of hell itself. And so, he became Demon. Think he prefers it to his actual name. Derek." I added when Emmie sat looking at me expectantly.

"I guess Fury is for something similar?"

"Fury got his nickname from the army. But yeah, he used to be a crazy bastard when he lost his temper. Army did a lot for him, though." I smiled encouragingly, not wanting to frighten her away.

"And you?"

I sighed.

"Indie is my real name. A shortened version of it." Emmie's eyebrow raised, trying to hide her amusement. "You saw my mother. She's eccentric. And my dad had to be high or something to let her name me. My full name is Indominus."

I caught the snigger and the way she bit her lip to stop her face from crumbling. The skin pulled into a flush of tiny lines at the corner of her eyes as she silently laughed at me, the golden freckles across her cheeks almost moving underneath the animation of her face. I didn't think I'd ever seen her laugh before. I'd watched her smile. Different smiles. The closed lipped adoration smile when she looked at her children, the nervous smile when she didn't know what her reaction should be, the smile that didn't quite grow the way it should where she was too scared to let herself be happy. And that just sated grin of satisfaction that I'd seen on her last night and this morning.

But the laugh, the curl of her lips and the crinkle of her eyes. That was something else, and it made me chuckle too, even though we were both now laughing at my expense.

"Apparently it means *fierce king*. Which is probably why he let my mother name me it. Not sure I lived up to that name the way he wanted me to."

"Why would he want you to be fierce?"

"My dad likes boys to be boys, and men to be hard. He once was a mean old bastard. Not as much as his brothers. He was probably the nicest out of the three of them, but he still had a reputation."

"And did that have anything to do with you joining the army?"

"Yes, and no. Some part of that was trying to escape the doldrums of the north east. I can't really remember whether I was trying to escape my father or show him I was the tough man he expected of me. It was 1993. Demon had just been born to my dad's new wife. My mother had eventually divorced him after years of him cheating on her. Hadn't taken him long to shack up with one of the women that hung around the bike club once she'd left him. And next thing you know, that one was pregnant."

"Yeah. It happens." Emmie's voice was suddenly quiet, her teeth worrying at her bottom lip again.

"Shit. I didn't mean to offend you, Emmie. My dad's relationships touch a nerve, even all these years later."

This time Emmie's smile was weak, an unhappiness setting in, and I realised I'd touched a nerve too. Whatever that was.

*****

"Mammy, I got all my spellings right today," the little girl that sat behind me in the crew seat of the van chattered happily.

"That's great, baby. Well done. And what about you, Luke? How was your day?" Emmie continued, straining to look over her shoulder at the sullen faced boy who'd said barely anything since we'd picked him up.

Luke shrugged. "Was ok. What's for tea? I'm starving."

"Don't know, yet. We'll have to see what's in."

The little street of council houses was quiet when we pulled up. Even the sparse cars parked on the road were almost completely gone. There was no one outside and not a curtain twitched. The garden gate to Emmie's house gaped open. Jumping out, I slid the side door of the van open, holding out my hand to help Lily out onto her feet and stepping back to let Luke clamber over the bench seats. He looked up at me, a hint of a scowl on his face, as if he was having to put some effort in to being annoyed at me. Then he walked off, leaving me standing holding the handle of the open door.

I followed up the garden path, Lily bounding away in front of me and Luke pulling the toes of the black leather shoes across the bumpy concrete. And right at the front Emmie paused, her palm outstretched, resting on the door, not moving, staring at something in front of her.

Chapter Twenty Five

Emmie

I would have barrelled straight in. I almost didn't notice. But the door seemed different, not quite in the frame. And when I looked closer, it wasn't in the frame at all. The wood around the edges was splintered, a huge chunk completely missing just around the locks.

Lily was right on my heels, happily skipping towards the door, her rucksack over her shoulder.

"Wait a minute, baby." I moved to turn, to look for Indie. But he was already there behind me. A sudden presence, carefully stepping around the small child, his arm outstretched, crossing in front of me.

"No, Emmie. Stay here till I know it's safe."

I nodded, my mouth suddenly dry, a tug of dread at the bottom of my diaphragm, watching him step into the house and leaving us behind.

“What’s he doing mam? Why can’t we go in?” Luke whined.

“I think we’ve been burgled. Indie’s going to check it’s safe.”

I could hear his footsteps inside, stomping over the laminate flooring and then moving away again, a hammer of booted feet on the stairs. Daisy barked furiously, locked away in the utility room, her voice shrill with urgency and a growl on the periphery. And then eventually the steps came back, growing louder, the tempo changing from heavy clods to a slower stomp.

The door yanked open.

“It’s not pretty,” Indie muttered, his voice low enough so that only I could hear. “But it’s safe.”

I swallowed, the acid in my stomach rising to the back of my throat. And nodded. Then I turned to the kids.

"Luke. Lily. Some naughty people have broken into our house. They've left a mess, and they may have taken stuff. When we go in, I want you to go to the lounge and sit down for me. There's probably going to be glass about, and I need to get that tidied up first."

Lily looked up, her grey eyes glossing over, her bottom lip wobbling.

"It's ok, Princess," Indie's voice purred, gentle and calming, as he dropped to his haunches in front of her. "We'll get it tidied up and then you'll never know it happened."

Luke stayed silent. Quiet tension on a nine-year-old's face. There was no hint he might cry, just an eerie stillness.

I followed Indie into the house, Lily's little hand gripping mine, waiting for the carnage to hit me. And carnage it was. The contents of the kitchen cupboards were all over the floor, cups and plates smashed where they had just been dragged out. Cereals scattered, Coco Pops and Rice Krispies spilled everywhere and crushed to dust, where someone had walked backwards and forwards repeatedly.

No room had been left untouched. They had been absolutely everywhere. The lounge had got off lightly, the cushions pulled off the sofa and dumped on the floor. Indie was already putting it back together.

"Look, kiddo. Good as new," he purred to the small girl stood at his side, as he patted the last cushion into place.

"I can't see Mr Morris. I left him here. Someone's taken Mr Morris!" Her voice escalated, panic rising.

"We'll find him, Lily. I'm sure he's here somewhere."

Upstairs was worse. The full contents of the airing cupboard had been pulled out, towels and bedding scattered across the landing, and I had to step onto them just to pass. I found Luke in his room, sitting on the floor. In his hands was a games controller. But that wasn't what he was staring at. Opposite him was his X-Box. The once rectangular box pulled apart. Gutted. He wasn't crying, yet his face was a mix of emotions. A concoction of unreadable expressions. Every feeling he was having right now all mixed into one, to the extent that I couldn't dissect anything at all.

"Luke," I said cautiously.

"My X-Box."

That was all he said. In every one of those few words, I could hear his pain. And I could feel it.

"I'm sorry," I whispered.

"Why? You didn't do this?"

I didn't. I hadn't. But I thought I knew who had. And that would be because of me. So yes. I had done this. There were no words I could offer to make any of this any better. To take any of his pain away. I couldn't tell him I'd buy him a new one. I had no money for that. We were managing now. Just. But there was little left for anything like a new X-Box.

The stairs creaked under a heavy weight. Indie's footsteps padded in long gentle thuds across the landing and then his frame blocked the doorway. I pushed myself to my feet, leaving my son sitting on the floor, nursing the broken bits of his X-Box. We said nothing, just a look, and I cocked my head sideways, beckoning for him to follow me.

In my room, the mess was even worse. My bedside drawers had been pulled out, all my underwear spread on my bed. If I was missing any, I wouldn't ever know. My room didn't have much. A few ornaments, a couple of pictures. And all of them had been smashed.

"Emmie…." Indie started.

But I stopped him, just putting my finger up in the air. A sign I needed a moment. A moment to get the anger racing through my veins under control, and to stop the spill of tears. To stop the swell of them at the back of my throat and the burn of them behind my eyes.

"It's Gaz," I said when I'd stopped the sobs from breaking out of me. "It can only be Gaz."

Indie looked tense. A flash of something across his eyes and the flicker of the muscle in his neck.

"Why?" He whispered, and for a second, I thought he was asking himself that question.

"I told you he won't ever let me go."

"But what kind of man does this to his own kids though, Emmie? Answer me that?" Indie paced the bedroom, stroking a hand through that thick greying hair. "No, don't answer, Spuggy. I know what kind of man. I was raised by one."

"Did your dad ever hit your mother?" I asked, shocked at the insinuation.

But Indie shook his head. "No, he didn't."

"Then you don't really know what kind of man Gary is. Your Dad may be a lot of things, Indie. A lot of things I don't know about. But is he a woman beater?"

Indie shook his head again. "No. No, he's not."

The bed dipped where he sat down beside me and for a little while we stayed there in silence, both of us staring at the smashed glass and broken ornaments on the floor.

"Mr Morris! Mr Morris!" The tortured screams got closer, the broken little girl with her broken pink unicorn running into my room. "They've hurt him," she wailed.

Lily thrust the bedraggled stuffed toy towards me, the white stuffing hanging out from where his stomach had been sliced open. Tears spilled down her face and welled in her eyes, and the back of my throat burned again.

"Shush, little one," Indie's voice was gentle.

He reached out for the unicorn, and she placed the thing in his hands. He turned it upside down, inspecting the damage.

"I know just the person who can fix him, Lily. Shall we go see her?"

I looked at him, not following the words, watching Lily nod sadly. Then he reached for me, grabbing my hand, his fingers entwining with mine.

"Come on," he said, getting to his feet, tugging me to mine. "Pack some clothes for you and the kids. Stay with me a couple of nights till we get this place tidied and secure. My boys will sort it out. I've got plenty of rooms, Emmie," he added, seeing the hesitation on my face.

"I can't leave the dog, Indie."

"Then she can come too."

*****

"I thought you said we were going to your place?" I asked, staring out at the pub we'd just parked in front of.

"This is my place." He grinned, a hint of mischievousness in his eyes.

"What is *The Dog on the Tyne*?" Luke asked from behind us.

"It's my pub. But it's also my home."

"Look at all those bikes!" I could hear the excitement rising in Luke's voice.

He was right. That was a lot of bikes. The same type that Indie had ridden. And the same type that had pulled us over on the way back from Holy Island.

"It's also the Northern Kings' clubhouse. So, there's already a few of us here."

And now I felt nervous. But Indie was already climbing out of the van and sliding the side door open to let Luke and Lily out. Lily looked as nervous as I felt, hugging the half-gutted unicorn into her chest and staring up at the building, whose paint work had seen better days. Indie had noticed too and dropped to his haunches at her side.

"There's a lovely lady in there that's going to fix Mr Morris for you. Would you like to meet her?"

Lily nodded. "Will she hurt him?"

"No, little one. She'll take good care of him. He'll feel so much better when he's whole again. You ready?"

Lily nodded again and Indie rose to his feet, towering over the little girl. But he smiled down at her, holding out his hand, and as she slid it into his, her entire hand disappeared.

I followed behind them, Daisy padding along at my side on her lead, and Luke behind us. Inside, the internal décor wasn't much better than the outside. The chairs were old, varnish peeling, and threads hanging from the seats. The floor was sticky, grabbing at my feet with each step I took, the faint smell of stale alcohol and fading nights out rising to my nose the further into the pub we moved.

There were a few people in. The big man with the long dark hair. Fury, Indie had told me. And two blond men. Identical blond men, who sat on either side of Fury, a pack of cards splayed out on the table and a scatter of half-full and empty pint glasses.

"You'd better have put money in the till for those," Indie grumbled in their direction as we passed.

"Nice to see you too, Indie," one of them called out, a hint of a laugh in his voice, raising his pint glass of gold liquid and fading froth in the air.

At the table next to him, another man sat by himself, smoothing his fingers over the glass tumbler he held in his hands. He'd been staring into the bronze liquid as we approached, but as we got closer, he looked up, chucked his chin and dropped his eyes to whatever was in that glass.

Indie stopped a few tables away from the bar where a group of people sat. Two men and two women. The taller couple glanced towards us, the man looking across from Indie to me, and then to the kids, his face as stoic as Indie's, his eyes familiar but not quite the same. The woman next to him was stunning. Thick rich brown hair and eyes framed with a bush of thick dark eyelashes. She was flawless, apart from a scar that ran almost all the way across her right cheekbone, the skin puckered and red.

"This is who is going to look after Mr Morris," Indie said as he stopped in front of the table, Lily's hand still tightly grasping his.

The other woman turned towards her and smiled. A big warm smile, like she was ecstatic to see the small child stood in front of her clutching an injured pink unicorn.

"Hi, there. I'm nurse Suzy," she said gently, playing a part that Indie seemed to have silently asked her to do. "Can I take a look at Mr Morris?"

Lily nodded her little head, holding out the now unstuffed toy towards the petite blonde woman. She waited for the little girl to plonk the toy in her hands and then turned him over, examining his injuries.

"Ok. We're going to need some new stuffing, babe. And my kit out of the cupboard in the back," she spoke to the man next to her, who immediately took to his feet.

He bent down to kiss the top of her head before moving away from us. And I watched him go, another one with long hair tied into a ponytail and a beard that hung a good six inches off his chin. On the back of the leather waistcoat were the same three skulls that I'd seen Indie wear. Their mouths opened wide in a hideous, gloating grin.

Chapter Twenty Six

Indie

Suzy unloaded her sewing kit out onto the pub table, Demon and Ciara shifting sideways out of her way as she spread her tools out. Then she looked up at the little girl, who was still clutching my hand and staring at her injured teddy unicorn with the deepest concern on her little face.

"It'll be as good as new in no time," Suzy said gently, pushing in a handful of the white fuzzy foam into its stomach.

"He. *It* is a he," Lily scorned.

But Suzy was unfazed, glancing up and giving the child a wide smile. "I'm sorry, Lily," she continued. "Mr Morris is going to have a small operation to mend his stomach. And then he's going to need lots of cuddles and kisses to make him feel better. Do you think you can help with that?"

Lily nodded enthusiastically.

"Do you know what I think he'd really like as well?" Suzy asked, her hand rummaging around in the pink unicorn's stomach as she pushed the stuffing into the right places.

Lily shook her head.

"I think he would like it if you helped with his operation. What do you think?"

Lily nodded.

"Come on and sit round here with me then," she said, a look of elation in her eyes as she patted the bench seat beside her.

The little girl slid in beside Suzy, and Suzy bent down towards her, saying something I couldn't hear.

"I forget how good she is with kids," Magnet appeared at my side. "I just wish I could help her have one of her own."

"Still no luck on the baby making project, huh?" I asked, watching the petite blond woman and the little girl with the dark hair working together on the toy lying pitifully on the tabletop.

"No, mate. Just seems every month it's a big fat negative."

"Better try harder then, mate."

"My dick is rubbed raw as it is. Any fucking harder, any more sessions, and the fucker will snap straight off."

"Fucking man up, Magnet. You've got a wife to satisfy. Stop whining about it." I patted him on the shoulder, a little bit of reassurance, and stepped sideways to Emmie, who was watching from a little way away.

"She seems nice," Emmie said faintly as I approached.

"That's Suzy. She's Magnet's ol' lady. Wife," I corrected when she looked at me with that question on her face. "Come on, I'll introduce you to my brother." I guided her towards the next table, to where Ciara and Demon had moved across to allow space for the operation to take place.

“This is Demon, my brother.” Demon looked up at me with a challenge but said no more. “And this is his ol’ lady, Ciara.” Ciara rolled her eyes but smiled at Emmie. “This is Emmie, my…err… girlfriend.”

“So, this is the woman who has been distracting our VP, huh?” Demon asked, a hint of a smile on his face. “If only you knew the things he had us doing… ow fucker!” Demon complained when I drove the toe of my boot into his shin.

“Ignore him, Emmie,” Ciara interrupted. “He’s just grumpy because Indie summoned him here before he’d had his tea. Demon is hangry,” she mocked.

“Maybe I’ll just eat you instead then, huh?” Demon leaned in towards her, grabbing at her lips with his, his tongue bulging out to launch into her mouth.

I turned, shaking my head, and beside me Emmie’s cheeks coloured, a tinge of pink at the show in front of her.

“Come on,” I nudged my elbow into her arm. “Reckon you could help me make up a room?”

Emmie nodded, her eyes drifting to the two people eating each other's faces on the bench. Young fucking love. As if Demon needed any more excuses not to visit our father. I guided Emmie towards the bar at the back of the pub and the door that led to the rest of my house.

Even with her light frame, the floorboards creaked under each step. The building was older than any of us really knew, the only clues the extra wide windowsills and the constant creak and groan as it settled or whinged each time someone stood on it. Yet now it seemed to sing under her weight, a different tune, gentle and rhythmical. Sweet like her.

The corridor led away past a series of doors, one leading down to the cellar, another to the industrial kitchen that was used only to cook breakfasts and the odd bit of catering when the club had an event on. Otherwise, it was just a lonely space of stainless-steel units. And then, almost at the very back, we passed through another door, opening onto a wide stairwell and an even wider set of stairs. And they creaked just as loudly as the rest of the place.

Crossing the first-floor landing, we passed the big heavy door to the room we held church in every week, the dark stained wood hiding the room where club politics played out, or thrashed out, as sometimes had been the case over the years. I guided Emmie quickly past, to the far end of the pub, till the landing ended at a series of windows. A door led off to either side and I ushered her through.

"Wow, this is a huge room," she breathed as she stepped inside.

"Plenty of space here for you and the kids," I waved my hand across at the four single beds. "Just need to get them all made up for you. Even Daisy can take her pick."

"Oh, we never let the dog sleep with us," Emmie replied. "She'll be ok downstairs."

"Well, she's as welcome up here as you are. If you want her to come up with you. Might give the kids a little feeling of comfort having her here too."

"Hmmm, maybe," she answered, not really listening to what I was saying.

"You ok, Spuggy?"

"Yeah. I…just…my house."

"I know it's a mess. We'll get started on tidying it up tomorrow. Demon and Magnet and a few of the others are going to secure it tonight. We'll have you all home as soon as we can."

She turned, her face tilted up towards me, her eyes scanning mine.

"Thank you, Indie."

We had beds to make, and the kids to settle, and I needed to go downstairs and give instructions, to mobilise the troops so I could get Emmie and her kids home again. But right now, I was lost in those beautiful eyes, the deep swirl of sea green. I nudged the door closed behind me, listening for the click as it closed. Then I reached up, grabbing a fist full of that apricot hair and pulling her into me.

She gasped, a mixture of alarm and arousal.

"Fuck," I whispered against the lips that were poised, just slightly apart, ready for my tongue.

And when I slid inside her mouth, I felt the little buckle of her body, the slightest of hints that her knees might not hold her weight. My tongue dashed inside, her mouth hot and wet, a sudden hesitation before she reacted, hers moving against mine, her lips plucking mine. And this time there was a sense of urgency in the way her mouth moved against me, her tongue swirling, her face pushing into mine.

Her hands swiped up my chest, fingers feeling over the muscles, hesitating in places, as if she now dared to feel my flesh. Then on my nipples she lingered, stroking across where they peaked under the light touch of her fingertips. I pulled away, taking a half step back, before grasping the hem of her top and yanking it off over her head in one quick movement. Emmie squeaked, folding her arms across her chest, that same self-conscious reaction to cover herself up.

"Don't, Spuggy," I warned. "There's nothing more I love to see than your skin. And every streak and scar in it. Now drop your arms," the last sentence came out more commanding than I had intended, but she bit her lip and dropped her arms to her sides. "Beautiful," I breathed, reaching out and hooking her left tit out of the cup of her bra.

Dropping my head, I sucked the nipple straight into my mouth, feeling the shudder from her body against my face as I nipped the sensitive little peak between my teeth. And then I teased the other one out, closing my fingers around it, rolling it between my thumb and forefinger as I circled my tongue around the other, blowing air across the top and watching as it tightened further.

"Indie," her voice was breathy, whooshing across the top of my head and disturbing my hair. "Somebody might come in."

"No one is going to come in, little sparrow." I trailed my lips down her stomach, sucking the skin into my mouth just as I stopped above her belly button.

Then, reaching for the waistband of her jeans, I flicked my thumb over the top, pulling both her jeans and her knickers down in one go. My cock throbbed against my own layer of denim, the heavy material rubbing torturously with each movement I made, or each thought I had about her. I pulled my t-shirt off over my head, watching her eyes cascade down my body, following my hands to the waistband of my jeans.

Popping the button, I pulled them down just to the top of my thighs, my hard-on bouncing free, smearing the pearly bead of pre-cum over the material. Emmie's eyes never left my crotch, and I noticed again how she fixed on my cock, her teeth pulling at her bottom lip, her face colouring in beautiful embarrassment.

"It's just a cock. And looks like cocks should."

"It just doesn't really look like what I've seen before… well, I've only ever seen Ga…"

She stopped, and now the embarrassment on her face had turned to fear.

Shit.

"I… I…I'm sorry. I didn't mean to mention…"

As my hand moved to her face, she winced, instinctively closing her eyes.

Shit.

"Emmie, baby. There's no need to apologise. I would never hurt you. No matter what you say or do, Spuggy. Please understand that. I will. Never. Hurt. You."

The knock on the door behind us broke the moment, and Emmie jumped again.

"Indie? You in there?" Magnet's voice came from the other side of the door.

"Yeah. Just a moment."

Emmie gasped, crossing an arm across her chest as she scrambled around for her clothes. I tucked my erection back into my jeans, pulling my t-shirt up from the floor and pulling it on over my head. Once Emmie was fully clothed again, I moved to the door, opening it fully.

"We have a problem, mate. Need you downstairs."

Chapter Twenty Seven

Emmie

Indie's hand wrapped round mine, guiding me out of the room as we followed the man with the long hair and the long beard. He strode out, big, long steps, an urgent pace, the floorboards creaking loudly under our collective weight. The man in front of us muttered something to Indie, but even at my half-stride behind him I didn't catch the words. But whatever they were, his hand squeezed round mine, releasing almost immediately as he realised his reaction and glanced sideways. I caught the corner of his eye before he looked away again, shielding his face and his expression from me. And now I was fearful, my heart gathering a rhythm deep in my chest.

We pushed back through the doors, taking us from Indie's home and out into the pub again. Ahead of us, a row of men stood. A row of patches on leather, multiple crowned skulls ghoulishly laughing at us. Suzy sat upright at the table, Lily cuddling into her side, her eyes wild. On her other side sat Luke. I couldn't see his face, Ciara's arm wrapped around him, crossing over his chest, guarding him from something in front of them.

My heart bounded faster because whatever it was, the men seemed to have created a shield wall and the women were protecting the kids. Daisy stood on the other side of the table, her attention on what everyone else was looking at. The fur at the base of her neck stood on end, and as we drew closer, I could hear a deep guttural growl coming from her throat. I closed my hand around Indie's, squeezing him tighter, the same tightness clinging to my neck, the steely fingers of fear closing around my windpipe.

Indie released me suddenly, his concentration on whatever was out there, and reluctantly I let him move from my side.

The movement of the two men must have caused a draught, enough to make the air circulate a little more, and now I smelt it. It was a burning smell, not that of wood, or of rubber, or anything particularly toxic, but it was familiar. Unpleasant. A memory formed, growing, the smell of burning when I was sat in front of a mirror, the memory of an ache in my arm, of holding something in my hand. And now I remembered that smell. The smell of burning hair when I'd left the tongs on it for too long, or when a strand of hair had wrapped itself around my straighteners and was slowly burning away to nothing. Burning hair.

I shuffled towards the table, to where my kids sat, Lily looking for me and Luke's face ashen with fear.

"What's happening?" I asked Suzy.

"Someone threw in a burning cut."

"Burning cut?" It made no sense.

"Yeah. They've set alight to a back patch and thrown it in. I saw movement, out of the corner of my eye, didn't really pay much attention, but then that smell."

"Burning hair?"

"Yeah, smells like it. But it's the leather burning you can smell, babe. Stinks."

"Who would even do that?"

"We dunno yet. But it's a signal. A slight against the club. My money's on another bike club. I just don't know who."

"There's a few around though, isn't there?"

"Yeah. But none stupid enough to enter Kings' territory to do this. So, it's either a club from out of the area, or a brand new one. Either way, it's not good news."

The smell of burning leather was now no longer my main worry. And neither was some prank by another bike club. But it was the inference that the Kings were not people to be messed with, and that sounded much more sinister than a bike club.

In front of me, the line of men in embroidered leather vests had swallowed Indie up. But then I heard his voice again. A low rumble at first and then something much more intelligible.

"Suzy. Ciara," his voice carried across the pub before emerging through the line of leather. "Take Emmie and the kids upstairs."

He was in front of me now, helping Lily to her feet, gently shoving Luke to his, as Suzy draped an arm around both of them, bowing her head to each and whispering something to them I couldn't hear. But I couldn't hear much now, because it felt like someone had put some of Mr Morris' stuffing in my head.

"What's happening?" I asked him as he got to me, his hand reaching down to stroke the top of the dog's head.

"Just something I need to deal with. I'll explain later. For now, I need you to go with the women and your kids and get upstairs." He ducked his head, kissing me lightly on the top of mine and then looked across at the other two women. "Ciara. Suzy. Show Emmie where everything is upstairs. I need beds making and the kids need some tea."

Ciara's eyes flashed, a stab of defiance, her scar pulling tighter over her face as she scowled. But then she relaxed, nodding, a silent agreement to obey.

"Come on, Emmie. We need to get out of here." She pushed her hand gently into the small of my back, ushering me towards the back of the pub once more. Beside me Daisy kept pace, silently padding, save for a last little grumble as the door shut behind us.

*****

Upstairs, the place was huge, a myriad of rooms tucked away behind doors that surrounded the landing. Suzy pushed through a door just off to the left of the stairs. I'd expected to see a dated room, a lack of investment like the rest of the pub, a room scattered with single beds, with worn carpets and mismatched furniture. But behind that door it stretched the entire width of the building, with smooth white walls ricocheting daylight that flooded in through a series of floor to ceiling windows.

Suzy's boots clattered off the wooden floor, that creaked no less than the rest of the floorboards in the place, but that had been stripped back, and smoothed right down, a thick layer of varnish giving the original floor a modern look, the only telltale signs of its age a slight unevenness.

"Wow!" Lily gasped, her head whipping back and forth. "This is huge."

"Kitchen is this way," Ciara pointed. "No idea what food Indie's got in like, but sure we can sort something out for the kids."

I followed to the left, leaving the sound of Lily's excited gasps as she explored the space above the pub.

"Ah man!" It was Luke I could hear this time, a little further away from Lily. "Look at this gaming console."

I turned, looking across from the kitchen of light-grey glossed units to where the nine-year-old boy was dwarfed as he stood in front of the biggest television I had ever seen. It was mounted on the wall at the far side of the room, the kitchen island, a table and chairs, and then a plush corner settee, all in between. To the right, nestled in the corner, was another unit with three flat screen TVs arranged in a horse-shoe shape, a leather gaming chair pushed up against the desk. And between the units were a series of speakers, tall, thick black boxes with four round circles embedded into them.

"It's like a cinema in here too!" Luke's voice continued to rise with excitement as he moved towards all of Indie's high-tech gadgets that were stored on the unit just under the television. "Wow, he's got everything."

"Think your son and Indie will get on well if they both like computer games," Suzy smiled, sticking her head back through the door, her arms full of bedding. "Ciara, put the oven on, will ya? The kids'll like turkey dinosaurs, won't they?"

"Erm, yeah."

"Excellent. Stick them some turkey dinosaurs and chips in, Ciara. Me and Emmie will get the beds made up."

"Indie has turkey dinosaurs in?" Ciara asked, mirroring my own surprise.

"Yeah. They're his favourite. Tell her Emmie. Indie loves that shite."

"I…err…I didn't know." I admitted, quietly, feeling that twinge of heat on my cheeks.

And what did I really know about him? I'd never asked him much about himself, or his favourite food, or what he liked to do when he wasn't hanging around hospitals. The tiniest of metallic tastes filled my mouth as I followed Suzy out of Indie's living room and across the creaky hall to the bedroom at the front of the property.

"It'll be ok," Suzy said suddenly, our footsteps making the landing crack and groan.

"Sorry?"

"What's going on downstairs? You look worried."

"Worried?"

"Yeah. I can tell. You're chewing on that lip."

"Oh."

"It'll be ok. Happens from time to time, but the lads will sort it out."

"Sort what out?"

"Just the usual bike club shit. Other clubs muscling in on patches and that sort of thing. Not had a burning one for a while, like. It's usually just cut up ones, or sometimes just the rockers off the back mailed to us."

"Rockers?"

"The bits with the writing on."

"Oh. Right. What does it mean?"

Suzy plonked the bedding on the first single bed, passing me a set and pointing over to one bed in front of the windows.

"Depending on which club is responsible for it, could mean a number of things. But normally someone trying to wind us up, threatening to take over our area. Don't worry. It's never happened. Well, not since the noughties."

"And what happened then?"

"Same sort of thing. The guys sorted it out. It was a good thing, really. It brought the bike clubs in the area together. And now we have the coalition."

"What's that?" I shook the sheet out, letting it fall from the folds and come to rest on top of the mattress.

"Like a bike club council. All the clubs have at least one representative there, normally two. They talk out any issues, rather than using their fists, and raise any problems they are having. Ste set it up. To keep the peace between bike clubs. It's lasted nearly eighteen years. As long as my marriage."

She smiled at me, stuffing a pillow into the white pillowcase in her hand. And despite the gentle, unassuming tone of her voice, I couldn't help dwell on some of those words. Of the thoughts of leather waistcoats being set alight and the need for a biker council to keep the peace. Indie told me this was a bike club, just a club, but now it sounded darker and more terrifying.

We were silent for a moment, concentrating on feeding a duvet into a duvet cover without losing the other end. Underneath was a low thrum of voices, men talking somewhere below us.

"There you go," Suzy said, smoothing the duvet onto the bed and tucking it in carefully. "They could just do with a teddy on the top. I'll go get the unicorn finished in a moment. Hopefully, it doesn't smell too much."

"Is there another set of covers there?" I asked, looking around at the two beds, now freshly made up.

"Another set? Thought you'd be bunking in with Indie?"

"I… I don't know that we've really given it much thought, actually."

"Don't worry. None of us are nuns here," she patted my shoulder as she moved towards the door. "And we won't judge you."

Suzy winked, pulling the door free from its frame, and waiting for me to step through.

Chapter Twenty Eight

Indie

The burnt leather cut lay smouldering on the carpet.

"Fuck's sake. Look at the fucking carpet," I kicked at the leather waistcoat with the toe of my boot, the carpet underneath singed and melted in parts. "I'm going to have to buy a new one now."

"If I'd known I just had to burn one of our cuts out on the carpet to make you replace it, I would have fucking set fire to mine years ago and taken the beating. Would have been worth it to see this tight cunt spend some money."

"Fuck off, Fury. Who's fucking cut is it, anyway?"

I glanced around at the crowd in the pub. At Demon who looked as pissed off as me, as the twins who stifled smiles, at Reap with a face like a slapped backside as usual, and to the faces of Fury and Magnet who shrugged in unison.

"Well, someone fucking check it then!"

Sighing, Magnet stepped forward, scooping it off the floor and holding the charred remains out. Inside somewhere would be a name. That was the rule. So, we could always point the finger at the idiot that had lost their cut.

"Looks like it was Beanz cut," Magnet answered, dropping the thing back into a heap on the floor.

"Anyone seen Beanz recently?" I scanned the faces staring at a heap of burned material. "Get him down here. What the fuck happened, anyway?" I asked Fury and Demon when Magnet stepped away, his phone to his ear.

"Heard a bike exhaust," Demon grunted.

"Harley?"

"Yeah. Thought it was just one of our lads. But they came barrelling in, didn't take their helmets off."

"There was more than one?"

"Yeah. Two. Maybe three. But I only heard the one bike. The cut was already alight when they charged through the doors and dumped the fucker on the floor."

I glanced at Fury.

"Anyone recognise them?"

"Nah," one of the twins piped up. "Nothing on their jackets. No colours or owt we could see."

"What you reckon, Indie?" Fury asked, toeing at the cut with his foot.

It could have been anything. Anything at all. But I knew what it felt like.

"Feels like someone prospecting," I swiped my hand across my face.

"But for who?" Twin two asked. I'd given up trying to tell the fuckers apart.

"None of the clubs in the coalition. Not sure even The Notorious would be that stupid."

"Dunno like," Demon muttered.

“Get that thought out of your head,” I pointed at my brother, even if he didn’t entertain the idea of us anymore. “You settled your beef with them at *Noise in the North.* Don’ think for a moment I’m going to give you any excuse to launch into anymore shit with them.”

“Then if it’s not one of the other MCs, then it’s probably someone forming a new club,” Fury turned to me. “And if they’re going round burning the cuts of the lead MC, I don’t reckon they’re gonna come over and sign up to the coalition like good little boys.”

Fury was right. These were the acts of defiance of the olden days. Of times long ago when new clubs were popping up everywhere we looked, and the existing ones were fighting for turf. My dad had stamped it out years ago, but not after we’d lost members, and more than enough blood had been spilled by every other club.

“We’re gonna need a coalition meeting, Indie,” Fury said to me, quiet enough that only he, Demon, and I could hear.

I nodded. I knew it.

"Ok. But it needs to be at *Trouble*. I'm not having the Notorious in here."

"If you reached out to them, it might cement relationships."

"You really think they'll not jump ship if the Bloody Hand are back? They're fucking rats that lot. They'll be the first ones to change allegiances."

"At least if you invite everyone here, we can show strength, open the beers, scout everyone out a bit. You lot can meet, and we'll gather intelligence. Enemies close and all that," Fury shrugged, flicking a strand of long hair back behind his ear.

"Fine. When Beanz gets here find out how he lost his cut. And Demon, whatever the fucking reason, you know what to do."

"Yeah, I do."

And with that, I left them to teach a brother a lesson whilst I went up to see my woman.

*****

I could hear the loud rumble of the computer games before I even opened the door. The room was dull in the fading light, a neon glow catching on the white table in the middle and the smell of a dinner I'd not eaten. The only things I could see were the back of four heads, all sat on the sofa as a green light bounced off the walls and the furniture and guns fired around us. For a moment I winced, the sounds of weapons firing too close a memory, pulling me back to a time of danger, of running for my life, sandy and thirsty.

Yet, whatever I'd seen during my limited time in battle was nothing like I'd seen on the streets of Britain in the middle of a biker war. There were no such things as honour and every such thing as every man for themselves as bike club pitted against bike club to wipe each other out and claim territory. And for the large part, those acts went unnoticed, if you bought off the right people and everyone kept to the code of silence.

"Hey. You all eaten?" I shouted over the bangs of explosions, the entire room feeling like it was vibrating.

Someone turned the sound down, and everyone turned to face me. From somewhere tucked away on the sofa, a little girl bounded, diving over the back of the big leather settee flapping a pink unicorn at me.

"He's fixed! He's fixed!" She shouted, waving the once dishevelled teddy in my face.

"Hey Princess! Mr Morris looks great," I took the stuffed toy from her, turning it over in my hands, unable to see any evidence of the sliced open belly of before. "Suzy did a great job."

"And me, Indie. I did it too."

"Lily was great. Make a good seamstress out of that one," Suzy agreed.

I patted the dark hair, glancing around.

"Any tea left for me?"

"No. But I can make you something," Emmie called, getting to her feet and making her way over to me. "We didn't eat all the turkey dinosaurs."

She smiled, not as wide as I had become used to seeing, a hint of nervousness in her face, but whatever emotion I was seeing, I loved it still. I wrapped my arms around her, pulling her to my chest. For a moment, she stiffened, as she often did when I touched her differently. As if every time I reached for her, I frightened her. But then she relaxed a little, the tiny slump of her body as she exhaled, the tension seeping out with her breath. And I rested my chin lightly on the top of her head, watching Magnet and Demon's women on the sofa, in the middle of a war game with Luke. Beside me, a child's arms wrapped round my leg, gentle but noticeable. For the first time in as long as I'd known, I finally felt like I belonged somewhere. Belonged to someone.

Chapter Twenty Nine

Emmie

It was late. Long after dark. Lily lay sleeping on the voluminous sofa clutching the pink unicorn and Luke yawned loudly, his eyes mere slits as he tried to concentrate on the game and beat Indie once and for all. They'd played on for another few hours, the games console alight with psychedelic pinks and purples, neon greens and bright blues. It was enough to induce a migraine.

"Time for bed, mate," Indie stood up after beating the frustrated nine-year-old for a countless time.

"No. I nearly did it this time. I nearly beat your score."

Indie chuckled, low and velvety, pushing his hand through his thick hair.

"Then you can try again tomorrow."

"Are we staying here tomorrow as well, mam?"

I looked at Indie, uncertain of the answer.

"Possibly. Depends how quickly me and the boys can get your house put back together."

"Please, mam. Can we stay tomorrow too? I like it here. Indie's stuff is cool, and he's got all these games and things."

Indie looked at me this time, shrugging his shoulders, a little grin on his face as if really, he was hiding his elation.

"Come on, bed," I answered, sitting Lily up.

"Here, I'll get her," Indie said, nudging me to the side gently and then scooping the sleeping child off the sofa.

I lead the way to the bedroom in the front, opening the doors and watching as he stepped through them cautiously, taking care not to catch her head or her legs on the frame. And for a moment I watched him with her, with both of them. The way he spoke gently and calmly, the way he cradled my baby in his arms, the way he'd played with Luke earlier, doing all the things their own father had never done with them. And I remembered the conversation I'd had earlier with Suzy, and the feeling of dread that trickled through me that he wasn't who I thought he was. That all of this I saw before me wasn't what it really would be like.

The door closed behind us softly, and he reached towards me, his arm wrapping around me, pulling me into him.

"What's wrong, Emmie?" he asked, dipping down a little, so he was more level with me.

I bit my lip, the spot I'd been worrying for the best part of the day breaking open again, a tiny hint of iron filling my mouth.

"Emmie? What is it?"

"Your bike club," I started, trying to choose these next words carefully. "You're really a gang, aren't you?"

"No. Why would you think that?"

"It was something Suzy said."

"And what was that?" Indie's jaw had tensed. The tone of his words changed.

"About the burning cut. That someone was muscling in on your patch. Patches. Territory. You're a gang, aren't you?"

Indie swiped a hand through his hair, drawing in a breath. And now suddenly I felt afraid of him, like I was going to regret speaking out loud.

"We're a bike club. Not a gang."

"What's the difference?" It was a whisper, words I had no business saying, but I did anyway.

Indie sighed; his face tight.

"We're not criminals, not really. We don't always do the right things by society's standards. But we are a family. People who live by particular rules, who are loyal to each other, look after each other."

He stepped forward, reaching out, wrapping his hands gently around the tops of my arms.

"We test the loyalties of people who want to join us, rigorously. We need to know we can trust them, that they won't disgrace the club's name, that they'll follow club and MC rules."

"But the patches? The talk about territory?"

"We've always had territory. And historically, it has been fought over. No different to neighbouring football clubs, or a spat about jurisdiction and the authorities. We just fight about it in different ways. Or we used to. My dad put a stop to that a long time ago."

His hands moved, cupping either side of my face, pushing up into my hair.

"Spuggy, we're a family. And we look after our family. From the boys in the club to the women they choose to spend their lives with. Once you're someone's ol' lady, we look after you. There's no death till we part. My dad's ol' lady, Tori, we'll look after her too. Even though some of us don't like her. We have to. It's in the rules. It's part of our code. We don't always do the right things, babe. But the wrong things we do are done for the right reasons. And that puts us way above any gangs or any mafia. That's what sets us apart."

I didn't know what answer I was looking for, but not that. The sincerity, the belief in the organisation, whatever that was.

“Come on,” Indie dropped his hands from my face. “Let me show you something.”

His fingers threaded through mine, engulfing my hand in his, and gently he tugged me back along the corridor towards that big open plan living space. But instead of going through the door in front of us at the top of the stairs, he took a right. That door opened up into another enormous room. Not as big as the room along the back of the pub, but big enough that it housed a never-ending table. The pitted mahogany stretched on and on, and I lost count at fourteen chairs nestled around it.

“This is where it happens,” his voice rumbled low and gentle from behind me.

“Where what happens?”

“Church.”

“Church? Oh… Church.”

I understood now. Sort of.

“This is where we hold the club meetings. Every member but the prospects attend. And every member gets to vote or has a say. Every member is listened to, maybe not agreed with, but their view is put forward for us to consider, fairly."

"Why not the prospects?"

"Because they haven't proved themselves fully. Once they have. Once we know they can be trusted to follow our rules, then they become fully patched members. And then they get their say. Until then, they only get to come in here if invited."

"What about the women in the club?"

Indie grimaced, like he was waiting uncomfortably for that question.

"That's probably one of the few rules you're not gonna like, Spuggy."

"Why? What is it?"

"The women don't get to come in here. The ol' ladies, for all we look after them, they're not patched members of the club. No women."

"Why not?"

"It's just the way it has always been."

"Does it have to be that way?"

Indie nodded, solemnly. "It's tradition. It's the rules."

"And who can change the rules?"

"Technically, the club. The whole club. Everyone has to agree with them."

"Then why not change the rules, Indie? If this isn't a gang, if this is a club, why not be more inclusive?"

He frowned slightly, a note of tension in his voice.

"It's easier this way. Women make more reasoned decisions in some ways. But sometimes their femininity and their passion cloud their judgement."

I drew a breath, ready to retaliate, but he continued, those rich brown eyes pinning me in place.

"What would you do for your children, Emmie?"

"Anything."

"Would you save them against all others?"

"Yes."

"Would you save them first before anybody else, without thinking about who else might be in greater danger?"

I let go of the lip that I was pinching between my teeth. "Yes," I whispered.

"And you should, Emmie. Of course, you should. But I assess the situation. I get those that need me the most out first. I think strategically and not just with my heart. In this room we need to make decisions for the club, to benefit all of the club. We need to be strategic. We don't need the passion of women to get in the way of that."

"You sound like you are fighting a war, not running a club."

Indie smiled. It was faint, sad, and full of meaning, but I didn't know what that meaning was.

"It's the rules," he finished, his voice quiet, final. "No women."

I folded my arms across my chest. "Any more rules I should know about?"

"That you shouldn't even be in this room."

"This room?"

I glanced around in the space that we stood, my eyes flitting between the pictures on the walls. It was a rogue's gallery. Some faces I recognised like Indie's, Demon's and Fury's, and others I didn't.

Indie nodded. "Only club members are allowed inside this room. Occasionally other clubs by invitation. But no women."

"Why? I can't see any secrets in here. Just all these pictures. Club members?"

"That's right. Past and present."

"Where are they now?"

"Some are dead, one or two left. But that's pretty rare."

"Why is it rare?"

"Most people join a motorcycle club for life. Very few choose to leave. Some are thrown out, others die."

Indie stepped forward until his body was touching mine, no space between us, and as I took a little step backwards, the back of a chair dug into my back.

"So, if I'm not supposed to be in this room, why did you bring me in here?"

"I wanted you to see it. To see the life I lead, Emmie. I don't want you to be scared of me, or the club."

"I'm not scared of you."

He dipped his head, his lips just brushing mine, so that I could feel the little wisps of air breathed against me, tickling at my skin.

"I don't want you to be scared of me, not ever."

His words were hot against my mouth, his lips following, plucking at me, sucking my bottom lip into his mouth as he stepped closer still so that the back of that chair was now burying into me. His hands moved against both sides of my head, pulling my face into him, his kiss deepening, my tongue battling to keep up with his. With each reaction, his lips became more forceful, taking what he wanted, what he needed. And that ferocity, that sudden assault on my mouth, the bite of the chair in my back, the surge of heat that raced through my veins. I needed him like this, too.

I needed to feel him inside me. Putting out the fire he'd created, not fanning the flames and leaving me to burn from the inside out. But we were in his sacred room. The room I wasn't supposed to be in. The room I probably should never have even seen. The flames inside me flourished, like someone had poured a load of petrol on them and as his lips grabbed at mine, as his tongue dipped and plundered, as his hands held my face there for him to take, I whimpered, loud and pathetic.

"Fuck, Emmie," he spoke against me, one hand moving from my face, the other sinking into my hair, grabbing a rough handful and pulling my head backwards, his lips and tongue landing on the exposed flesh of my neck.

I shouldn't like this. I didn't use to like this. But with Indie, it was all so different. Just the swirl of his tongue on my skin did something to me. Like I'd never been touched. But maybe I hadn't? Not like this. Not in a way I actually enjoyed.

I gasped again as he sucked down onto my skin, his fingers brushing my stomach, grabbing at something. The material pulled up over my head in one quick movement, and my first instinct was to cover up the marks on my stomach.

"No," Indie whispered against my lips, tugging my hands away.

Indie's other hand slid over my stomach, and this time I stifled the wince, biting back the words that told him to get off that sagging part of me. His fingers moved up my body, reaching round my back and then he flicked them, my bra pinging free, his hand sliding straight into the gap he'd created, rolling a nipple between his thumb and forefinger. Gasping, I let my head loll back, his lips and tongue replacing his fingers, his other hand moving over the other breast, teasing my nipple into a tightened peak.

Reaching for him, I let my fingers glide under the t-shirt he wore, feeling over every bump that was covered by tight, tattooed skin. Indie stopped, taking his mouth from my nipple, wisps of cold air attacking the very end and making me shiver involuntarily. Then, over his head, he peeled his own t-shirt off, his muscular body absorbing shadows where the ink covered almost all his skin in a dancing pattern of colour. The silver-grey hair on his chest, caught in the light, shining, the same hair swirling together to form a line on his stomach, and down under the waistband of his jeans.

My fingers wandered over his skin, following the flow of the ink, brushing over the definition of his pecks, the scars hidden in the ink, the skin rougher where the flesh hadn't properly healed. Like mine. And then over the faint ridges of his stomach, settling just above the button of his jeans.

"You want them off, Spuggy?" he asked, his voice hinting at the smile within it.

I nodded, my teeth raking across my lip. Indie's fingers swept over the top button, pinging it free with one deft movement, the zip scraping angrily as it was ripped open. He pushed the jeans over his hips, the trail of hair down his stomach expanding to his groin, dark grey, with flecks of silver, and then as his jeans cleared his arse, his erection jumped out, its angry head peering at me.

Reaching forward, I stroked my fingers over the top, a bead of pre-cum ready and waiting, the head engorged, mushrooming out from the shaft. My fingers only just closed round it.

“I love seeing your hand on my cock, Spuggy,” Indie spoke from above me, his voice thick. “Makes me look so much bigger.”

“It is,” I whispered, not looking up to meet his eyes, fixing my stare on the swollen dick in my hand like it was the first time I’d touched one.

“Alright, Emmie. Trousers off,” Indie’s words were a command. A sudden thud of pressure hit me square between my legs, my stomach clenching. “Now.” His impatience was growing, and his words laced with something raw.

I let go of him, pulling open my own jeans, sliding them down over my thighs. Indie stepped onto them, holding them with his foot as I tugged my legs out.

“And the rest Spuggy. Don’t make me rip them off.”

I shouldn’t like those words he used, the threats they contained. But instead of scaring me, instead of making me feel defeated, belittled, out of control, I felt exactly the opposite. And so, I looked up at him, meeting his eyes and the hunger on his face, and smiled.

“So, it’s like that then, huh?” his voice was almost a growl, a low rumble, a demonstration of the size and power difference between us.

Indie reached for my shoulders, spinning me suddenly, and now I was facing the wall of framed photos that looked more like mug shots than a member’s gallery. He stepped in behind me, kicking my legs apart, pushing my shoulders down. My nipples twinged, hardening against the cold of the wooden table.

“I’m gonna fuck you like this, Spuggy. From behind. I might get rough. Tell me now to stop?”

He was asking permission. Asking if he could do what he wanted. I should be scared, but I wasn’t. Inside, my stomach was on fire, a sense of need building, a static between my legs. I needed him to touch me, to enter me, to fuck me. I trusted him. For the first time, I trusted this man to look after me, even bent over the table, vulnerable.

“I’m gonna need an answer little sparrow,” his fingers ran over the top of the fabric covering my pussy, making me whimper stupidly, a signal for him as he tugged my knickers to one side, pushing the tip of a finger gently inside me. "I need an answer, Emmie."

"I don't want you to stop," I breathed, his fingers sinking lower, my pussy clenching round him.

"Good girl." His thumb swirled my clit and my hips moved back into him, feeling his cock against my bum.

Indie slid his fingers from me, holding me over the table, pulling my knickers down my legs. Then behind me I felt the brush of his hand as he guided himself towards me, sliding the head of his cock back and forth, feeling his way until it sank inside, little by little. Then with a groan, he pushed forward, forcing inside, forcing me open, my body clenching hard, an involuntary motion I didn't think I would truly get over. His hand tightened in my hair, pulling my head backwards, a prick of pain in my neck.

That pang should have made me stop him, made me hate what he was doing, but my pussy pulsed in response, a fresh surge of energy forced through my veins. Indie bent his head forward, his lips plucking at my skin, the scrape of teeth, and then a sudden fullness as he pushed inside and stilled. And now I could feel him flush against me. His groin against my bum, the hand in my hair forcing my head back, another hand in the small of my back, keeping me from getting away. But he stopped, his breathing ragged, his fingers smoothing over the skin just at the top of my pelvis. I squirmed slightly, tilting my hips back into him, a little signal for him to move.

"Careful, Spuggy. I'm not sure I can move right now."

"Why? Am I doing something wrong?"

"No Emmie. Everything about you is so right. But this little pussy is killing me, and if I move right now, I won't be able to hold back."

"I don't want you to hold back, Indie." I never would have thought those words before, and now I was saying them out loud, almost begging this man to hurt me.

He dipped down, kissing my neck again, swirling his hips slowly, so that I felt every thick inch of him move within me. And then I realised I didn't need him to hurt me, no matter how much I wanted it, because every time we were like this together, he made me feel alive. He circled those hips again, and this time I couldn't hold back the cry that slipped through my lips.

"That's right Spuggy. And now I'm going to fuck you hard."

He pulled out, just a little way, and then slowly back in again, carefully building a rhythm. And then again, and again. No faster, just steady. And with each slow movement, I could feel him inside, pulling and pushing through my flesh, awakening every nerve ending in my pussy, sending a thousand tiny signals around my body. Then he pulled back again, stopping a moment as my flesh relaxed, but then suddenly he moved, ramming back into me hard, really hard, the top of his cock hitting me, my cervix stopping him driving it any further. And I did cry out, a gasp of pain, a wail of pleasure, the two sensations mixing into an alien cocktail.

Indie didn't stop, grunting behind me, thrusting and moving, his fist tightening in my hair, his other hand gripping my hip. And now he was muttering, half under his breath.

"Fuck. Fuck. Fuck." His hips moving in the same rhythm, my unintelligible cries mixing with his chants.

The heat building inside me was excruciating, and with each connection with my cervix, my body shook, my legs feeling like they couldn't take my weight. He moved closer to me, the hand moving from my hair to round my throat, his fingernails gently scraping across my skin, his other hand snaking around the front of me, reaching for my clit.

"I can't stay in control much longer, little sparrow. I'm going to need you to come for me." He pushed his thumb against my clit, sending a bolt of electricity up through my legs, and I shouted something that made no sense.

Indie pumped faster and harder as my strangled cries filled the room, his fingers rubbing and pinching at me, and now my body moved on its own, my hips sinking back to meet him, trying to take him deeper and then pushing my pussy into his hand.

"Oh God, Indie," my voice filled the room.

"Come for me, Spuggy. I want to feel you."

I looked up, my eyes struggling to focus, but what I could see were the faces of the club members in the frames on the walls, watching me being fucked by their vice president in their most sacred room. Indie rubbed at me again, and my legs shook, my toes tensing, my fingers scrabbling for something to grab hold of on the table in front of me.

"Ah fuck," I breathed, the sensation hitting me hard, my whole body shaking before going limp underneath him.

Then he took his hand away, putting both on my hips, as I lay flat on my front helpless, Indie's cock pounding into me from behind.

"Good girl, Emmie," he breathed through gritted teeth.

Chapter Thirty

Indie

Her moans and cries drove me wild, the sound of her voice filling the room, her bare tits against the table, her arse on display, at an angle where I could watch my cock sliding in and out of her. I'd wanted to take the time to fuck her hard, to bring her to the edge time and time again without letting her go fully over. But every time I sank my cock inside her she whipped that control straight from my grasp and I became a grunting, rooting lunatic that could barely keep themselves from coming too quick.

It was even better in this room. My only real rebellion against the club rules I helped to enforce. A rebellion against a lifetime of servitude to a lifestyle I had been born into. A lifestyle I could never escape, no matter which way the club voted when my dad's death finally came. I'd never really meant to do that in here. I'd only wanted to show her what I could, the things that wouldn't make her run for the trees, the things that wouldn't make her liken us to some cowardly street gang and her abusive ex. Yet there had been things I hadn't told her. Because if she heard them, she never would want to stay with me. With the club. And I didn't think I could live without her. Not now she had opened my eyes to what I really needed and opened my heart up to something other than the loyalties and ties of this brotherhood.

Now, for the first time, I could understand Magnet and the things he'd done for Suzy over the years. For the pain he suffered when she hurt, the fear for her life in the dark days of a war not that long ago. I felt it all. Consuming darkness, constant worry combined with the deep pull of longing. It wasn't just lust; it wasn't just the need to sink inside this sweet pussy over and over. It went much deeper than that, something I had no words yet to explain.

She was so much younger. So less experienced. But none of that had mattered over the last few days. And suddenly, I realised that in trying to save her, she had saved me.

Emmie panted underneath me, her own orgasm fading away, her heart slowing. I could feel it bounding round her body as I leant over the top of her, my hand still wrapped around her neck, my dick softening slowly inside her. Above, the framed members of the club looked down at us, judging the founding members of my family watching me break their rules right here in front of them.

I'd loved it even more in this room. In the place she shouldn't be in. It was like I'd sacrificed her on an altar, our altar. In the Northern Kings Church, I'd fucked my old lady, willingly breaking the rules. My dick twitched, a spark jolting in me.

"Indie?" Emmie whispered, uncertainty in her voice, a shake in her legs.

I pulled out of her, spinning her over onto her back, pushing her thighs open wider, spreading her open for me to stare down at.

"What are you doing, Indie?" she asked, her voice weak, nervous. The sound ringing in my ears and sending another message to my cock.

I reached my hand down between us, gently gliding over her, her pussy lips still swollen, still wet from moments earlier. Still ready for me to slip back into. Instead, I dropped to my knees, grabbing her legs and pulling her closer, so her arse balanced right on the edge of the table. She smelt delicious. Her scent was heavy and musty, womanly. I remembered the way she tasted the other night. A slight tang and a tiny hint of something savoury, sitting on the very end of my tongue, almost stinging but not quite.

I pushed my face between her legs, inhaling a lungful of the smell of her, closing my eyes and dwelling on the scent of her pussy. The pussy I'd just fucked. The pussy I'd not yet emptied myself into because of the condom I'd just rolled off. I dropped that on the floor too, letting its contents spill onto the carpet.

"Indie? What are you doing?" She squeaked, wriggling, trying to sit up.

"I'm not finished yet, Spuggy," I spoke into her, feeling her squirm under the movement of my lips and the hot air rushing against her wet folds. "Now, be a good girl and I might just let you come again."

"Indie…."

“Shush. The only sounds I want to hear from that mouth are you screaming while I eat you out.”

I pushed her thighs outwards, my fingers sliding up in between, her slick running out to meet me, her scent heavy against my nose. Gently, I teased her lips apart, spreading her open for me, for my tongue. I took one long lick. All the way along her slit, ending at her clit, which I sucked into my mouth. She moaned loudly, leaning back on her table and tilting her pelvis up to the ceiling. I licked again, then sucked against her lips, alternating quickly, each little movement making her gasp. Then I stopped at her clit, flicking the end with my tongue, waiting for that little wriggle of her arse before sucking it into my mouth. She whimpered now, a sweet pitiful noise, and I slid a finger inside of her, crooking the tip and then worked it in and out of her, my lips and tongue playing with her little nub, teasing and assaulting it.

Emmie moved her hips against my face. It was involuntary. I could tell. Her mind sinking into an abyss of pleasure. Using my face and lips and tongue to satisfy herself. Shit, that made me rock hard. I moved my finger from her pussy, her hips stopping suddenly, like she'd only just realised what she was doing.

"Don't stop little Spuggy. I want you to ride my face. I want you to rub your pussy against my lips. I need you to come all over me."

"I can't," she whispered.

"You just were, Emmie. Do it again, or I won't let you come at all."

"Please don't."

"Then you know what to do, little sparrow."

I dropped my head into her again, pushing my tongue inside of her now, thrusting and sucking, taking the place of my finger. Emmie clamped her legs round my head, scooting her arse just that little closer to the edge, her hips moving tentatively. I pulled my tongue out and started on her clit, swirling and licking and sucking. Sucking it hard into my mouth and then flicking the end with my tongue, and now her hips moved. It was slow at first, a gentle rocking. Then I felt fingernails scraping my scalp, a little gasp of breath as she pulled my head into her, her own body moving with me now, her pussy thrusting into my face.

"Oh God, Indie," she cried out. "I can't do this."

But she could. She was. Her pelvis moved into me, each long lick of my tongue, each thrust into her, and she held me tighter and tighter, her hips moving faster and faster. Her pussy rocking backwards and forwards across my face, covering me in her juices, gasping and writhing over my tongue, my mouth, my nose, my chin. And now she was fucking me, using my tongue and lips as she wanted, panting and gasping as she rocked her orgasm out on my face.

"Shit, Indie," she shouted. It was loud, and high pitched, and beautiful, and fuck, it made me so damn hard. "Shit, shit, shit," she repeated with each rock of her hips, her hands wrapped in my hair, forcing my face into her like she would suffocate me completely. And I was so up for dying this way. Fuck me.

Her grip on my hair loosened, her arms dropping to the side of her, the muscles in her thighs relaxing, and the tiny trickle of something warm running over my lips.

That was fucking amazing. Eating her out on that table, defiling the rules of the Northern Kings in front of their very faces, knowing every one of them would have had that fantasy at some point, and I was probably the only one to have lived it out. But I wasn't done yet.

I guided her up, pulling her towards me as I kicked a chair back a little way from the table and pulling her into my lap. She squirmed a little on top of my hard-on, but she was so wet, so well worked in that already her pussy slid over the tip of my cock, and she let out that little gasp that I was coming to love. Emmie closed her eyes, biting hard on to her lip, lowering herself a little further, my cock slowly sliding home for the second time that night.

"Emmie. I don't have a condom on yet. I need to get another." I scooped up my jeans to fish about in the pocket.

She slid down further, halfway down on top of me now.

"Shit. Wait. I don't have another. I need to go get another."

"I. Can't. Wait," she panted, her eyes closed.

"This isn't a good idea, Emmie." She took another inch, her flesh squeezing my shaft hard, forcing blood around my body, and clearly away from my brain.

"I don't care," she whispered, as if she was drunk. "I just need you inside me. Right. Now." She dropped the rest of the way down on top of me, and this time it was me who shouted out, under the onslaught of the pussy that pulled at the flesh over my cock.

"Fuck, Emmie," I grunted as she moved her hips backwards and forwards, the same motion as before, but on my cock now, not my face. "What about birth control?" I gasped as she slid up and down my shaft, her hands grabbing at my shoulders.

"Yes. There'll be no babies. I promise."

"We should still use a condom."

"I know."

But she kept going anyway, and now any last ounce of sense I'd had left had gone. The only thing my brain could think about was the beauty with the apricot hair who'd impaled themself on my dick. I sat still for a while, relishing in the feel of her hips moving against me, sliding up and down my shaft, taking every bit of me before lifting herself off. She was taking her pleasure first. I could see that, and I was going to sit here and watch her get off on my cock. Her eyes stayed closed, her teeth never leaving her lip, as she concentrated on the feel inside her body. She moved quicker, her breaths coming in rocky bursts, a gasp and a moan as she built up her orgasm. Her pussy gripped me tightly with each movement, a pressure building in my balls. My hands moved to her hips, gripping hard.

She was nearly there, nearly ready to come undone all over my cock. And this time I was going to fill that beautiful little pussy full of my cum. Emmie moved away, pulling herself off me, but this time as she started her descent, down on to my shaft, I tipped up to meet her. She gasped a little, her mouth suddenly opening. I helped her up again, feeling for her pussy sitting right over the head of my cock, and this time I pulled her down on me hard.

Emmie cried out, her eyes shooting open, and for a second, I thought I'd hurt her, forced her down on me too hard. But the cry quickly turned to a moan, and she was pulling off me again. And now I tilted my hips just as she hit the bottom of my shaft, forcing into her, pulling her down onto me at the same time.

"Oh, fuck!" she shouted loudly.

"You going to come, Emmie?"

She nodded, and I helped her up my length, yanking her back to me, again and again, her voice filling the room with shouts and cries so loud that I thought we might even waken the dead members. Fuck, she was fantastic. She finally let go. Finally relaxed with me and what a beautiful fuck this was going to be. And just as I pulled her down on me again, I felt her body shake, and her hips rock into me, her head lolling backwards. Her pussy clenched hard, and I pulled her hips over me, following the rocking movement she was making as the last of her orgasm erupted over the top of my cock.

She was fucking amazing when she came like this, when she let go of the fear she'd always been holding onto. Then I rocked my hips, pumping up inside her, guiding her helpless orgasming body over my cock, until I felt the sudden tightening of my balls and the surge of hot come shooting out. And fuck, it felt so good to finally release inside her. I pulled her up and down the shaft, grunting like an animal as the last of my orgasm ebbed away and I'd filled her. Fuck.

I'd been awake for a little over an hour. I wasn't used to someone else in my bed, and every time I'd turned over into her, I'd woken up. A jolt at first, a sudden stab of panic, but after a few more times, it merely woke me. Now, I lay with my stomach against her back, my arm draped over her lightly. I would have tucked my body into hers more snuggly, but pushing the raging hard-on I was sporting against her would not make the damn thing go away. I knew how much sleep Emmie didn't get, and the few hours we'd caught when I eventually carried her tired, naked body out of the club's chapel, was going to leave her drained all day.

Her hair tickled my nose, coconut and soap mixing with the gentle heat rising off her naked body. Daylight crept through a gap in the curtains, and even that tiny slither of light lit up the plain room enough that I could see her. Her eyelashes were darker than her hair, not quite black, more dark auburn, resting lightly over her cheeks, and her lips lay gently together. They were thin, but well-shaped, proportionate to the delicate features of her face, the bottom one fleshier. But it was the dusting of light-gold freckles on her cheeks that stole the show, making her look younger than she was, an immortal innocence.

The door clattered suddenly, before banging off the wall and ricocheting.

"Mam! Mam!" The little voice called.

"I'm telling you; she'll not be in here."

Emmie jolted, sitting upright, clutching the duvet across her chest, her eyes still glazed from sleep.

"Mammy! You're in here. See. I told you she'd be in this room, Luke."

"Hey baby, what's up?"

"We'd lost you!"

"I'm sorry, Lily. Go back to bed. I'll be up in a minute."

"I'm starving." The little voice moved closer. "Mammy, who's that in there with you?"

"Go get dressed Lily, I'll be out in a minute."

"Is that Indie?" Lily squawked.

"Urgh! That's disgusting," Luke's voice now. "Come on, Lily."

Footsteps moved quietly over the carpet, the slight creak of the floorboards underneath the only real sign the intruders were retreating.

"Sorry about that, Indie," Emmie muttered, turning over towards me.

I reached forwards, pushing my hand against her cheek. I didn't care about the noisy intruders. She was here with me. And that far outweighed any early morning wake-up calls. Something vibrated next to us, loud and annoying. Maybe I didn't welcome early morning calls. Reaching out for my mobile, I dragged it off the nightstand, but the vibration of a phone ringing wasn't coming from mine.

"Think that's yours, Spuggy."

Emmie wriggled sideways, picking up the mobile and sliding the green button across, the incessant vibration stopping immediately.

"Hi," she answered with a note of familiarity.

"No. I wasn't on shift yesterday.... No, I haven't lent it to anyone.... Oh God...yes, yes...I see.... I don't know how that could have happened.... wait.... no...I was broken into yesterday. Some stuff was taken.... Yes, a big mess...No I didn't ring the police.... Yes.... Yes.... Ok. I guess I just wait to hear from you then."

Emmie ended the call, but didn't put the phone down. Instead she stared at the black mobile in her hand, her face now pale.

"Emmie?" I turned her towards me. "What is it?"

"I...I've just been suspended!"

Chapter Thirty One

Emmie

"Emmie. I'm sorry, we have to suspend you while we investigate this. I hope you understand?"

Those words. My lip wobbled; my stomach dropped.

"I guess I just wait to hear from you, then?" My voice was shrivelling up to a squeak, anxiety gripping at my throat.

I didn't understand. Not really. Indie was watching me intently, his eyebrows pulling together and wrinkles forming across his brow.

"Emmie?" He pulled me towards him. "What is it?"

"I…I've just been suspended!"

"What? How?"

"There's been some drugs stolen from the hospital. And a load of nitrous oxide."

"So?"

"When they've run security checks, my security pass code was the only one accessing the areas where those things have been taken from."

"Well, it obviously wasn't you."

Indie was angry. I could hear it in his voice, see it on his face. I'd never seen him angry before. Frustrated, tense, but never angry.

"My house. Not much was taken. Just ripped apart. A big mess. They… he will have been looking for my pass."

Indie scowled again, running a hand through his hair, a couple of thick wayward tufts bouncing back up to stare sideways at the wall.

"I always thought it was Gaz and his mates," I continued. "I knew he wouldn't stay away. Even with your guys watching my every move, he found a gap."

I'd always feared that the few short weeks he'd left me alone had would end. It was the disappointment that hit me first, a sudden surge of darkness, despair, knowing I'd never be able to shake him off.

"I should never have called the lads off."

"What do you mean?"

"I called them off watching you. About a week ago. The lads needed to get back to some normal lives and with me being close by, I thought you'd be safe."

I could see the anguish in his eyes, on his face.

"But they didn't stop. Indie. Right until yesterday morning, there's always been a car outside on the street."

Indie stared at me, his eyes flitting across my face.

"Can you describe the car?"

"Uh, yes. It was small. A Corsa or Fiesta. Can't remember the colour."

Indie scrubbed a hand over his jaw, the tiny scratch of stubble on his skin just audible.

"That wasn't any of us. Your description of the car doesn't sound like anything my boys would drive."

My stomach tensed, acid swirling suddenly, and the burn of bile rising at the back of my throat.

"Don't worry, Spuggy. Your house, your job, your ex. I'll sort it all out. I promise."

"How Indie? How can you sort any of it?"

I was growing fond of this man, of watching him with my kids, of spending time with him, of lying in his arms all night after we'd spent long hours of the night having sex. But he made big promises, promises he couldn't possibly keep. I smiled, encouragingly, like the way you do to a child when they tell you they're going to be a famous footballer when they grow up, or a princess.

He reached forward, pushing his palm against my face, the tips of his fingers in my hair.

"I will sort it, Spuggy. You'll see. But for now, you're just going to have to trust me. Do you trust me?"

"I trust you on a lot of things, Indie."

"That wasn't what I was asking. Do you trust me?"

"I trust you'll try. And that's all you can do."

A floorboard creaked, and then the door banged against the wall again.

"Oh God," a woman's voice shouted.

"Tori! For fuck's sake!" Indie barked, anger resurfacing. "What are you doing here?"

"What are *you* doing in bed with your dad's nurse?"

"It's got fuck all to do with you who I have in my bed. Now fuck off downstairs."

His words leaked venom, their harshness even making me recoil. But the woman they were aimed at didn't flinch, leaning a shoulder against the wooden flame.

"I've come to talk to you about your Da."

"Then you can wait downstairs till I'm ready to talk to you about it."

"And why are there kids in your kitchen?"

"Tori, I'm not going to tell you again. Downstairs. Now."

Tori shrugged and turned, leaving the bedroom door gaping wide open. I clutched the duvet cover around my chest, staring at the space the woman had been.

"Fuck's sake," Indie muttered, swinging his legs out of bed and grabbing a pillow to cover his groin. He padded to the door, pushing it back into the wooden frame with a forceful thump. With his back to me, I admired him. The tattoos didn't continue, his skin bare of ink. But as his arms moved, so did the muscles in his back, skin pulling tightly over the lumps of hardened flesh. And just above his pelvis were two little dimples leading the way to a pert bottom and to the right cheek, which had a star-shaped wound on it.

"Your bum, Indie. Is that another scar?"

"Checking my ass out, huh?"

"No. Yes. Maybe."

"Fury shot me."

"Fury did it? Like friendly fire?"

Indie chuckled, a release of tension, the smile lines reappearing at his eyes, and the dimple in his chin evident.

"No. He was messing about with a gun. We were both drunk. It was a long time ago."

"A real gun?"

"Aye. A pistol. He'd bought one off a guy. Wanted to know if it worked."

"So, he aimed it at you?"

"Nah. The bloody thing didn't fire. Not at first. He'd stopped pointing it on the targets he was supposed to be aiming at, and started messing around with the gun, working out why it was a dud. Whatever was stuck, he unstuck, and it fired right into my arse. Couldn't sit down for a week. You can imagine the shit the lads gave me for it."

But even with the lightness in his voice and the laugh that sat around the edges of his words, there was a sense of darkness. A half-truth. Something he wasn't going to tell me. And maybe I didn't need to know. He'd been in the army. He had wounds. So, I stopped asking questions I didn't know whether I wanted the answer to, such as why Fury bought a gun in the first place.

Indie padded away to the far side of the room, disappearing behind a door, the sudden sound of water cascading over a hard surface.

"Want first shower, Spuggy? Or we can just share?" Indie asked, poking his head back into the room.

"I…errr… I don't mind."

"Then I reckon we should share. Saves on the water bill."

"No. You just go; I'll jump in after."

Indie turned, then stopped, stepping back into the bedroom.

"If this is something about you being naked in front of me, then I'm not accepting first shower."

"It's not that."

"Is it not? Then prove it. Get over here."

"I…," I looked around, at a room with mirrored wardrobes, my clothes nowhere to be seen, a duvet too heavy to swipe off the bed to cover myself with.

"Tick Tock, Spuggy."

Indie stepped towards me, absolutely naked, the light streaming in reflecting off the mirrors on the wardrobe doors so that not even a shadow covered him. His tattoos bulged over muscles, his skin perfect, his scars hidden mostly by ink. But they weren't the same scars as mine. He didn't stop or slow down, marching towards me as I sat clutching the duvet over my body.

"On your feet, Emmie," it was a command, a tone I'd heard him take with his club members, but never with me. "Now."

My stomach leapt and tightened and leapt again and I stared at the hand he stretched towards me, waiting for me to place mine in his. He wasn't going away. That was clear. And I didn't think he was going to let me stay covered by the white quilt. But if I ran quick enough and stared straight ahead, at least I didn't need to see myself.

Pushing back the covers, I leapt out of the bed, fixing my eyes on the bathroom door and ignoring the palm offered to me. One step. Two steps. Two more and I could make a dive across the remaining space. Yet, as I took that next step, I felt fingers close round my wrist. A sudden pull.

“Please,” I whispered, not daring to look to my right, shaking at the grip on my arm.

“Emmie,” his voice was a low warning.

I shook my head in answer. An answer that was ignored. Indie pulled at me, almost rough enough to spin me towards those wardrobes and into his body. I could feel him against me. Skin on skin. His warm flesh against my back.

“Open your eyes, Emmie.”

I bit my lip, taking a deep breath, and did as he wanted. He stroked a hand under my breast, cupping it, his fingers reaching for my nipple.

“You have beautiful tits.”

“They’re small and they sag.” I desperately wanted to look away.

“They’re perfect. They fit right into my hands. They’re fleshy. I don’t expect them to stick out and poke me in the eye. These have fed babies. They’ve provided a better service than anything my body could do."

"That's not true. You were in the army. Fighting. Protecting our freedoms."

"I was killing while you were bringing life. There's no joy in what I did."

His hand slid down my stomach, fingers stroking over the hideous red lines that spoiled my skin.

"These are better medals than I ever won. You grew two healthy children. You're a brilliant mam…."

"I can barely provide for them. Some days I struggle to find money to feed them. What life is that?"

"They're strong, healthy. They don't even realise that you struggle because they never feel like they have nothing."

"Luke knows. He knows most of his birthday and Christmas gifts are second hand. I can see it in his eyes."

“And he knows he still has Christmas and birthday presents.”

“And time. I never spend time with my own kids, because I work every extra shift to make sure I can afford just to feed them. And when I do have time, I can’t afford to take them anywhere or do anything.”

“They just need a mother’s love. You’re still there with them. When my mam left, Dad fought for custody. With the power of the Club and his contacts behind him, she really had no chance. Do you know what I was doing growing up?”

I shook my head, watching him watch me in the mirrors, not letting my eyes stray from the reflection of my body at any point.

“I was being made into a soldier. Not to fight for Britain. To fight for the bike club. To beat a man with my bare hands. I was made to watch my Da and his brothers decide about what punishments to dish out onto our own members, never mind competing bike clubs. And all in the name of power.”

And that was the dark side of the bike club.

“Thought you said you weren’t a gang.”

"We're not. But we've done tough things in the past, especially under my uncle's rule. It's better now, mostly. The life is easier. Not as vicious as it once was. My Da took the club in a better direction. He never wanted to be president. But when Ade died, he was voted in over his own brother. And now when he dies, they'll vote me in. And I don't want the title either."

"Then why don't you quit?"

"I can't. It's not something we do. Remember, I told you there is no death do us part?"

"But last night, you said some members had left."

"Very few have. In extreme circumstances. One was kicked out. Everyone else died. Yet they're still a part of the club. Their faces are still there on that wall. But this isn't about me, Emmie."

He gripped my jaw suddenly. His fingers were gentle, but there was a determination behind them as he turned my face back to the mirror.

"Look at yourself, Spuggy. This body is incredible. Every time I look at any part of you, I want to fuck you. You're the most beautiful person I've ever met. Inside and out."

His hand slid further down my stomach, his fingers tickling my skin with their gentle descent. Then they came to rest at the very top of my mound. Inside, my pussy clenched, desperate for his touch. He turned his head, his lips brushing my ear.

"I want you to stand every morning and look at yourself naked. I want you to see what I see. I want you to see why you drive me insane."

He pushed against me, the bulge of a hardened cock against my back, his fingers sinking lower in front, cupping underneath. I tried to wriggle away, to turn my face away, his hand slipping lower.

"Watch yourself, Emmie. Watch yourself be fucked by my fingers."

He pressed against me, his eyes fixed on mine in the mirror. "Look, Emmie."

He moved again, a finger sliding inside. Moving in and out slowly three times, and then he filled me with another. I gasped. I watched my face scrunch. Another finger, stretching me, making my heart pound and my expression change again. His thumb pressed against my clit, and I frowned, biting down on my lip. And then he let loose, pumping his fingers in and out, his thumb moving over one of the most delicate parts of my body in a tortuous, rapid rhythm. My moans came loud, but I didn't shut my eyes, instead I watched my mouth open and close, gasping, moaning, gaping. His hand pounded between my legs, and my legs shook. I could see it in the mirror, the little vibration of my flesh. Moving my legs further apart, letting him get deeper, my cheeks flushed with red, my brow wrinkled. My eyes opened, then closed again, no one body part able to stay still as he thrusted and pushed, hooking the top of his fingers suddenly and pushing against the front wall of my pussy.

I cried, my hands moving over the top of his, pushing him back into me, helping him pump my pussy with his fingers. And I stood writhing against his hand, coming on his fingers, watching myself fucked by a man nineteen years older than me in a mirror. Fuck. Shit. Indie. My body shook hard, my insides clenching around him and in the reflection, he smiled at me.

"Good girl," he purred.

Chapter Thirty Two

Indie

"Luke, Lily. What do you want for breakfast?" Emmie called to the back of her kids' heads.

Luke had already lost three lives on the games console as it was, and now insurgents surrounded him. It really didn't look good.

"Luke's gonna die again, mammy. And he still won't give me a turn."

"I've got stuff in for pancakes, Emmie," I called out, watching the young boy wave his weapon, surrounded by the enemy.

"Pancakes?" Emmie asked, opening the cupboard in front of her.

"Yeah. Always have stuff in for pancakes. Granted, it's out of a packet. Bottom cupboard, just there," I pointed.

"Ah, man. I can't get past this level. Indie, you got past this level?" he called, his eyes fixed on the giant television in front of him.

"Yeah, mate. Ages ago. I'll show you how to do it later. Get your breakfast," and then I turned to Emmie. "I need to go downstairs and talk to Tori. She's been waiting for me for nearly forty minutes. She'll have either drunk all my drink or shit in the sink just to piss me off."

"Would she really do that?"

I smiled. "Nah, babe. I was just being dramatic. But she'll probably chew my ear off. Better get it over and done with."

Although when I got downstairs, she'd helped herself to coffee, the coffee machine now lit up like a Christmas tree.

"Fucking hell, Tori man. What have you done to this?"

"I dunno. Pushed a few buttons till something came out."

The dark-haired girl moved to the doorway and crouched down, coffee cup in hand, her other feeling over the charred patch in my carpet.

"What happened to your carpet?"

"Some arseholes tossed a burning cut through the door."

"Really? Who's was it."

"Beanz."

"Beanz? Is he ok? How did they get hold of his cut?"

"Seems the daft fucker lost a spare one."

"Didn't know he had a spare," Tori commented.

And for a moment, something rang in my head, something I couldn't quite grasp.

"No. Neither did I." But this conversation was club business we were encroaching on, and that wasn't a discussion with Tori, no matter who's old lady she was.

"What are you doing here, Tori?"

"How long you been fucking Ste's nurse?" There was a hint of tension in her face.

"Tori," I warned. "You wanted to talk to me about my dad?"

"Yeah. He wants to come home, Indie. The hospital says they can get him comfortable and then he can be nursed from home."

"Ok."

"Well, I thought it would be better if he came here to the clubhouse, rather than our house."

His house, not hers, but I didn't correct her.

"Why? Surely, he wants to be in his own home?"

"Thought it would be for the best. Plenty people round here to help, and he can stay involved in the club a bit more. It would be where he wanted to spend his last days, Indie. And besides, if we've got a live-in nurse, reckon that would be even better. It's not like she's got a job to do anymore. Heard she got herself suspended. Might as well be useful to the club."

I stepped back, the sudden pang of rage making my fists twitch. I'd never been keen on the woman when Demon first brought her to the club, and even less so when she moved onto my father when Demon dumped her. None of us had expected it to last, but a leach like Tori wasn't going to go away easily and somehow my dad had become besotted with her. I would never hit a woman. Never. And never the old lady of the President of the club. But my fucking God, if this woman didn't push my limits.

"Ok, whatever. We'll set him up in his usual room."

"Good. Oh, and Indie?"

"Yes?"

"He wants to go to the Howl."

"What?

"Yeah. This weekend. Reckons it'll be his last rally, and he wants to be there, Indie. Reckon I could get him there in the car. Don't think he'll be able to ride his bike. But at least he'll be able to go."

"Fucking hell."

"Well, what do you think?"

"I think it's a crazy fucking idea." I swiped my hand across my face. A cold rally in the middle of Northumberland was no place for a dying man. But then, maybe that's what his thinking was, anyway.

"It's his last wishes, Indie."

"Yeah, I bet it is. If the fucker snuffs it in a tent, I'm not tying his dead body on the back of my bike to get him home. You'll be bringing him back in the car, understand?"

"Roger," she answered, touching her hand to her forehead in mock salute. "Thanks, Indie. I appreciate it."

"Yeah, whatever. Now, if you don't mind, I've got some kids to get to school."

"Someone's got you wrapped round her little finger, huh? Got you playing the part of daddy already, she has. Is that what she calls you, Daddy? You're old enough to be hers."

I didn't need to say the words 'fuck off'. She could see them in my face when I turned and walked towards her, the limits she was pushing against becoming more and more frayed. And whatever I felt inside must have been displayed all over my face, because she threw her cup onto the nearest table and bolted out of the door.

*****

"How's Emmie's house looking?" I asked the men sat around the table.

"It's secure. We've put an alarm system in. We paying out of club funds for that?" Fury asked.

"Yeah, mate. I'll get you some money."

"Do we not get to vote on that, Indie? Just we don't even know this woman and her kids, and now you want to go spending club monies on her."

The table went silent, an energised hush, and all faces turned to stare at the bald-headed, Beanz.

"Actually, you're right. We should take a vote," I answered, anger straining in my veins. "As part of Beanz's punishment for losing his cut…"

"I didn't *lose* it. Some fucker stole it."

"For the punishment of not realising weeks ago that his cut had been stolen when his house was broken into. Shows how much riding you been doing lately," I added, watching the man across the table frown at me. "I put it to the brothers that he will pay the sum of…how much was it, Fury?"

"Five hundred, mate. Parts and labour."

"Ok. Five hundred pound fine."

"But I've already paid the price," Beanz whined, blinking a few times as the fat, black eye on the left hand-side of his face watered.

"Votes?" I charged on, ignoring the protest. "All in favour."

All but one person held their hands in the air.

"Beanz. Five hundred to Fury, on behalf of the club."

The bald man said nothing, his bruised face sullen, the one eye that wasn't swollen shut, dark with anger.

"Now, about cuts. Who else has a spare?" I glanced around the table.

The twins slowly held their hands in the air, followed by Magnet and a few others.

"Fuck's sake. I want all spares handed back to Suzy. No one has a spare, understand?" I glanced around the table to see the curt nods from the offenders. "You will look after your only cut. You will know where it is at all times. If it's not on your backs, it's locked away. No one else touches it. And if you lose the fucker, or damage the fucker, there's a price to pay, physically and financially. Don't be a Beanz."

I glanced around the table, listening to the muttered 'ayes'.

"Good. Now onto the Helmhiem Howl. Ste wants to go."

"Ste wants to go to the Vandals' rally?" Big Red asked.

"Apparently so."

"Is that a good idea? I mean…." The big red-headed, bearded club treasurer drifted off.

"Nope. But who am I to step in the way of a dying man and his last requests?"

The rest of the room shrugged, but I didn't miss the looks they shared with each other.

"Magnet, Fury, Demon. Stay back a minute. Big Red, the rest of the clubs will arrive shortly for the coalition meeting, get the women to get the bar running and be hospitable, but I don't want any of these fuckers stepping out of line."

Chairs scuffed against the carpet, the floorboards straining from multiple footsteps, and when the door closed into place, I turned to the remaining men.

"What's up Indie?" Demon asked, knowing a fresh set of instructions was coming his way.

"Emmie got suspended this morning?"

"From work?"

"No. The fucking ceiling…."

"We don't need to know what you were getting up to last night, mate," Fury chuckled, Demon and Magnet joining in, and I glanced to where they stood midway down the table.

To where I had spread her open last night, fucking her roughly, with no regard for any of the club rules. Just the thought of it today already sent blood rushing to my cock, and getting a hard-on in front of the lads would do nothing for my club cred.

"Her security pass was taken in the break-in. It had to be. Her pass had accessed the areas where the drugs and the laughing gas were stolen from. The hospital has suspended her while they investigate. I want those investigations concluding quickly to get her back to work. Find out who owes us favours or who we can lean on to get her cleared."

Magnet and Demon shot a look at each other, a mix of exasperation and uncertainty. We had contacts all over the place. Some who'd been on our books for years and others that we'd covered up for or held dirt on them. I suspected hospital management wasn't any of those. But I'd promised Emmie I would get her job back, that I'd put everything right and I would, whatever it took.

Fury and Magnet wandered out, Demon loitering.

"What?" I asked him roughly.

"Not sure how we're going to get her job sorted, mate. That's out of our league. We can bribe and blackmail. I can frighten as many people as possible, but I've no clue how to convince a load of people in suits to lift a suspension. She's innocent in all this. Why not let it play out?"

"Because I can't stand seeing how much she's suffered at the hands of this prick of an ex. How the kids suffer. I want this all to go away."

"What about the Viking then? He owes us his life. I reckon that's a pretty big favour to call in."

"And what are we going to ask him to do?"

"His mafia mates can sort the job situation out. Cian has a way with the authorities and a link in with the police. And V can sort the ex out."

"I'm not killing her ex, Demon. He's the dad to her kids."

"Not much of a dad if he beats their mother up. V knew that as much as I do."

"She would know it's me, us, if I order a hit. I don't want to lose her, Demon. I know you can appreciate that."

"Ok. Whatever."

Demon left me alone, and I slumped back into the chair at the top of the table, listening to the purr of voices in the pub below me as it filled with bike club members from all around the north east of England.

*****

The chapel was bursting at the seams, the first time in as many years that we'd held a coalition meeting on anywhere other than neutral ground. Two representatives from all the bike clubs sat around the table or leaned against the walls where there were no chairs left. There was a buzz, people muttering and talking in low voices as the last of the clubs piled in.

"Is someone babysitting Demon?" I muttered to Fury, sitting on my right-hand side.

"Aye. Magnet and Reap are keeping a close eye on him. Him and Thrash have squared up to each other already."

"Fuck's sake. The last thing we need right now is any more beef with the Notorious. Although I'll bet they're behind the business with the cut."

"Me too, Indie. But that needs to be kept between us for now."

I nodded, standing to my feet.

"Thank you, everyone, for coming here to the Northern Kings' clubhouse for the coalition meeting this month. We're pleased to host this for the first time in years. There'll be food served afterwards. Help yourself."

The room vibrated in a low grumble of voices. Thank yous and acknowledgements. To the MCCs, this was an honour to be allowed into the sacred room of an MC. For me. This was a ball ache and a risk. But here we were.

"Just the other day we had a threat against the club," I started after regular coalition business concluded. "A burning cut was thrown through the pub doors."

I scanned the faces around the table and those that lined the walls. Shock, confusion, and some showing nothing at all.

"Any clues who was responsible?" Tomahawk, the Valhalla's Vandals president, asked.

"A few men on bikes. Unpatched from what we could tell."

"And the bikes?" Brie asked, the voice of the Angels and Demons president coming from the far end of the table.

"One Harley, a Harley copy, and some scrappy sort of scrambler."

"Sounds like the sort of shit prospects would do," Brie continued.

"Not for years, though. We stopped most of that fuckery after the last war," I answered, trying to pay close attention to the faces of the members in the room.

"The Hand has been sniffing around for weeks. And we've had issues with unmarked riders trailing us," Tomahawk continued. "This sounds like a new club prospecting. The Hand have previous for starting up new clubs to target the existing ones in the area."

"And just putting pressure on clubs," Tez interjected. "Some of the MCCs have had their bikes stolen. One from Tyne Thunder just a few days ago. Police haven't got a clue who took them or where they've gone."

"Aye, those bikes are long gone, Tez, mate. They'll swap the plates and grind the numbers off the chassis. But that definitely sounds to me like a new club prospecting," the old Angels and Demons president addressed the room now. "We used to do that years ago. Part of the initiation of a new club. But normally, an existing club would sponsor you, support you, because it supported their interests in taking out others. Which means someone in here is helping a new club be born."

The room fell into a static hush, heads turning to look at their neighbour, to look for a reaction, any hint it might be them.

"Brie, this isn't MCC territory. There's no way any of the MCCs would get in on this shit. We know the consequences," Tez's voice held a note of panic.

"This stinks of the Bloody Hand," Tomahawk added. "Their visit the other month was never about keeping up old alliances. It's all about a takeover in England."

"Fuck's sake, Tomahawk," it was Thrash this time, the Notorious VP, his own president, keeping quiet. "You and your conspiracy theories. It's probably just another club trying to get some purchase. I suggest we find out who they are and invite them to the table."

"Not before we teach them a lesson in MC etiquette," Fury grumbled.

The bang rang out around the room, Tomahawk rising to his feet, a whole note of tension sweeping everyone's faces. I grabbed Fury's arm, just as I felt the little movement beside me, stopping him from rising to his feet as well.

"I'm telling you, the Hand is back. They are already testing our security. Who else here has had break-ins or attempts at break-ins?" Tomahawk asked angrily.

Hands rose around the room. Every bike club president, MCCs included, held an arm in the air.

"A war is coming," the huge Vandals' president with the braided dark hair growled. "Make sure you're on the right fucking side of it."

Inside my stomach, a vortex had opened, whirring and pulling at my insides. We'd won the last one. Not without some serious casualties. But those old Kings' members had nearly all gone, and our firepower wasn't what it was. I didn't know whether we could withstand another one. And I was about to pull Emmie and kids right into the middle of it. I wasn't sure I could let myself do that.

Chapter Thirty Three

Emmie

Men in leather spilled through the pub doors, the big space below Indie's rooms filling quickly. Outside, the air rumbled with exhaust after exhaust. A cacophony of voices, deep, guttural calls of motorbikes.

"Can I go see the bikes, mam?" Luke asked excitedly.

"No, sweetheart," Suzy interrupted from where she sat beside Lily, helping her feed fabric into the sewing machine. "Not tonight. There's a lot of people coming in here right now. You're probably better going upstairs and playing on the computer."

"But Indie's too busy to play with me," Luke whined.

"He'll come and play when he's finished some meetings. Why don't you take Lily up and put something on that you can both play? I'm sure Daisy could do with some company," I prodded, hoping to coax the kids from the ever-filling pub, the noise of gruff voices and expletives filling the space.

"I could take Daisy for a walk?"

"I've already walked her, Luke. And it's getting dark."

The young boy huffed, looking defeated.

"Go with Luke, baby," I said to Lily. "I'll be up in a minute."

The kids retreated slowly, eventually disappearing behind the door that led up to the living quarters above the pub. Another group of men moved passed us, with backs of embroidered runes surrounding a Nordic helmet.

"They're the Valhalla's Vandals," Suzy spoke almost into my ear.

"I recognise them. They were the ones that stopped us on the road back from Holy Island."

"That's their patch. They hold one of the biggest geographical areas, covering nearly all of Northumberland."

"Are they mean?"

"Not really. Tomahawk, their president is intense, and Flat Pack, their VP, he's eternally pissed off with us."

I glanced over at the men. The president was tall. Super tall, and wide, consuming the space he stood in like a dark cloud on a thundery day. He had a patch of long dark hair, braided into a bunch of plaits that fell down his back, the sides of his head completely shaved. I couldn't see much of his face, but when he turned to talk to the smaller, older, grey-haired man beside him, I could see crops of tattoos on the exposed skin on the side of his head. Runes to match the embroidery on the back of his cut.

"Your kids are beautiful," Suzy said from beside me suddenly.

"Oh…err…thank you. They can be a handful. But can't all kids?"

Suzy smiled sadly. "I don't really know. We don't have any yet."

"You sound like you're planning to, though?"

The blonde-haired woman nodded. "Yes. But so far, we're not really getting anywhere."

"They'll come. They might just take time. Some people take longer than others to fall pregnant."

"We've been trying for four years," she said, just loud enough that I could make out the words.

"Oh. I'm sorry."

"Did it take you long to fall pregnant with yours?"

I bit my lip, knowing my answer wouldn't help this woman feel better. I'd heard the same grumble for years from my mother.

"No. I hadn't planned for either of them."

Suzy nodded, saying nothing, but she couldn't hide the defeat in her eyes.

"Have you seen the doctor?"

"Yeah. Had tests and everything. Can't find anything wrong with either of us. We've tried fertility drugs and all sorts. Just not IVF yet."

"I hear that's supposed to be effective," I offered, feeling her sadness seeping into my skin.

"Yeah. It's expensive. And because we don't have any diagnosed problems, we can't get it on the NHS. Magnet is saving up hard, though. So, hopefully, we might get a chance soon."

*****

"Hey, Spuggy," Indie said softly, the bed dipping under his weight.

"How did your meeting go?"

"Yeah, well, no one got punched, so that was a win. Hey, do you reckon you can get your mam to watch the kids at the weekend?" He quickly changed the subject. "The Valhalla's Vandals rally is on. It'll be chilly this late in the season, but would be a weekend away."

"Hmmm," I snuggled against his warm, bare flesh. "A weekend spent in a tent in the cold and probably in the wet?"

"Uh-huh."

"How could I possibly say no?"

"Yeah, but your mam could."

"I guess. I'll ask her. See if she's not on shift, whether she would have them."

Indie kissed the top of my head.

"It would be good to have you there. But it'd also make me feel better having someone to hand just in case my dad has a turn."

I jolted upright.

"What do you mean?"

"My dad, he's coming to the rally, too."

"Indie…"

"I know. I know. It's a stupid idea. But it's in his head that's what he's going to do. And well, he's dying anyway. It's not like we're taking him to Disneyland to go on the rollercoasters."

"I get why you want him home, Indie. But a rally? A tent? Dying or not, it's really not a good idea."

"I know, Emmie. I'm not for it. I've told Tori we'll bring him home at the first sign of him deteriorating. And she's taking him up in the car. So, he'll not be riding the bike up."

Indie pulled me down into the crook of his arm, his flesh warm, and I snuggled against him, listening to the sound of his heart beating in his chest, my own mimicking a similar rhythm.

*****

"I didn't expect the rally to be so big. It looks like those music festivals I've seen on TV," I muttered to Indie as I passed him another long, thin black pole.

It had rained on and off the entire ride up north, and the air grew cooler as we moved closer to the Scottish Border, sea air tussling with cold clouds blown down from the mountains by a north-easterly wind.

"Us bikers like a party. And we don't get to do it often enough."

"Do you have rallies all year round?"

"No. It gets too cold for a tent in the middle of winter and even fuelled on alcohol and other stuff. We're not that mad. This is the last before winter.

The *Frostbite Frenzy* is the first one afterwards. In March, in the Lake District. More torture and a survival challenge rather than a party."

I glanced across at the tent not far away. Magnet and Fury were building it, but it wasn't for them. Tori, Ste's dark-haired girlfriend, sat in the driver's seat of the car, watching the men work, and Ste shuffled about, chatting to another group who'd ridden up at the same time as us. I couldn't catch the badge because it wasn't on their backs. Some sort of Thunderbolt embroidered on the left side of their jackets.

"They're Gateshead Thunder," Indie answered, even though no words had left my mouth. "Tez, the President was one of us a long time ago."

"He was allowed to leave?"

"Yeah. Extenuating circumstances. If anyone earned a get out free card, it was Tez. Anyway. He couldn't stay away from the life for long, so he took up with an MCC Gateshead Thunder. They're pretty close to us. Friends."

"They wear their badge on their front."

"Yeah. That's because they are an MCC. Sort of affiliate bike club. They'll meet up, have a drink, subscribe to some rules and values, but they don't take it as seriously as we do. Guess that's the difference."

In the time I watched, passing poles and tent pegs when Indie needed them, tents had taken over the landscape. The wet green field was full of a myriad of shapes and colours, and the gentle rain which landed softly on the grass now tapped onto taught polyester and nylon.

"Who the fuck are they?" Fury asked, sidling over to where Indie hammered in the last of the pegs, pulling the porch of the little tent tight.

Craning my neck, I followed where the men stared. All I could see was another band of bikes riding across the field. I counted ten, maybe less, packed tight with panniers and tents tied to the back. They were all single riders, dressed in the usual black leather and black helmets, riding in the same formation that the Kings had all the way up here.

The riders passed us slowly, all heads turning in our direction. The slow movement meaningful. Threatening. And on their backs as they crawled away from us was a fan of cards, aces, the ace of spades sitting prominently on the top.

Chapter Thirty Four

Indie

"When the fuck? How? Who created those?" my father panted, as he stopped at my side, dislodging the little bottle of oxygen that hung off one shoulder, and dumping it beside the seat he then collapsed into.

"Judging by the back patches, I'm guessing the Aces."

"And who the fuck are they?"

Emmie shifted nervously on my other side, and I slid my hand over hers, clasping her fingers with a little squeeze. It was supposed to reassure her, a little signal that it was all ok, but her arm felt heavy, her fingers rigid against mine.

"Reckon you can go unpack the sleeping bags and stuff into the tent now that it's up, Spuggy?"

She looked up at me, uncertainty swirling in her eyes, and slowly nodded, slipping her hand from mine and approaching the bike to scoop what she needed out of the big leather panniers.

"I'm pretty certain they're a street gang turned bike club," I answered my father eventually as we both stood watching them set up camp not far from us.

That wasn't a fluke, either. The proximity of the camp was supposed to be a threat in itself. A blatant disregard for the lead MC in the north east of England.

"I'm guessing since I know fuck all about this, that they haven't declared themselves to us. Or had those patches signed off by the coalition?"

"No. The last dealings we had with them was when Demon roughed them up, Emmie's ex in particular."

"Emmie's ex is an Aces gang member?"

"Yeah."

"And why have you never told me this before now?"

"It wasn't relevant to anything."

"It's fucking intelligence, that's what it is. You know I'm not dead yet, don't you?"

"Aye. Unfortunately, you're still here chewing my ear off."

"Aye. And I'm still the president. I should know this shit."

Ste turned and shuffled back to his tent, slinging the little tank back on his back as he went.

"Reckon they're responsible for the burning cut?" Fury asked, taking my dad's place at my side.

"Yep, reckon the odds are good on that. Makes sense now, new bike club and all. The question is, did they think this thing up themselves or has someone put them up to it?"

"Gotta be put up to it. Even a common fucking street gang wouldn't pull this shit unless they thought they had someone behind them. Is Emmie's ex here with them?"

"Dunno. Can't see fuck all with those helmets on. Hope not. I wanted her to have a good weekend, let her hair down for a bit."

"She will. Seems to get on with Magnet's ol' lady."

"Dunno whether she'd have had a choice. Suzy saw those kids and swept right in on her, like some crazy old cat desperate for her own litter."

"Sure that's not what you see an all? A ready-made family. Looks good from where I'm standing."

"Shut the fuck up, Fury. Emmie is the woman I've fallen in love with. She has kids, they come with her, the whole package. If she didn't have any, then we'd stay that way. This is not the life for kids."

"You know you're blind sometimes. This is one big family. We fight, but we take care of each other. And if one of us dies, there's always someone else to step up and help. Couldn't be a better place to be in my eyes."

"Then they need fucking checking."

*****

The rain didn't stop, the wet field quickly soaking my boots every time I made a run from the marquees to a scran van or to take a piss. But it had dampened no one's spirits, not least my father's who'd sank beer after beer like he might actually die tomorrow.

"You know he really shouldn't be drinking," Emmie shouted above the heavy beat of the music on the main stage.

"Yeah, I know. But I guess he doesn't have long left. Don't know whether he'll make it to the Frostbite rally. Might as well enjoy it like it's his last."

Emmie quieted, turning her face back to the stage, her body shivering against me slightly and then stilling. I wrapped my arm around her shoulders, pulling her in close, feeling that little shiver again.

"Indie?" Emmie asked, quieter now, so that I'd barely heard her, the sound almost an afterthought. "I really don't think he has much time left. He hasn't been eating much, like barely anything, and the disease has really progressed in the last few weeks."

I'd seen changes too, but I was trying my best to ignore them. He was so thin now, even the pot belly caused by nightly alcohol had receded and his breathing had become so noisy that he'd never be able to pull off any covert operation. But I'd seen something else in his eyes. Resignation maybe? And I thought this weekend he was happy to dance with death, to push his body to the last, because now he was ready to go.

"Do you think he'll be in much pain?" I asked suddenly.

"When he goes, you mean?"

"No. Now. Do you think he is feeling pain now?" Emmie was silent, thinking, her hesitation a fraction too long. "The truth please, Emmie. I don't want comforting. I just want to know."

"Yes," she said. "From what I understand, these last stages can be excruciating. Not just from the cancer that fills his body, multiplying daily, but also from the organs inside him, which are still struggling to work and are slowly shutting down, failing."

We sat quietly then, listening to the sounds of the band. The rhythm changed, the tempo slowing. A guitar being plucked for the first few notes, and then a wind instrument joining in, slowly building, quietly creeping up, gently coaxing us into a different rhythm, slower. '*There's a lady who's sure all that glitters is gold.*' I'd always found these lyrics haunting. But tonight, each chord struck against my ribs with a blunt, heavy force. My chest filling with emotions. Anger, anxiety, desperation, sadness. The crowd in front of us rocked slowly, holding a partner or wrapping an arm around the man next to him, pints held in the air. '*And she's buying a stairway to heaven.*' When the last lyric sang, and the *Led Zeppelin* copy of *Stairway to Heaven* ended in all its haunting glory, he turned to look at me from a little bench just off to my right.

Chapter Thirty Five

Emmie

I watched Ste get weaker and weaker as the weekend went on. He'd put on a good show, chatting and joking, doing his best to appear like the man he once was, and either people played along with the façade or hadn't really noticed. The weather hadn't been kind, with only a few dry hours a day. Most of the time, we traipsed through soggy grass, trudging through ever-increasing mud to go anywhere or huddled in marquees to stay out of the worst of it.

When we packed up on Sunday morning, I wasn't disappointed. I was desperate for a warm shower and my pyjamas. I watched Tori lead Ste to the car, packing him in the driver's seat, as members of the club took their tent down for them.

"I'm going to get Ste home," Tori said as she approached Indie, swiping a hand slowly down his arm. His eyes tracked her before shrugging her off. "He's feeling exhausted now."

"It's called a hangover, Tori. We get it. You want us to pack all your shit up and then you can scarper without having to lift a finger," Demon grumbled, forcing the expanded tent fabric into a bag that seemed much too small now for it to fit, the knees of his jeans soaked from wrestling with it in the wet.

The rain had started again, heavy smatters on the remaining tents, and now our cover was minimised. There was no choice but to get wet while we packed up.

"I fucking hate these wet rallies," the man they called Reap grumbled loudly from the side of us.

"Really?" the ever-grinning Magnet chipped in. "I think I might have even seen you smile once last night."

"Nah, you had too many pints, Magnet. Reap never smiles, not even when he's thinking about wanking himself off over his prison mates," Demon corrected, and the man with the dark red, cropped beard shot him a look that was darker still.

"Reap's been in prison?" I asked Indie quietly, as I crouched down beside him to help him roll the tent up.

"Yeah. Got out on good behaviour coming up a year ago. Long story about what he went in for. Definitely one for another day. But put it this way, he still blames Demon for getting him put away, hence why we keep them apart as much as possible."

"Was it Demon's fault?"

"Yeah. Guess it was kinda."

There were those questions again, the ones I didn't really want an answer to. The ones where ignorance was bliss.

The ride home was quick. The formation breaking several times from what I could see in the mirrors as Indie led a furious pace. We had no one flanking us, just wet road on either side, and loads of spray and I didn't know how Indie could even see. The wind had picked up by the time we'd been on the road for a few minutes, driving the rain hard into our faces and dampening the leather suits we wore.

My fingers throbbed, my toes already starting with a cold tingle, and I watched the countryside fly past from the shelter of Indie's back.

As we approached Newcastle, the line of bikes got smaller, riders peeling off to go their separate ways, until there were only the two of us left. We pulled into the pitted car park of *Dog on the Tyne*, the bike engines rattling noisily in the wet air. There were only two other vehicles, Tori's car and Indie's van. The bike lurched to the side, my stomach going with it, my arms tightening around Indie for that second or two that it felt we were going to tip over. His chest vibrated, a noise I could feel but not hear and he patted my hands gently, before wriggling free from my grasp.

"I hate that bit," I muttered as I pulled my helmet off, a rush of cooler air and damp hitting my already cold face.

"You get used to it, Spuggy. You just need to be on that bike more."

Demon and Ciara followed us into the pub, Indie pushing through the heavy double doors.

“Dad!” I heard him say from in front of me, and I stepped sideways to peer round him, catching a glimpse of Ste slumped at a bench seat next to the bar.

“I tried to get him upstairs,” Tori spluttered, panic clear in her voice. “But I can’t get him back on my feet by myself. He’s too heavy. And he’s just too tired to walk.”

Ste was grey, more grey than usual, his breath coming in shaky rasps, not quite a rattle.

“Don’t move him yet,” I instructed, reaching for his wrist, and pushing my fingers into the little indent just beyond the main tendon.

Indie and Demon muttered between themselves, a heavy, urgent drone of deep voices behind me.

“Shush. I need you all to be quiet while I take his pulse.”

The room dropped into silence, and I concentrated hard, eventually finding a weak, thready beat.

"Indie," I looked up at him. "We need to phone an ambulance."

"No!" Ste tried to sit up, his voice as weak as his pulse. "No ambulance. I'm just worn out. Just need an hour or two to sleep. Get me upstairs, boys."

He pushed up from the bench seat, wobbling and falling back. I glanced at Indie, his face the same old stoic, and I couldn't tell what he was thinking, wondering whether he knew what was really happening here.

"Come on, dad. Let's get you on your feet," Indie looked at Demon, tilting his head, and Demon moved to the other side of the Kings' president.

Between them, they hoisted him carefully to his feet.

"Ciara. Pull that table away," Demon instructed, and I watched the tall, brown-haired beauty with the scar drag the heavy pub table out of the way so that they didn't have to manoeuvre around it.

"How bad is he?" she asked quietly as they slowly moved, step by step, guiding the dying man to the back of the pub.

I shook my head, not needing to say anything for her to understand.

"Shit." she swiped her hand across her mouth. "It's the first he's seen him in months. I don't think either of us expected him to look so poorly."

"He's had infection after infection. That won't have helped. But none of this is nice to watch."

"How do you do it?" She asked, the men disappearing down the long corridor through the door, Tori following close behind. "Look after people who are dying, I mean."

"It's an honour that I get to look after them in their last days. And it hurts every time they go. Every time. But some more than others."

We stood in silence after that, listening to the floorboards above our heads groan and creak, and eventually Ciara sat down at one of the tables.

"Where did you and Demon meet?" I asked, hoping to fill the silence with distraction.

"Funny story that. He ripped my wing mirror off my car. Yeah, I know, utter knob huh?" she continued when I looked at her in surprise. "Still haven't forgiven him for that. Even if he did eventually save my life."

She laughed gently, her face breaking into a smile, the thick scar hugging her right cheekbone.

"They're a good bunch, really," Ciara continued. "Just emotionally inept sometimes. Ste brought them up to be hard. Fighters. But Demon's different, on the inside, at least. Indie, well, you never really know what he's thinking. He probably ought to be a poker champion."

The door clanged against the wall, ringing out loudly through the pub, Demon charging towards us.

"I can't stay here," he said urgently, Ciara already rising to her feet. "I need to go."

Ciara gave a wry smile.

"Come on then. Let's get out of here. See ya later Emmie."

"Indie asked if you would go up," Demon's voice muffled, half lost under the helmet as he secured the strap under his chin.

The stairway was dark, the persistent rain and cloud stealing away any light, and it was almost as if the weather knew what was coming. As did I. That heavy note of dread settled into my stomach as I wandered towards the low muffle of voices, following the drone of conversation until I pinpointed the room they were in. This one was to the right, the opposite side to the room Indie called the chapel. Leaning my ear to the wooden door, I listened for a few seconds. The only words I could make out were Tori's.

"He must have some meds we can give him..."

I knocked tentatively and waited. Footsteps clumped louder until the door was opened and I could peer inside.

"You don't need to knock, Spuggy," Indie greeted me, tipping his head in wordless invitation, and I followed him into the room.

It was as plain as the funny room on the front with all the single beds, yet this one had only one king-sized bed, in which Ste sat, half propped up by pillows. I could hear the rattle of his chest as I got closer, the sickly grey of his skin.

"Can we give him more meds?" Tori asked.

"More painkillers, yes. He has some oramorph prescribed. Can you get some of that?"

She nodded, "it's in the car. I'll go find it."

Ste tried to smile, but every breath tugged at his throat, a gargling noise coming from inside.

"What's happening, Emmie?" Indie asked.

I turned him away, trying not to let Ste hear these next words.

"I know what's happening," he gasped. "Just tell him, Emmie."

I nodded, taking Indie's hand. "It's time."

"What do you mean, it's time?"

"The final stages, Indie. Your dad is going to die."

"I know that." His tone was clipped, emotions welling to get out.

"No. Soon. It's going to happen soon. Could be a few hours. Could be less."

"No. How? How can it be so soon?"

"You need to be with him now, Indie. I'll stay if you want me to, or I'll just be along the corridor. We'll make him a bit more comfortable."

Indie nodded, reaching for the hand that lay at my side and squeezing it gently. He took a breath, composed himself and turned round, sitting down on the corner of his father's bed. I moved out into the hallway, leaving them alone, watching Tori climb back up the stairs.

Chapter Thirty Six

Indie

"Emmie said to give him these," Tori distracted me from my father's breaths.

For once, I was thankful for the sound of her voice. Normally, it was enough to make my ears bleed. Not today. Today she masked the crackling rattle coming from my father. Every time he breathed in or out, there was a gurgling, like he was constantly drawing on a crack pipe. Yet each breath came differently. Shallow and gasping, then for what seemed like minutes he didn't seem to breathe at all.

And his eyes. They would spring open every so often, like he was suddenly shocked or jolted awake, but they barely seemed to focus on anything. This time when they opened, he stared straight ahead, his brown eyes dull, looking more like glass.

"You're here," he muttered, his voice faint.

"Yes, Ste," Tori spoke. "We're right here."

"I didn't know whether I would see you again. You look different."

"No. Just the same, babe. Same old me."

"And you. You're here too."

But he looked straight ahead, and I didn't think it was me he was talking to.

"Indie's right here, baby. Right here," Tori reached for his hand.

"Not you, you stupid bint," my father's head snapped towards Tori. "I'm talking to them."

Tori's lip wobbled, her eyes filling up, and she dropped his hand, getting to her feet and rushing out.

"I know she's a waste of space. But she's been a bit of fun." His face moved back to the spot in front of him, talking to the people only he could see. "Can you give me a few minutes? I need to talk to Indie first."

Then he turned, looking at me, a faint smile coming to his lips. His chest rose and fell, like he was heaving after a long run, every breath more and more laboured.

"You take good care of our club, son," the last word left him gasping, a horrendous wet gurgling, like he was drowning. "I know you don't want to be president, but, trust me, you are the best man for the job."

"I don't want it, though. I don't think I could ever make the decisions you could. I don't want to make those calls."

"Now look here," he sat forward momentarily before falling back against the pillow. "There is a war coming. Whatever you think you can do to avoid it, it won't be enough. If the Hand gets a foothold on English soil, they'll wipe the Kings out, our families with them. They tried that the last time. We only won because we formed the coalition. But not everyone of those clubs wanted that."

He paused, breathless, his fist pulling on the duvet as he closed his eyes. "Keep a close eye on the Vandals. If anyone will stab you in the back, they will."

"Because of Flat Pack?"

"Partly that. But Tomahawk wants control of the north east and the stupid fucker is as paranoid as they come. His own distrust will make him take a stupid decision. Keep the women close. The Hand will go after them."

And that cemented that decision in my mind, the one I'd thought about some nights ago. The one that stabbed me in the heart the moment it had slipped into my consciousness.

"Indie, if you're thinking of cutting her loose, don't."

I opened my mouth, partly in surprise, partly to argue.

"She's too good for you, son, but it's too late to let her go now. You took her to the rally. You paraded her as yours in front of all those other clubs. You've marked her now. Anyone who wants to get to you will target her to do that. You owe it to her to keep her safe."

"You let mam go. Where were you on that?" I shouldn't get angry with a man on his deathbed. I really shouldn't.

"I didn't just let her go. I was a fool to treat her the way I did. It's the biggest regret of my life. We could have just stayed together. She would have forgiven me, but she never would have forgotten. I moved on. Taking another ol' lady meant your mam was free of the club. I bought her that cottage on Holy Island. Her favourite place."

"I never knew that," I whispered.

"Why would you? I never told you. It was the safest place for her. I freed her from the club. The only real way there was. And it wouldn't have been that easy for people to target her. It worked Indie. In my own way, I kept your mam, my Grace, safe."

He coughed suddenly, a loud hacking cough that seemed to go on for minutes. I stood up, not sure what to do. In the end, I think I might have shouted for Emmie. But I didn't remember doing it. Maybe she'd heard him coughing, because suddenly she was there with us.

"What's happening? What's happening?" I could hear the panic in my voice, but I couldn't stop it.

She nudged me to the side gently, propping my father upright, pulling an extra pillow under his back. And still he coughed, fighting for every breath like he was choking, his hands scrabbling over the covers.

"Shush. It's ok Ste. Just try and breathe for me," her voice was barely audible over the sounds he was making.

His hands moved to his chest, clutching and clawing at it, panic rising in me as fast as in him.

"Emmie. Please!"

"You're ok Ste. I want you to concentrate on my voice. Breathe in. That's it. Breathe out."

He coughed again, racking and gurgling, but it wasn't as loud as before. Quieter. And then another cough. Softer, his hands relaxing against the bare skin of his chest. He closed his eyes, the fingers of his hands balling and straightening, his chest wheezing and whistling. The breath sounds slowing until it was only the rattle of his chest I could hear.

He settled back, falling into the pillows behind him, staring ahead once more.

"They're proud of you, you know," he said again, his voice fainter.

"Who, Dad?"

"Ade and Si."

"Really?"

"Aye. They say you're a good lad. You're what this club will need. A true warrior is one that has survived many wars."

We sat silently for a while, his hand resting in both of mine. The rattle in his chest neither improving nor getting worse, but his eyes closed more and more. There was a creak at the door. Tori. I wanted to tell her to leave, that she wasn't welcome. She'd only known him a couple of years. I wasn't offering her any of my time with my father. But I'd let her sit quietly on the other side of him.

His eyes fluttered open once again, his voice a whisper, barely audible. "Tell Demon I always thought of him as mine. Even though I knew he really wasn't. I'd always seen Si in his face, from the very day he was born."

He drew in a breath, the rattle in his chest stilling, the hand that had grasped mine relaxing. Then he exhaled. And then nothing. Not another breath. Not another movement. Jolting to my feet, I looked down at him, then across to Emmie. She shook her head gently, her eyes filled with sadness. I stared for a moment, watching. Waiting for him to breathe again, or his eyes to open, or something, anything. Anything to show that it wasn't yet his time, that he hadn't just come to the clubhouse to die. That this wasn't it, that it had been a dream, or an intrusive thought in my head. And around me no one moved, or said anything, as if waiting for me to let loose the first tear.

Carefully I scooped both arms across him, resting one hand on top of the other, my hand lingering on top of them for just a little while, in case the movement should wake him up. And then, when it didn't, I bent down and kissed him on his forehead, his skin still warm on my lips.

"May the heart of the Harley beat eternal. May the roar of the Kings never die. Goodnight dad."

I didn't look up, not at Emmie, not at Tori. I walked away. As I turned down the corridor towards the stairs, I heard the high-pitched wail. Shrill. Desperate.

Chapter Thirty Seven

Emmie

I watched the man I'd nursed for weeks close his eyes for the final time. The room went quiet, the noisy gurgle of his chest and the persistent wheeze gone in an instant. The rest of his body relaxed, a strange stillness descending on him, his face no longer tense, no longer braced against the pain, his lips lightly pressed together.

Time passed slowly, Indie staring at Ste, as if waiting patiently for him to wake up, his face as stoic as ever, giving nothing away. Beside me Tori stood quietly, unsure what to do next.

Then slowly Indie moved, carefully reaching over Ste's body and picking up an arm, moving it across his chest. Then he repeated the same with the other arm, lying them so Ste's hands crossed. Indie left his hand there for a moment, before leaning down and kissing the man on the top of the head.

"May the heart of the Harley beat eternal," he said quietly. "May the roar of the Kings never die." Words that meant something to him, and Tori too, as she hiccupped suddenly beside me.

Indie stood a few seconds longer, then turned and walked away. I followed him. I wanted to wrap my arms around him, tell him I knew how hard that was to watch. I hadn't made it out the doorway when behind a cry rang out. Loud and painful, and the woman I'd left behind in the room broke into loud sobs.

But I didn't turn like I should, to offer comfort and kind words. Instead, I went after the man who'd shown such strength and at the same time such vulnerability.

He was downstairs when I found him, clutching a glass of bronze liquid, staring at the double doors of the pub from the middle of the room.

"Indie," I called tentatively, but he didn't look round, or flinch, or turn his head towards my voice.

And he didn't move as I approached him, or when I slid my hand into his. His fingers squeezed round mine, letting me know the gesture was appreciated. And we stood there in the silence, the only movement between us was the glass he lifted occasionally to his lips.

Eventually, he tugged his hand free and touched his face. He might have been wiping tears, or scratching at his cheek, but I gave him the privacy he needed, keeping my eyes fixed on the doors in front of us. Outside, the rain pelted the windows, the wind now roaring round the property ominously, as the universe wept down upon us. And whatever those words meant that I'd heard Indie whisper, it was like they taken a life of their own, filling the air with that same roar.

"I need to ring Demon," he broke the silence, the rain outside not retreating from its attack on the pub.

Turning away, he sat at a table, pulling out his phone, pressing a button and holding it to his ear. I couldn't hear Demon on the other side, but Indie drew in a deep breath, and I could only guess the call had connected.

"Demon… look…yes he has."

Indie fell silent again, and there was no sound of another voice, no one in the background. I sensed they were both there, connected by their mobiles, pensive.

"Yes, please, Demon," he said eventually. "Make the call. Follow the protocols."

He slipped the mobile back into his pocket and sat staring at the table.

"We need to notify someone, Indie," I said, sliding in beside him.

"Why?"

"It's also protocol when someone dies at home. There'll unlikely be an inquest as his medical records show he was dying, but someone official needs to attend. Do you want me to ring them, the ambulance?"

He nodded, lifting the short, stubby glass to his lips and taking a sip.

"An ambulance. He's fucking dead. What's that supposed to do?" It was Tori's voice breaking through the quiet.

I opened my mouth to answer, but a growl erupted from beside me, a darker noise than any I'd ever heard from him.

"Speak to her like that again and I'll throw you the fuck out. I don't give a flying fuck if you were his ol' lady, you'll be out of here on your arse."

"Indie," I cautioned, knowing his anger was something else.

The woman stood in front of us turned around, disappearing back through the door that led to the upstairs rooms.

"I'm sorry," Indie muttered, raising his glass to his lips again. "I didn't mean to get so angry."

"I understand, I really do." I'd seen it all before. Anger, tears, shrieks and wails, and nothing. Everyone grieved differently. "There's no right or wrong way to deal with this, Indie."

But what I hadn't seen was biker grief, because soon men poured through the double doors dressed head to toe in leathers, their waistcoats with the embroidered emblem on the back. Every one of them walked to Indie, clasping arms and hugging him tightly. Some stayed longer. Saying something to him, words that he didn't seem to reciprocate, only listened to, offering nothing back of his own.

Eventually, there were faces I recognised. Magnet, Fury, Reap, the identical twins. And much longer after everyone else, Demon. The men clasped hands, standing close much longer than anyone else, words exchanged that I didn't try to make out, letting the brothers, or half-brothers, or cousins, or whatever they were, have some time.

I hadn't seen Suzy come in, or Ciara, but suddenly they were there too, behind the bar, handing out glasses. Glasses that no one drank from. Fury handed one to me, a short, stubby tumbler with bronze liquid.

"It's whisky," he said when I stood staring into the liquid. "Ste's favourite. Just swallow it in one, like a good girl." He winked mischievously.

Indie and Demon approached the bar, each taking a glass, and the chatter that had filled the room dissipated until there was total, utter silence.

"Ste Carter," Indie stated loudly, raising his glass in front of him. "President of the Northern Kings. Let the road be winding and the pace fast."

"May the heart of the Harley beat eternal. May the roar of the Kings never die."

The chant filled the building, eerie and haunting, stinging my eyes and filling the back of my throat. Those words I'd now heard for the second time, words I was appreciating, making emotion swell inside of me. No one in that room dropped a tear, and for a few moments, the glasses remained raised. Then, when Indie brought his glass to his lips, chucking back the thick liquid, the rest of the room, man and woman, did the same. Quickly I copied, the liquid burning as if it had been alight, and I did my best not to bring it all back up.

The ambulance crew appeared just as the last biker was leaving, me, Indie and Tori the only ones left. The coroner's office arrived shortly afterwards, tending to the body, and Tori leaving after that.

Indie said little, locking the doors of the pub behind them and then guiding me up the stairs to the rooms above. He said nothing as he got undressed, sinking into bed beside me, his body warm, but his mind distant. I scooted closer to him, moving up against the side of him, and he held out an arm, pulling me closer. And that night we fell asleep in silence, the house that would usually moan and settle long into the night as quiet as we were.

*****

"I need to go see my mam," Indie said, his voice flat. "I'll probably be gone a few days. You can stay here if you want."

"No, it's alright. You need some space and I need to tidy the house up and get the kids back into their home."

Indie passed me a cup of coffee, fresh from the machine in the kitchen.

"Fury will be over in half an hour. Your car's all fixed. I've asked him to pop it over."

"Ok. Take care," I mumbled, as he thrust his arms into the leather jacket, pulling the waistcoat with his back patch on over the top.

I spent the next two days tidying up, trying to find something to do now I didn't have a shift to work. I didn't have to rush the kids into school, and I'd even taken Daisy on a proper walk. Now she lay at my feet, cuddled up at the bottom of the sofa, the kids long in bed and the TV droning away in the background as my eyes drooped with tiredness.

I must have dosed off, because suddenly at my feet was a low growl, Daisy sitting up suddenly, her attention on the door from the lounge. My attention was there too, straining my ears over the sound of the television, watching a shadow to see if it moved. But there was nothing. Daisy relaxed, curling back down at my feet, tucking her chin over her feet. The clock on the TV stand ticked gently, almost ten-thirty. I should go to bed, capitalise on all this time I had to sleep, not lie here on the sofa half-watching a TV programme I wasn't really interested in. Daisy sat up again, her ears pricked. And now I did hear something. A knock on the door. A short sharp tap.

"Shush, Daisy. You'll wake the kids." I told the dog that landed on the floor as lightly as a cannon ball.

My new door had a peephole, the image in front of me distorted. Men in bike leathers. Indie and some others, I presumed, and I opened the door.

I presumed wrong.

Chapter Thirty Eight

Indie

It was hard to focus on the run up to Holy Island, my mind drifting off, the heaviness in my chest from the dread building within me about what I needed to do next. I was lucky the roads were reasonably straight, because several times I couldn't remember riding the last few miles.

When I got to the edge of the causeway, I had to wait. The tide hadn't quite gone out, the water receding but not having cleared the road enough to proceed. And now, without the rumble from the Harley's exhaust, or the feel of the vibrations under me, my mind had nothing at all to distract it. The air was chilly today, the nip on the coast even icier, and the wind from yesterday hadn't quite blown itself out. I tried to focus on the numbness of my finger ends, the throb in my toes and the fresh sea air against my face, where I'd slid my visor up.

The wind had pushed the clouds away, a bright blue sky offering compensation for the rain that battered the clubhouse long into the night. My eyes felt dry, and despite the lack of tears that I'd shed, I felt like I'd cried all night. I was tired, and it felt like my eyelids were stuck to my eyeballs after every blink. Emmie had slept lightly, waking every few hours to check I was still there, and I'd spent most of the night staring at the ceiling and listening to the wind and the rain.

Now in front of me, the road cleared. A few more minutes and the causeway would be clear enough to ride over, and the next agonising thing I had to do would begin. Maybe I should wait a bit longer, sit and watch as others made their crossings. Listen to the shouts of the gulls and the purr-like ring of the curlews wading in the retreating water.

Taking a deep breath, I turned the ignition, the big bike coming to life beneath me and for a moment drowning out all other noise, the deep voice of the engine the only thing that rang in my ears. I released the clutch; the bike moving forward onto the wet road, and I chased the rest of the North Sea from the causeway.

I could see her in the snug little lounge reading something, a half-drawn painting standing to the other side of the quaint little log burner. She was probably just finishing breakfast. She'd always been late to eat, getting up to pursue a sunrise and then falling back to sleep until late. I stood a little while watching, delaying giving the message I was here for, putting off having to say those words. They'd been long apart, but I'd always got the sense she'd still loved him, and I thought I could never understand why, not until now.

Somewhere a clock chimed, deep and resonating, urging me to do what I'd come to do. In the street, the metal door knocker clanged loudly.

Mam's door opened with a clatter, the door vibrating and the knocker striking the plate again, just a little less loud than before.

"Indie," she greeted me with happiness, and then a frown. "I wasn't expecting you."

"I know, mam."

And she knew too, her face changing from elation to worry in an instant. I followed her inside, letting her lead me to the kitchen. I let her fill the kettle and then settle it on to the stove. It didn't seem right to stop her preparing, and I suspected she knew the news that I had come with.

"It's Dad..." I started, unable to keep my voice from trailing off, getting stuck over a lump in my throat.

"He's gone, hasn't he?"

I nodded. I'd been able to say those words to Demon, but I couldn't say it to her. She turned away from me, moving to the sink. Her hands gripped the ceramic basin, and her head dipped down in front of her. And that first sob hit me so much harder than I'd ever expected. I let her cry, her shoulders shaking, her back to me, my first real tear trickling down my face. Then the rest came, like a dam had just been breached.

Mam turned and walked towards me, wrapping her arms around me like she used to do when I was a kid, and my dad wasn't watching. We stood like that together for a long time until the shrill scream of the kettle pulled us apart and the moment subsided.

"I never stopped loving him, you know," she said as she handed me the cup of tea.

"I don't think he ever stopped loving you, either."

"I know."

"He said something at the end. That he let you go to keep you safe?"

She smiled weakly.

"In his own stupid way, he thought he was protecting me. I just wished he'd thought about that before all the women. I couldn't stay in the club after that, knowing that the next one who walked through the doors might end up in our bed. I don't think he could help it. If we'd been normal, I could have just walked away, instead I had to be partially hidden so that those enemies he'd made wouldn't come after me too."

I stayed silent too long after that.

"If you're going to bring Emmie and the kids into this, just make sure there are no more wars. It's up to you to change things now, Indie. The club doesn't have to be run the way the Carters always did."

I wished she was right. But the way the club was run was the least of my worries. We needed to avoid being wiped out by the Bloody Hand first. If we disbanded the club, we were still targets, and while we were the Kings, we still had an army.

*****

The last few days in the cottage hidden away on an island were surreal. We talked and reminisced and I spent two hours stood outside, an icy sea wind whipping around us as I passed her brushes so she could capture the anger of the waves attacking the outcrop of rock on which Lindisfarne Castle stood. I was ready to get back to normal now, or at least as close to it as I could get.

The fire in the log burner crackled gently, filling the little lounge with a swell of heat. The soft low lighting glowed a delicate orange, the flowery chintz of the tasselled lampshade in the corner casting animated shadows around the space. I could see why she loved this cottage and the island, locked away from everyone, trapped by the sea.

My phone rang, a noise I'd not heard for nearly two days, the shrill music out of place in the idyllic cottage. Emmie. I smiled and pressed the button.

"Hey Spuggy."

Silence.

No, not quite silence. There was background noise.

"Emmie?"

I strained my ears. The background noise was a voice. A male voice, one I didn't recognise. I couldn't quite make out the words. It sounded like something said through gritted teeth. But I could make out the next noise.

"Please." Emmie. It was her voice, strained and frightened. I only needed one word to hear it.

And then she shouted out, half scream, half wail.

"What is it, Indie?"

“When does the tide go out?” I asked my mam, knowing she recognised the look on my face, one she had seen before.

“Not till the early hours.”

Fuck.

And down the phone, I heard her cry again.

Chapter Thirty Nine

Emmie

The door burst open as soon as I'd unlocked it, throwing me backwards, nearly knocking me off my feet, but not quite. There were three of them, but it was the one at the front with the dark hair and cold blue eyes that I noticed the most. The same eyes as Luke and Lily.

"Where are my kids?" he grunted, pushing past me, the two others following and shutting the door behind them.

"What are you doing here, Gaz?"

"I've come for my kids."

"What? Why?"

"They're coming with me."

"No. Why?"

"Because you and me need a little chat. And I know you don't want them to hear that. Now if you wouldn't mind getting the kids."

Beside me Daisy grumbled a low warning, the two men that Gaz was with glancing at her and muttering between themselves. I patted her on the head and then went upstairs, gently waking Luke first.

"What's happening mam?" he asked, sleepy eyes not really able to focus on me.

"I need you to get up and go with dad. I'll get you tomorrow."

"Why? We've never stayed at dad's in ages. I don't want to go. Tell him I'm not going."

"It's ok. Just for tonight. Hurry, please."

When I brought two sleepy children down the stairs, Gary was pacing back and forth between the kitchen and lounge.

"I don't want to go," Luke whined.

"Come on, mate. We'll have a great time. Now go with Darren and Shaun and get in the car."

"I don't want to go, mammy. I want to stay with you." Lily hugged my leg, and I watched the tension build on Gary's face.

"Please kids, just go with your dad's friends. I'll pick you up in the morning."

Lily dropped her arms, scooping up Mr Morris and following Luke out of the house, the door closing behind them, leaving me and Gaz alone.

"What the fuck have you been telling my kids, Emmie?"

"Nothing, Gaz. Nothing I swear."

"You been convincing them that old man biker of yours is a better dad? You been calling him daddy too? Is that what you've been doing, you dirty little slut?"

I was going to try to reason with him, plead with him, tell him Indie was on his way over. But the fist that flew into my mouth knocked those thoughts right out of me, snapping my head backwards and I went staggering with it.

Crumpled on the floor, I wiped my mouth where the sting was developing. Blood swiped across the back of my hand. Gary moved closer, and I scuttled back. Daisy barked.

"Bet you like it rough you whore," his leg swung forward into the middle of my stomach, the toe of his boot connecting right in the softest part, pushing my diaphragm upwards and the air out of my lungs.

I needed to curl up in a foetal position, protect as much of me as possible. But somewhere, Indie was at the end of a phone. And that phone was on the sofa in the lounge. I tried to push to my feet, but my stomach felt like it had gone into cramp, and I struggled to even get to my knees.

"Stupid bitch."

I expected another blow, but instead I heard him scream this time, a big lump of brown hanging off his arm, snarling like she was a wild beast. Pushing through the thick, thumping pain, I crawled to the lounge, reaching out for the mobile. My hands shook, my fingers trembling, barely able to type in the key code, desperately scrolling for his number. Daisy yelped. Then a second yelp. And then a whimper. I pushed the call button, looking over my shoulder just as the lean, towering shape got to me, grabbing my hair and yanking me backwards.

My legs moved as he dragged me back to the kitchen, my heels scrabbling for purchase, pricks of pain where the hair was ripping out of my scalp and then he flung me sideways.

"Please," I shrieked, tears streaming down my face.

But the words only made him worse.

"I bet you begged him, didn't you?"

His toe crunched into my ribs. I shouted out. A yell of pain.

"Begged him to fuck you."

His foot connected with me again. The searing hot blast of pain hit me like a missile. I screamed.

"I told you, no one else can ever have you."

Another kick. A sickening crack.

"And that's exactly what I'm going to make sure of."

The foot struck me again, my body in agony, and all I could do was let out a silent cry. Gary crouched down beside me, grabbing a handful of hair, pulling my head back.

"You're so fucking pathetic. The kids will stay with me and before you fucking say it, the police are gonna blame him. They're gonna think that he's the one that's done it to you."

He waved a leather cut in front of me, the back patch on the back a blur. Then he stuffed it into my face, moving it left and right, making sure he'd covered it in my blood, before throwing it on the floor behind him. The foot came at my face this time, dull, heavy, full of force. Then a second time. My head whirled, everything going black. But the blows stopped.

I thought I saw him move away, but it was hard to tell among the shadows that collected in front of my eyes. It had gone quiet. It was calm. Somewhere nearby a dog whimpered.

Chapter Forty

Indie

Frantically, I scrolled my contacts, the first attempt not connecting.

"Fuck!" I shouted, moving into the kitchen and trying again.

The phone beeped at me, the signal bars showing a cross.

"Fuck's sake!"

Throwing open the door of the cottage, I ran out into the street. One bar. But it wasn't enough to connect. I ran further, out into the dark, away from the houses, out into space. Two bars. Come on, come on.

"Hey Indie," Fury's voice was calm.

"I need you to get the boys and get to Emmies," I shouted.

"What? Why? What's going on?"

"Just fucking get there, Fury."

"Indie. You need to tell me more than that. I need to know which ones to bring."

"Fucking all of them."

"Where are you?"

"Stuck on the Island. Tide's in. There's no way I'll reach her in time. Just get over there. She's being attacked."

"By who?"

"Fury…" I warned.

"I need some intel. By who?"

"I dunno. Probably her ex. But I don't know. Just get to her, Fury. Please."

The phone went dead.

I jogged back to the cottage, my chest tight and my heart pumping, and a red-hot anger bubbling over. Mam hadn't closed the door behind me, but she was standing in the doorway when I got to it.

"What's going on, son?"

"Move, please. I need to pack."

"Indie." Her tone was sharp enough to stop me in my tracks. "You can't go anywhere until the tide goes out. So, you may as well tell me what is going on."

She ushered me inside, closing the door behind me.

"Emmie. She's being attacked."

"What? How do you know?"

"That was her number that rang me. I could hear her in the background, crying and screaming."

"Oh, God. Have you called the police?"

I shook my head. "I called Fury."

"Jesus, Indie. Don't you think the police are a better idea?"

"Why? So, they can do fuck all like the last time?"

"What do you mean, like the last time?"

I hadn't realised I'd followed her into the kitchen and now I watched as she yanked back the curtain from the unit under the deep ceramic sink, pulling out a bottle.

"Her ex is abusive. He'd been beating her for years. She'd tried the police, and it did nothing. Just some stupid injunction which was as much fucking use as the paper it was written on. I thought I'd sorted him out, the ex. But I guess a broken face and ribs and a warning weren't enough to stop him."

Mam poured a dash of whisky into each glass.

"I'll need a bit more than that if you expect me to wait until the tide goes out, or I'm just gonna fucking swim across."

"Language!"

"Sorry."

I paced the cottage, clutching the glass of whisky to my chest, taking the odd sip, but constantly checking the display on my phone. Nothing. Crickets. Absolutely fuck all from anybody.

I walked out into the street again, watching the signal bars increase, and tried Fury again.

"Where the fuck is he?" I muttered into the night, the waves gently lapping against the shore just a little way off. The sound should have been soothing. But it was irritating, and all I wanted to do was lob stones out there, at the sea that stopped me from getting to her, and the waves that rubbed it in.

The phone rang. Shrill in the damp air, making me jump and nearly dropping the fucker.

"Fury?"

"Mate."

"Where is she?"

"We've got her. But she's in a bad way."

"Where's she now?"

"In the ambulance. We had to call one, Indie. She's really messed up."

"Who was it?"

"Don't know yet. But one of our cuts was there. I've taken it."

"Whose fucking cut was it?"

"Beanz's cut."

"I want Beanz waiting for me in the clubhouse when I'm back."

"Indie?"

"What?"

"There's another thing?"

"Fucking spit it out then?"

"She was muttering something when we got there. She could barely speak. But we think she said he's got her kids."

Another stab hit me hard.

"Then it has to be Gary. I want to know where he lives. I'll be back as soon as I can get off this fucking island. I want everyone ready to go when I get back."

"Who's everyone?"

"You, the twins, Reap, Magnet and Demon."

*****

I'd been sitting at the start of the causeway staring into the darkness. The night sky was clear, millions of stars twinkling, and with less light pollution from the island, you could see so much further out into space. It would have been a beautiful place to sit and watch the sunrise. But I was desperate to leave, my eyes straining, searching for any sign I could cross before the safe crossing times.

Eventually, the display on my mobile ticked over. 2.45 am. The time Northumberland County Council said it was safe to cross. And cross I did. The wheels of the bike hissing, spray kicking up from receding waters and puddles that trapped the north sea, just like it had done to me. I wasted no time pushing the Harley over the wet road and up the other side, leaning into a corner of the windy road as much as I dared with the heavy bike. This was the one night I regretted my choice of ride, wishing for something faster, something that could break the 100mph barrier quicker and didn't sound like it was having a heart attack, or leak oil like it was mortally wounded afterwards.

It was the quickest I'd ever made it home from Lindisfarne, testing out the Harley's top speed down stretches of the A1, slowing for the speed cameras, and I was lucky that there had been no police around to clock me.

The clubhouse was lit up like a Christmas tree when I roared into the car park, hardly letting the bike safely settle onto the kickstand before jumping off and running inside. Magnet, Fury, Reap and the twins were sitting around a table, coffee cups spread out. Reap had a swollen eye and a cut on his eyebrow, but the rest seemed unscathed.

"What the fuck happened to you lot?"

"Kids are upstairs," Fury muttered, holding something against his jaw.

"You've been to Gary's and got them without me?" Adrenaline and anger surged, pushing together, a volcanic eruption waiting to blow.

"We didn't need a murder tonight, Indie. What's happened to Emmie is going to attract a lot of police attention that we can't just get rid of. It won't just get swept under the carpet. So, we went ourselves and took the kids."

"We still had to shake the information out of the Aces," Magnet added. "They weren't too forth coming with it. Lucky for us, half of them had knocked themselves out on fuck knows what."

"Yeah. Hospital issued drugs and laughing gas. They'd cut some of the drugs up. But seems they'd started sampling," Reap sipped on his coffee.

"Are the kids ok?"

"Bit shaken up. Don't understand what's going on. Suzy's up there with them."

"Where's Demon?" I scoured the pub, and I hadn't noticed his bike or van outside.

"Him and Ciara have taken Emmie's dog to the vets. It's taken a kicking, too."

"And Beanz?"

"Dunno, Indie. We called at his and he's nowhere to be seen."

"We good to start on something stronger now, Indie?" Fury asked. "Might be good to have an alibi. I want to be tight when the police come calling."

I nodded and then left them to it, walking through the pub to the big industrial kitchen at the back and checking the doors were closed. Then, taking my mobile phone from my bike jacket pocket, I scrolled through the contacts till I came to an entry with only one letter. The phone rang for a while, taking its time to connect and making me pace backwards and forwards.

"Indie. It's five o'fucking clock in the morning."

"I'm sorry, V. Need to call in a favour."

The man on the other end groaned.

"What do you need?" he asked after a moment's hesitation.

"Someone gone. And an alibi."

"When?"

"In the next week or so."

"Ok."

"Also. Ste died a few days ago."

Silence.

"Shit, cuz. I'm sorry," he said eventually. "Anything I can do?"

"No. But if you're here on business, you can stay for the funeral. If you want to."

"That depends whether the Kings will come after me once it's over."

"Assuming I stand for president, then no."

"And why would you not?"

"I'm not sure this life's for me anymore."

"Well, when you've decided, you can tell me whether I can attend at the graveside or in the shadows. Call me in three days. I'll be needing some intelligence on that mark."

The phone call cut off.

Chapter Forty One

Emmie

I breathed carefully, packing clothes into a holdall and stuffing the well-read magazines in with them. My left-hand side ached, even with a cocktail of painkillers and my face was only just going down, but I still couldn't properly open my left eye.

"Hi, Emmie," The voice was unfamiliar, well rounded, but made me jump all the same. "Sorry. I didn't mean to frighten you." The woman at the door held her hand towards me, taking it away again when I continued to stare at her with one eye. "I'm one of the senior management team here. I just wanted you to know that the enquiry into your misuse of a pass has been stood down. We understand you had a break-in that night in question. I have your police crime number."

"I…I don't have a crime number. I didn't report it."

She frowned. "Strange. The police themselves gave it to us."

"So, does that mean I'm no longer suspended?"

"Yes. You're completely cleared. I understand you'll be on sick leave. But when you're ready to come back, we're ready to have you."

I turned away from her again, finishing stuffing clothes into the bag. Behind me was a shriek. A beautiful light squeal of delight. The little girl rushed at me, and I braced myself for the pain she was about to inflict when she bowled straight into me. But she stopped just in front of me, carefully walking the last few steps and tentatively wrapping her arms round my legs.

"Mammy! I missed you."

"You only saw me yesterday."

"I know, but now you're coming home. And I get to cuddle on the sofa with you."

I smiled weakly, the thought of going back to the house sitting heavily in my stomach.

Indie and Luke brought up the rear a few strides behind, lightly arguing over some new computer game they'd been playing and who was better at it.

"Ready to go home?" Indie asked.

"Yeah."

But I wasn't ready. Not to go back there. To the house that held such beatings. Where he would find me again. I cradled my side at the throb that wouldn't go away, despite the painkillers I'd slugged back.

Indie's van was filled with the excited chatter of the kids' voices. Lily had scored ten out of ten with her spellings, she told me. And Luke still babbled over whatever level he'd just cracked on the latest game that probably involved shooting something. Their voices faded in the background. White noise. Pushed away by the panic rising in my chest each mile we crept closer to home. My hands clutched the handle, my fingers squeezing the hard plastic.

Eventually, the van pulled into the street, slowing to a stop at the garden gate. I looked at the house and then at the handle I was holding, then watched the kids bicker in the crew seats behind us. Indie's fingers touched the back of my hand, sliding slowly over me, squeezing my fingers until I couldn't pick at the loose thread on my jeans anymore.

Then he started the van again, pulling away from the curb. I glanced across at him, not understanding, unable to ask the question. He patted my leg and smiled gently.

"I've a better idea," he said, then glanced over his shoulder at the kids. "Fancy a little holiday?"

*****

The log burner crackled, the little lounge filled with heat, and three of us squeezed in on the mismatched flowery sofa. Grace bent over the easel the other side of the fire.

"That's it," she said, her hand just covering Lily's. "Just a bit more shading here, and then a swipe of white paint there. Perfect."

Lily jumped up and down, squeaking with delight.

"Look! Look mammy! It looks just like Mr Morris!" She lifted the canvas block from the stand, tilting it for us to see in the dull orange glow. His head look like it was swollen, and he seemed to be missing a leg, the unicorn of rainbow colours not proportionate to the rest of his body.

"That's cra…."

I nudged Luke hard.

"That's incredible, baby. Well done."

She smiled, elation all over her face in the form of pink paint.

"Think it's time for bed now, you two," Grace ushered them onto their feet and up the stairs in the corner of the room.

They were right at the very top of the house, in the attic bedroom nestled in the eaves. I'd envied them at first, jealous of the views from the little windows, looking out across to the craggy rock and the castle sitting on top of it.

"You know, they've never ever had a holiday before," I murmured, snuggling in against Indie, the logs burning in front of us making me sleepy.

"They can have plenty more holidays, Spuggy. You know I've never been to Disneyland? I've always wanted to go. Got an excuse to go on those rollercoasters now."

Indie kissed the top of my head.

*****

The gentle shaking woke me, my eyes struggling to open, and when they did, it was still dark. My heart jolted, beating frantically, and at first I didn't know where I was.

"S'ok, Spuggy. It's just me."

I sat bolt upright, willing my eyes to adjust to the darkness, a very faint light filtering in through the windows.

"What's wrong? What's wrong?" I couldn't keep the panic from my voice.

"Nothing. I just want to show you something."

"What time is it?"

"Just after 6.30am."

"It seems so dark."

"Not for long. Come on Emmie, I need you to see something."

I dressed as quickly as my injured body would allow, shuffling down the stairs, my side aching with each tentative step. Indie helped me into my coat, before stuffing his arms into his leather jacket and carefully prising the door open.

Clasping my hand, he led me down the street and out towards the shoreline. The sea lapped gently against the beach, a slow rhythmical sound, hypnotisingly inviting. Behind the castle on the rock, the first streaks of dawn peeked through, stroking the night sky with gold. Slowly, those streaks morphed into a semi-circle, pushing up from the horizon, seeping reds and oranges across the sky. The shape grew outwards, exploding, filling the horizon with colour, the castle just a black shape in the foreground.

I could feel Indie at my back. Then he wrapped his arms around me, carefully at first, terrified he'd hurt me.

"This is beautiful," I whispered, watching the sun grow larger in the sky in front of me.

"Just like you, Spuggy."

"What happens now, Indie?" I asked the question that had been squatting in my head for days.

"We watch the sunrise till there's no doubt it's morning. Or someone gets cold."

"No. I mean for us."

"What do you want to happen, Spuggy?"

"I want to live without fear. I want to wake up in your arms every morning. I want to stop jumping every time you reach for me."

"Some of that will take time." Indie kissed the top of my head. "Some of it, living without fear, I can never promise. Because I wake in fear most mornings, worried that this is a dream, that this won't last. That you see me getting old and get bored?"

I whipped round to face him, instantly regretting it, but also ignoring the burn in my side as I reached up and wrapped my arms around his neck.

“I like bored, Indie. If we could be bored together, that would make me very happy.”

Indie kissed me tenderly, lingering on my lips.

“I won’t ever try to be a father to your kids, Emmie,” the words struck me hard. But I promise I’ll be the best role model I can be. I just want to know whether you want me, Emmie, in all my greying glory.”

“Indominus Carter,” Indie flinched at the words, and I couldn’t stop the creep of a smile. “Of course I want you. I’ve never felt so very alive, and occasionally nearly dead. But I wouldn’t turn the clock back. These last few months have been a whirlwind. A very exciting and sometimes scary whirlwind. But I’d do it all over again, just to be with you.”

Indie smiled, pulling me into him as he dipped his head. A pain shot through my side, and I gasped.

“Sorry, little sparrow. I forgot,” he murmured against my lips.

“There’s one more thing,” I added, pulling back slightly. “Just before I left the hospital, a woman called by. Management. Apparently, the investigation into my security pass has been dropped."

"That's great news, Emmie." Indie didn't look as surprised as I'd thought he'd be. "I always knew they would clear you."

"Yeah. She said the police provided a crime number from the break-in. But I didn't report it to the police, which was odd." Indie's face stilled, almost expressionless. "It made me think. How different my life is with you in it. How you make me feel. I'm not going back to being frightened all the time, and for once I'm going to be brave. I'm going to divorce Gary."

Indie's lips pursed, a slight flicker of tension.

"I'm not asking that you marry me, or anything like that. That's not what it's for. I just need to take that first step to being free of him. Mills was his name, not mine. I'm plain old Emmie Smith."

And then relaxing, Indie smiled, big and beautiful, the russet of the sunrise catching in his deep brown eyes making them almost dark gold.

“You know, when I first met you, I knew I wanted to save you. Seems it was you that saved me, Emmie Smith.”

I pressed my lips to his, feeling the warmth of his flesh against my cold face, his tongue darting out to meet mine, hot and wet, his arms wrapped protectively around me. If I had to live this same life all over again, just to get back here, then it was absolutely worth it. And in that moment, I had no regrets. Only hope. I thought I’d known hope before, but I hadn’t. Now, cradled in Indie’s arms, dawn breaking around us, I knew what it was. True hope.

Chapter Forty Two

Fury

"How is she?" I asked Indie as the club house filled up for one of the most important church meetings in club history.

"Sore. And tired. She's not sleeping well. So, neither am I."

Indie looked as tired as he sounded, his face gaining an extra couple of wrinkles in the last few days. A mix of looking after Emmie and the kids he'd suddenly acquired, and the impending vote which would toss him into the position of president of the Northern Kings MC. A position only I really knew he didn't want. Yet, what we all knew was that there was no one else fit enough for the job. To guide us through the turmoil springing up around us.

"Angels and Demons lost a bike last night," I added another grey hair to that thick mop on his head.

"Shit."

"No intel. But we probably all know anyway. Speaking of which, when are we dealing with the problem with Emmie's ex?"

"It's already in hand, mate."

I stared at him waiting for him to tell me, and Indie watched me, waiting for me to get it. And I thought I did but it was a really bold move.

"The Viking?"

Indie nodded.

"Why?"

"Because if I do it, I won't be able to keep it clean. I want to rip every finger off his hands and ram them down his throat. I want to make him suffer, to know what real fear is like. To feel excruciating pain. But instead, V will make it clean. Or at least cleaner than I'm capable of. It has to be a solution, not revenge, however much I want it."

I understood, I really did. I'd felt the same anger when I'd seen her lying there on the floor, her pretty face battered and broken, the rattle coming from her chest. And still she spoke to me, begging me to go get her kids, because he'd taken them. And beside her lay her dog, and even as I approached the pair of them, and it couldn't struggle to its feet to defend her, it still growled, a low savage noise, intent perfectly clear.

"How is the dog?" I asked.

"She's getting stronger. The bastard broke its leg as well as its ribs. But sounds like it half degloved his arm. Demon has been looking after her. Apparently Kinobi has taken a real shine to her, and Ciara to it."

"Never thought I'd see the day that Demon settled down with a girl and two dogs, like."

"Nor me."

"I knew you always would. It was always just a question of who. I'd half thought if things hadn't worked out with the Viking's lass, she would have been the one for you. Never saw Emmie coming."

"No. Neither did I. Now reckon we should get it over with?"

*****

The chapel was quiet. Apprehension filling the air around us and Indie sitting at the top of the table as vice president, tense and strained. I sat to his right, watching the many faces of the men that joined us. Round, thin, bearded, grey, young, battle worn and war virgins. There was a muttering, voices talking in low tones, coming together to form a low drone. Indie's hands clasped together on the table in front of him, short fingernails digging into skin, tightening and relaxing, and for once the stoic mask of the man with the most control, was slipping. For once he was human.

But it was that control that we were voting in. That calmness. That ability to make decisions under pressure. Not just any decision, but the right one. He might not know it. But he always had been the right man for the job. Whether he wanted it or not.

"Brothers," Indie's voice scattered the mumbling, everyone becoming silent. "On the passing of our president, Ste Carter, we are here to vote for a new president. Nominations please."

"Indominus Carter," I said the words without hesitation, feeling Indie shift uncomfortably beside me.

"Seconded," Big Red's deep voice boomed.

"Any other nominees?" Indie spoke sullenly.

Brothers glanced at each other, wondering whether anyone would suggest someone else. No one moved. No one spoke.

"Then we shall vote," Indie continued. "All in favour?"

Hands shot into the air, the room filling with 'aye' and the gavel fell. The decision made. Destiny fulfilled. A military leader for a biker war. Because we all knew it was coming.

What's Next?

The Northern Kings MC Series (best read after the Northern Sins Saga) reading order:

1. **Demon** – https://mybook.to/NorthernKingsDemon
2. **Indie** – https://mybook.to/NorthernKingsIndie
3. **Fury** – https://mybook.to/NorthernKingsFury
4. **Chaos & Carnage** – Coming soon
5. **Jazz** – Coming Soon
6. **Reap** – Coming soon

The Northern Sins Saga reading order:

1. **Red for Revenge** – https://mybook.to/RedforRevenge
2. **Kiss for a Killer** - https://mybook.to/NSKissforaKiller
3. **Devil in the Detail** - https://mybook.to/DevilintheDetail
4. **Taste of Temptation** - https://mybook.to/TasteofTemptation

Keep up to date with new releases, get access to bonus scenes and exclusive giveaways by signing up to my newsletter:

https://nikterry.link/newsletter

or go to my website:

https://nikterryauthor.wordpress.com

Follow my Facebook page to learn more about me and join my reader group.

https://facebook.com/nikterryauthor

About the Author

I can't remember a time I haven't written stories. I wrote my first short story collection at six years old and they went a lot like this:

Once upon a time there was a goat. The goat was good. The goat met a witch. The witch was bad…..

Well, you get the idea, but the imagination, creativity and story structure was there, even when I'd barely learnt to read and write.

I then took to writing thrillers and fantasy series, none of which I have ever published but are sitting, patiently waiting to be given some attention at a later date.

My very first fascination with romance came from the absolute best series of my generation – Buffy the Vampire Slayer. How I loved bad-boy Spike and how angry I used to get with Buffy over some of her rubbish romantic choices (I only approved of Angel when he lost his soul). Then there was Cole and Phoebe in Charmed and later Bella, Edward and Jacob in Twilight (I was strictly team Jacob by the way – he was much more my type – I think you're getting the picture).

One day I stumbled into the steamy romance genre (before EL James made Romance so very sexy) and bought a book that looked like a fantasy story – which it was – but with extras. I remember reading it on the commute to work and hiding it in a newspaper because I was worried about what people would think if they read it over my shoulder, because that's what I always did to others. I also remember coming across that first scene totally not expecting it and turning bright red when I realised just what I was reading. But I quickly became hooked and I've read so many in this genre since, falling in love with the passion, action, and angst and the adrenaline rush of a hot scene.

Then, just before the Great Pandemic of 2020 (this will sound much more dramatic in ten years' time), I decided to see if I was capable or writing such scenes. It seemed I was, and my hubby was happy to 'sense check' them with me. Now, between us, we have released the first book in the Northern Sins Saga, set in the North East of England where we live with our two daughters, two cats and three ponies.

I'm really excited to get you all on board the steamy romance train with me because what a ride this is going to be!

Printed in Dunstable, United Kingdom

79204182R00282